Hurricane

Hurricane

A NOVEL

By

Elaine L. Allen

Perfect Perceptions Publishing
www.perfectperceptions.wixsite.com/elainelallen
perfectperceptionspublishing@gmail.com

ISBN- 13: 978-0-692-79537-8
ISBN- 10: 0-692-79537-5
LCCN: 2016956805

Published by and for Perfect Perceptions Publishing
Cover Art: Najla Qamber for Najla Qamber Designs
                www.najlaqamberdesigns.com
Edited by: Patrice Harrison for Little Pear Editing Services
                www.littlepearediting.com

Manufactured in the United States of America

This book is dedicated to the memories of everyone who couldn't wait to see the sun shine after the storm

***Acknowledgements:** Sometimes the best material develops from experience and it takes a little bit of tack and know how to make it entertaining. Special thanks to my 1st round BETA readers: Angelique Long, Elizabeth Francavilla, Cinnamon Thompson, Kina DeShazor. I was hungry for feedback and y'all gave it to me…*
To my supporting cast; Crystal, Aimee, Shalom, April, my momma; Elaine, and my inherited momma; Abby. I love y'all for keeping me grounded, focused, and on point.
My babies; Aniyah and Amir who are watching everything I do and are taking notes. I still wear a cape for them and am ready to get into action in a sec.

If you or anyone you know is suffering from depression, PLEASE SEEK HELP!

To my readers, I want to say, THANK YOU for taking the time out to allow me to entertain you with words.

The Storm

Who should I run to...

Chapter One

*C*LICK... CLICK... CLICK... CLICK... CLICK... the nauseating sound of metal locking into place caused bile rise up in her throat, but fear of the consequence kept her from spitting it out all over his face. Instead, she swallowed it down, burning like a fiery trail of acid as it slid back down her throat. Click... click... click... the chain wrapped around the bed frame linked to the leather collar. Trapped.... She breathed as the mattress dipped beneath his weight, that sick feeling rising again as his muscled arms wrapped themselves around her waist. Paralyzed... Her throat, raw from screaming, torched from swallowing bile could not carry a single sound. It was useless; no one would hear her. The beating of her heart, so loud, it almost drowned out the voices in her head as they asked questions of survival and gave quips of encouraging words.

She squeezed her eyes tight as he breathed in her scent, his nose touching the nape of her neck.

"So ripe..." he drawled out, one hand traveling from her waist to in between her naked thighs. "Sooo mine," he added with a wicked *laugh of distinct pleasure. It did not seem to matter that she was dry or that she had begun to cry as he rubbed at her most intimate place.*

She shivered, all hairs on her body standing at attention. "There's always a silver lining," she murmured aloud as darkness overtook her.

The eyes of twenty-nine-year-old Dr. Sharae Jones opened with a jolt a second before her alarm blared its daily wake-up call. She rolled over to emptiness, taking note that James had never made it home from the night before. Sharae rolled her eyes. She detested waking up alone, sweaty, and in fear from the dreams that made her nights sleepless and her days restless.

"You're safe," she murmured before moving. Fifteen years, iron bars, and four states separated her from that danger. "And apparently alone," she added.

Old demons, new ones... they all make you feel like shit. I guess you can only be disappointed by someone else's actions if you give them the power to actually disappoint you.

James had spent another night working and disregarding her need for his time. She often attempted to soothe her need and her own loneliness by reminding herself that building his studio and music production company were important to both of them, the home they were constructing, and their future. The thought was easier to bear than the actual acceptance of his constant absence and what it meant to their relationship. He'd sent her a quick text the night before saying that he wasn't going to make it home as expected and that he was sorry. She'd texted him back "ok" and that she loved him, and had even called, but he hadn't responded to that either.

The lack of response sent her heart into turmoil because in her mind they weren't floating on the trusting waters of honesty and fidelity. The constant nights out, the vibrating cell phone, the quiet calls taken in other rooms, along with the fact that he never left his cell phone out anymore and took it with him even when he went into the restroom, or that he sometimes didn't answer his phone when they were together were all signs that something was going on. Sharae knew that they were signs that all women should wake up and pay attention to. When she'd brought them to his attention, James had sworn up and down that he was working, and the calls and her suspicions had nothing to do with his reality. He'd even gone as far to tell her that if she trusted him, she would believe him.

Believe him? she thought. *Hmph, not as far as I can see.*

Stressed, Sharae flicked on the bathroom lights and looked at herself in the bathroom mirror. Through blurry hazel eyes, she could see the haunting shadows of her nightmares and the puffiness beneath them that traitorously revealed a brief crying jag the night before.

Sighing, Sharae turned on the shower faucets and tested the temperature of the water with her fingertips. She peeled away her nightclothes and stepped into the bathtub and shower. She adjusted the shower curtain so that water wouldn't hit the floor. For a minute, she leaned into the shower wall, letting the hot water strip away that layer of fear, disappointment, and nighttime worries.

It was there that Sharae felt free to let a fresh rush of tears go, sure that they, like the shower water, would be washed down the drain and soon forgotten. The tears would be, but the memories of what had been done to her would not.

Sharae chastised herself as she glided the sudsy washcloth over her body. Years of therapy had taught her to be strong, and strong women did not cry in her book. She then challenged her mentality, but let her mind give way to the rationale that strong women were able to identify a weakness and then spend an allotted time mourning over it. When her shower was over, so was her period of mourning. Sharae had learned early in life that time waited for no woman, and she did not have any expectations that the rule would change for her.

It was the reason she awakened every morning at five a.m. to hit the gym when more than a third of the people she knew were still cuddled in bed beneath their sheets.

The soft sounds of early morning radio personalities from her favorite station joked carelessly about last night's episode of American Idol. Sharae stepped on the scale she'd placed in front of her dresser as a daily reminder to weigh herself. She nervously bit her bottom lip in anticipation of seeing the numbers drop since yesterday morning. A confident smile appeared as the number displayed itself. She was down one pound, with ten more to go. All the hard work of eating right and working out was paying off. If she didn't get pregnant, she'd vacation in the Caribbean this December, in a two-piece bathing suit, she mused hopefully.

Sharae closed her eyes for a brief moment to imagine it. She could already feel the heat from the sun basking all over her honey-toned body, a body that she'd spent the last year perfecting. She had literally spun, ran, squatted, and kickboxed her ass off to shed the excess fifty pounds she'd gained from the contentment of her relationship.

At five feet eight inches tall, Sharae carried the majority of her weight in her hips, thighs, and behind. It was an inherited family trait. She grew up receiving admiring looks from men who made it known that her body's resemblance to the coke bottle was attention-getting. *It was also the reason you attracted him...* the dark recesses of her mind threw back at her.

Sharae shook her head to clear it of negative thoughts. Her light brown skin was a shade darker than what most people considered "redbone", but she was easily referred to as light- skinned.
Meticulously organized, she removed her sports bra and underwear from their designated drawers and then sprayed them with some soft fragrance that was a mix of lavender and honey she'd fallen in love with during her youth. She forfeited smoothing lotion over her entire body, applying it only to the areas she knew would be seen in her black capri workout pants and form-fitting lilac t-shirt with the words; *Top Model* stretching across her breast. As Sharae stretched her arms over her head, the five silver bangles she wore every day danced and clinked around

her wrist. She wore simple, star-cut one-carat diamond studs in her ears. Her left hand was adorned only with a thin platinum band that represented her promise and commitment to James. One day, it would be replaced by an engagement ring and then eventually a wedding band.

With the night terrors now behind her, Sharae grabbed her favorite everyday bag— the brown Gucci Sukey tote, her gym bag and then made her way down the stairs. She stepped into a pair of retro Nike Bo Jackson cross trainer sneakers at the front door and quickly walked to the back of the house and into kitchen to retrieve a half-frozen bottle of water.

Finally, ready, Sharae stepped out into the brisk August morning air. There was a slight chill to it that carried a cool breeze. It crept up the back of her thighs to her spine, tickled her cheek, and caused the long black tendrils of hair to dance around her face. Briefly, she looked up into the darkened sky. The weather forecasters were calling for showers and were tracking a hurricane heading up the east coast. Sharae could feel it.

There was a storm brewing...

Hurricane Irene was coming...

Sharae hesitated before closing the door as she completed her mental checklist to ensure that her morning haze had not caused her to forget anything. She'd hate to have to go through her day without the necessary items or make an unnecessary trip back home once she was in the city.

The iPhone she carried beeped, alerting her that she'd received a text message. Once she was settled in her car, she looked at the message and rolled her eyes as she read,

Good Morning, Baby. I know you're on your way to the gym to work it out. Sorry, I didn't return your call last night but I was fuckin' around with Troy and Shiz tryna mix down some tracks. Love you.

"Lyin' Nucca," she murmured as she turned the key in the ignition of her car.

Immediately, Sharae turned up the car stereo to blast Philadelphia rap artist Ms. Jade's single, *Why U Tell Me That*. She nodded her head to the beat as Jade heated up the track with a story of a woman's heart turned to stone. There'd probably be a nice note in her mailbox, requesting that she keep her music down in the morning when she returned home from work. She sucked her teeth at the thought and backed out of her driveway.

Her cell phone rang as she shrieked her custom-painted black-on-black 2009 Jaguar down the street of her quiet suburban block. She needed the hype music as she feared her worries would follow her to the gym and throughout the course of her day. She glanced down at the caller ID and saw that it was her best friend King. Sharae contemplated ignoring him but knew that he would call again if she didn't answer. Never mind the fact that he would see her in less than twenty minutes. He had no sense of time or respect for hers.

"Good morning, Beautiful," King's deep voice greeted. "Can you turn the music down?"

"What's up, King?" she responded, reaching to adjust the volume.

"Just wanted to let you know that I'ma be late for our workout session," he explained to her as he rolled onto his back in his bed. The woman beside him stirred and snuggled into his side.

Sharae sighed; she detested tardiness when it came to her dollars but made a regular practice of it in her own life. "What do you mean you're going be late?"

King cleared his throat and braced himself for her attitude. "Rae, I didn't get in until after twelve a.m. this morning."

She ignored his excuses and went in on him. She needed to kick something, to wreck something, to balance her emotions. "How is this your job, and you slacking?"

"I'm tired as shit—"

"It's cool," she said with disappointment. She had been looking forward to their kickboxing session to relieve some of the stress she'd been feeling. "I have my music, but know that you owe me two extra sessions this week."

"Nawl. I'ma be there," he yawned, sitting up. King dragged his hands over his face and glanced down at the woman lying beside him. He got out of the bed and moved around the darkened room. Kyrie was about to be pissed that she was going to be rudely awakened and sent home so he could meet Sharae at the gym.

"Where are you going? I thought you said we were going to sleep in," Kyrie purred as she sleepily looked up at him.

Kyrie knew that King thought she was sleeping, but she had been listening since the moment she felt him reach for his phone in the dark. An instant pang of jealousy twisted in her stomach. She hated that she couldn't roll over to him when the sunlight crept through the blinds in the mornings because he was always rushing off to meet Sharae.

"I gotta meet Rae at the gym. You wanna go, and we can come back here and lounge 'til my next appointment?"

Kyrie frowned, "You know what time it is? I don't think so, King." She wanted to roll over and just get lost in the massive king-sized bed but knew that he wasn't having any of that. King had a rule that all guests exited his house when he did. No one had a key to his place except for Sharae.

Kyrie was still trying to decipher if she'd used it for matters that extended beyond them being best friends. For the life of her, she couldn't figure why the two of them weren't dating each other.

When King had introduced his best friend Sharae to her, she had been surprised because, in her opinion, Sharae was beautiful and successful. From her observation, they were comfortable in each other's personal space and had even completed one another's sentences. She only assumed that since they'd know each other for over ten years that they were oblivious to their reactions to one another.

Kyrie frowned as she thought that Sharae must have been blind or completely happy with her man to not have attempted to hook up with King. He was *fine*. His skin reminded her of dark chocolate; the hair on his head was a dark sea of waves, and he'd let his facial hair grow a little longer than a natural beard. King stood six feet three inches tall, was lean like a basketball player, and his body was toned perfectly.

It surprised her that King had been single and that there had been no drama with other women since they'd began dating six months before. Single black women were always on the lookout for handsome, heterosexual, and successful black men to snag as their own. With the way their relationship was progressing, this just might be Kyrie's opportunity to get hers.

"I could have stayed home for all of this," she pouted as she climbed to the edge of the bed. She rose to her knees in front of him. King sent her a sideways glance with a bright smile that showed off his pearly white teeth. "And miss out on all this good dick this morning?" he smirked as he stepped closer to gather her up in his arms.

"Ummm. You 'bout to pass out some more?" she inquired as she let her arms settle around his neck. Her eyes sparkled in anticipation. He glanced at the clock and grinned back at her. "I got a lil' bit of time," he murmured, coaxing her onto her back.

Chapter Two

*T*ime always seemed to tick several seconds slower than normal on Friday afternoons. Hating your job only added to the time slowly passing by. Sharae stared at the colorful abstract art painting that hung directly in her line of vision from her desk. She wondered if she stared at it long enough, would she disappear into it. That dream had her out of sorts. It made her edgy, moody, and sad. It had been more than a year since she'd had her last one. More than fifteen years had passed, and she could still feel the heat of his breath on the back of her neck. The stench of Egyptian musk still had the power to make her insides curl.

Leave those thoughts in the dark...

There is so much light, honey...

Where, though? she wondered.

Ripping children away from their families was taking a toll on her life. When she'd started working at the Department of Human Services six years ago, she believed in their mission of promoting safety, permanence, and the well-being for children and youth who were at risk from abuse and neglect. A Master's and Doctorate degree later, Sharae was still not doing what she'd set out to do. Her dream had been to save at-risk girls from falling prey the streets and show them how to become successful regardless of their past experiences, their upbringing, and/ or environment.

The consulting position with the Commonwealth of Pennsylvania to develop welfare to work program initiatives had not gone as she'd expected. Although the position was very demanding, she'd dedicated a year of hard work and a limitless fountain of fresh ideas, pulling from several referenced employment theories. The PPIPC method was her most success trial using statistics of the under and unemployed which identified potential careers based on personality profiling in combination with the client's actual skill set. The EET method focused on enhancing the education and technical skills of its participants to become gainfully employed in their prospective or ideal careers. The outcome of her employment methods had not been as successful in this pool of subjects as it had been in her original pool of participants. When the 4th quarterly statics report had come back showing a steady decline in participation since her program began, Sharae was released from her contract. From the backlash she was receiving, her understanding was that the state of Pennsylvania disagreed with her implementation of the programs to get Philadelphia's welfare population employed.

The goal of the federal government was to reduce the number of families relying on federal funds to support their everyday life sounded like they had the people's best interest at heart. Their plan lead others to the road of self-sufficiency was a fanciful dream but a far cry from becoming reality. It hurt to chalk up the experience as a failure when she'd seen both employment methods work during her research for her thesis. Hundreds of unemployed people could be thankful to her for their current employment. She'd set up the personality profiling at local unemployment offices and had begun completing assessments and made successful matches. Based on her last polling ninety-four percent of the participants in her first and second run trials still held their positions with their matched employers. The result of that alone was enough to have garnered interest from every employment agency in the city.

This experience humbly— if not embarrassingly had taught her that what worked for one population didn't especially mean that it would work for everyone. In theory, there was an employment method supposedly that fit every type of person. But everything worked perfectly, in theory, she reasoned. It was when she put that theory into practice that the truth revealed itself. She felt that the state hadn't given it enough time to work. She wasn't overly sure that they wanted it to work.

It pricked her nerves that no one paid attention to the fact that the economy was on the brink of destruction. None of them took into consideration the participant's mindsets. She knew that they all felt that they were going to walk away with jobs that paid enough for them to provide for their families without assistance from the state. She also knew that the likelihood of people obtaining the successful careers they wanted was based on each person individually.

Sometimes, I just want to sprinkle some common sense on these heffas.

Sharae shook her head; she knew the answer laid in changing people's perceptions of success and instilling some ambition and drive into the hearts of the city's poorest and most hopeless citizens. She knew that she needed to be proactive instead of being reactive, which lead her back to educating and mentoring young women.

When the time was right, she would actively start Girls Living Out Successful Starts at Youth, to be known as GLOSSY; a mentoring program she'd developed that paired a female teen with a successful female adult in various fields with the intentions of instilling hope in their hearts, as well as creating an action plan for a better life. She had an extensive list of contacts and willing friends ready to participate.

Sharae smiled as she rolled around the ideas of what she envisioned for GLOSSY and all its participants. All she had to do was take that step. It would be a very large undertaking, and she had to admit that fear of failure held her back. Drawing from all that she had experienced in life and her current situation, Sharae came to the conclusion that failure was but a stepping stone to ultimate success.

Considering that, for all intents and purposes, her program with the state had been a failure, Sharae felt the hundred-thousand-dollar salary they paid her for the year was compensation enough to heal her heart. That was her story, and she was sticking to it.

Given the opportunity, she would show the world what she was capable of. She didn't want to waste another moment living for other people and subjecting herself to their dreams while putting hers on hold. One day, the word GLOSSY wouldn't simply be a reference to how shiny a person's lips were. Girls would be educated in the fine arts, literature, and given the opportunity to add culturally diverse experiences from the opera and ballets to spoken word forums and sold out Broadway shows. The dream was to add a layer of gloss to their already shining and make them stand out as bright as a star in the evening sky.

She bit her lip nervously as she contemplated signing the resignation letter she kept in the top drawer of her desk under her portfolio. She glanced at the wooden frames that hung from her walls that held her degrees, reminding her of her accomplishments. She closed her eyes and was soon brought back to reality by the vibration of her cell phone.

"Hey gurl," she answered her younger sister Ava.

"Can you tell me why your cousin is getting married during a hurricane?" Ava's even- toned voice came through the cell phone.

"I'm so sure that they planned this before they knew about the hurricane. It's indoors, so it's not gonna bother me none. Are we still going to the mall?"

"And you know that," Ava answered cheerfully. "You think you can get me that Gucci bag we saw last week?"

Sharae frowned and looked at the phone to ensure she was hearing her correctly. "Hell no! I keep telling you when you get a job and are responsible enough to stop living off your refund checks, then maybe I'll get you something Gucci, or Louis-like."

At the age of twenty-three, Ava was completing her final semester of graduate school to obtain her Master's Degree in marketing management at Drexel University. She was very spoiled and misguided if she was operating under the impression that Sharae was going to take over her parent's pampering now that they'd moved permanently to Phoenix, Arizona.

"Please? I can get Mommy and Daddy to give you half," she pleaded.

"If you'n get outta here. If you can get them to give you half, then you need to have them replace my shoes."

"Which ones?" Ava asked hesitantly, praying she didn't want the Madame Butterfly pumps by Christian Louboutin back. The peep toes had become her favorite shoes during the past summer.

"All of them," Sharae answered quickly with an aspirated sigh. Ava had at least ten pair of her designer heels tucked in their boxes hiding in her closet. Ava wanted to assure Sharae that they been put to good use but assumed that Sharae wouldn't understand. Ava knew that she still saw her through eyes of the sister who was almost seven years older with different tastes in music, theories, and literature. She had yet to see the young adult who had completed two successful internships in each of her undergraduate majors or realize that the website and blog she ran was a part of her building her brand. Ava wanted to remind Sharae that playing her part as the older sister and sometime benefactor was necessary to the success Ava was certain Sharae wanted for her.

With that in mind and no shame, Ava pleaded a little bit more, "Please, Rae? I was also thinking that you could get me something to wear to the wedding."

13

"Girl, you shot out for that one. I know you better have some money later on, or you are going to end up being very sad."
Ava laughed. "Don't be like that, Rae. You know I love you. See you later when you pick me up."

Sharae smiled to herself; as much as she loved her little sister, she was confident that her parents had slipped in the time between their births. She guessed the age difference had something to do with it. The sense of responsibility that had been instilled in her seemed to be severely lacking in her younger sibling. At times, she seemed to be more of a mother figure than a sister. Ava was so carefree, that none of Sharae's warnings about life and responsibility had yet to reach her.

"Okay, baby," Sharae said, clicking her phone off. She smiled; being Ava's big sister had saved her life. In her most desperate years as a teen, Ava's need for attention and approval had kept Sharae engaged in what it meant to truly love without limits or reservation. For that, her heart was always soft, grateful, and unwavering with unchallenged affection.

Sharae briefly contemplated contacting Dr. Trainor to request an emergency session this afternoon to discuss her nightmare. Deciding against it, she opted for human entertainment instead. Sharae used her telephone to log into her Facepage profile. Social networking always had a way of helping the day pass by quickly. She scanned the feeds for updated news on her friends. She checked her inbox messages and accepted a friend request from Daneen Roberts. Sharae rolled her eyes as she looked over the young woman's page to discover if she actually knew her.

In her opinion, the profile picture displayed the light brown-skinned woman as a blonde, weave-wearing, purple lip-looking, poorly-aged female. Sharae scanned through a couple of her pictures, read a couple of her feeds which noted that she was continuously chillin', and determined that she didn't know her. She saw a post in which someone affectionately referred to her as Goldie and laughed.

"Hoes on Facepage be burnt out," she murmured to herself as she scrolled over the pictures. The young woman was provocatively dressed with dollars bills over her body in one picture. In another, she had a bare shoulder exposed with the name Semaj scrolled in cursive across her left side of her chest. A couple of the other pictures looked like they were advertisements or promises that the dimly lit room resembling a vampire's den could turn into a strip joint for the right price.

Sharae shook her head and narrowed her eyes.

Why the hell is this trick tryna friend me? Just as she began to scroll through her feed to dissect it, the phone began to vibrate in her hand. She saw that it was James and she smiled. "Hey, Babe," she cheerfully answered.

"Sup, gorgeous?"

"Waiting for five o'clock to come. What are you doing?"

"Standing outside your door," he told her.

Despite the fact that she was still upset, a lazy smile appeared and spread across her face. "What are you doing standing outside my door?"

James entered the room, walked directly over to her, and bent to kiss her lips. "I've been so busy these last couple weeks that I didn't realize how much I missed you."

Sharae tilted her head to the side as she eyed him suspiciously, "You missed me? I can't tell."

James eased his hip onto the corner of her desk and leaned in for another kiss. His lips captured hers, and he nibbled on her bottom lip before his tongue delved into her mouth. Sharae reached up to run her hands from the base of his neck to rest on his cheeks. She let her tongue dance with his before she pulled away. Sharae's hand fell, and she lightly pressed his chest to bring him to a halt.

His kiss had the power to make her heart melt, to make all her issues with him disappear. James's hand was rested on her cheek as the pads of his thumbs brushed across them in a circling motion. His fingers began to roam in her hair.

"Of course, I've been missing you, Rae. Waking up and going to sleep with you, rolling over to you in the middle of the night, loving you."

The scent of his Dolce and Gabanna cologne wafted through her senses. Lost in his trance, Sharae smiled. "What are you up to?" she questioned him, feeling that familiar spike in her blood.

"Nothing. I realized that I don't spend enough time telling you how much I love you," he smoothly replied, dropping a kiss to her forehead.

Sharae tilted her head back so she was able to look him in the eyes. "It's not in the telling but all in the showing," she informed him.

James stepped back, giving her an opportunity to study him. His brown eyes were bright, but the lines beneath them told her that he had worries. The dark waves of his hair were beginning to be infiltrated by gray. At thirty-five years of age, he still had a very young and handsome face. It was clean-shaven except for his neatly-trimmed goatee. He was tall; if asked, he would extend his six-foot-two-inch frame to six-feet-four-inches. His body was lean like a basketball player's. "So, that's why you been acting all funny?" he asked

"I'm not acting funny. I'm restless. I'm tired," she responded defensively. *I had a nightmare and need your arms around me to protect me.*

"This shit is stressful, Rae, and you're one of the only things that keep me going. I know I haven't been at home as much, and we haven't spent that much time together, but sacrifices have to be made in order for us to get this bread," he went on to explain.

Guilt chipped away at her attitude; she knew that he was stressed. The knowledge of that stress kept her from mentioning her own loneliness and insecurities about their relationship.

The initial sacrifice had been their quality time. It was hard for her to adjust to him not being readily available as he was still working full time as an engineer for SEPTA and going straight to the warehouse where they were building Horizon Studios. Due to the constant demand of opening a new business, James was never around.

Promises for quality time were issued but never delivered. She'd accepted that it was going to be a strain on their relationship. Sharae guessed she'd prematurely made the assumption that it had to get better. When he'd taken the leave of absence from work, she'd been excited because it would allow him to be home more often. When that had not happened, she bit her tongue and didn't complain because this journey was very time-consuming and she was either going ride with him through it all or get left on some curbside. She believed in his dream as passionately as he did and was willing to invest her time and devote herself to helping him make it come true.

Somewhere along those lines, the distance and lack of communication had placed doubt and fear into her heart and mind. That, combined with the multitude of tale-tell signs of cheating, was enough for her to question his faithfulness. Now, every word he spoke from his mouth was being scrutinized. She battled with herself daily because she loved him and wanted to believe him.

"I know, babe. We all about gettin' the bread," she said, wrapping her arms around his waist and laying her head on his chest.

"You come first, and everything that I do is for us."

"I know," she repeated. Not wanting to dwell on or even go into the loneliness she felt, she decided to change the subject. She stood up, adjusted her navy-colored pencil skirt. "We're supposed to be going to the mall later to see if we need to make any last minute outfit changes for the wedding. What are your plans for the evening?"

"Have a couple sessions lined up. It's real nutty that your cousin didn't invite me to the wedding."

Only married people were invited with plus ones to naturally bring along their spouse. All of the couple's unmarried friends were only issued an invitation for one regardless of their relationship status. That had been a unanimous complaint among her family. She

17

understood and didn't complain, though. King and Ava would both be there to keep her company.

"They didn't have enough money."
He did a flagging motion with his hand. "It ain't 'bout shit, though. I'ma be busy at the studio most of the day anyway."

Quickly disappointed, Sharae came to the conclusion that this would be a perfect excuse for him being at the studio. She knew that it would lead to him being there all night. Sharae quietly said, "Working hard. You know they're forecasting a hurricane, right?"
Irked by her own reaction, Sharae turned her back to him as she walked over to the office door. She had no clue why she walked there, but she needed the distance and didn't want to give him the opportunity to detect the shift in her mood. She leaned against the door.

"Unt uhn; come here. Looking all fuckin' good," James told her as he caught the brief change in her eyes. He followed her to the door.

"What?" she asked, a little breathless as James caught her wrist within his grasp. Her heart began to race as he stood in front of her. The hairs on the back of her neck stood up when he gently backed her up against the door.
Excitement registered in Sharae eyes as the weight of James body pressed into her chest as he leaned down and joined her lips with his.

Sharae allowed his lips and tongue to explore her mouth as she felt her resistance begin to fade. She assumed that he was trying to soothe her worries in the only way he knew how. Sharae had come to the conclusion that he used his dick as a bargaining tool to fix all their relationship problems and issues. Sex had always made her agreeable and pliable in the past. He'd break her off with some of the good loving and assume that everything would be okay. She'd become accustomed to that in the first year of their relationship. James still had no idea she knew his strategy.

As much as he thought he was, James was no different from any other man when it came to this matter. In her opinion, they were all the same. And at this point, if he wanted to play the "*fuck and make me feel better game"*, then she'd go along with it and hoped there would be a happy ending to it.

Yes... a voice purred.

Fuck him and let him make us feel better... the more cynical voice added.

Sharae listened to the voices and turned her head to break the kiss to give him the impression that he was going to have to work for it. Just then, he went in for her neck. She closed her eyes so they could roll around beneath their lids while he fed from the crook of her neck as if he were a vampire. Her intense attraction to him had her hands reaching for his belt to undo it, then to the zipper so he could tug his jeans down his legs. James let out a frustrated grunt as he reached behind her to lock her office door.

Sharae let her head fall back while she gathered her thoughts as she felt James' hand pushing her skirt up her thighs and then pulling and all but ripping the lace of her Victoria's Secret underwear. She moaned as he expertly lifted her off her feet and made himself comfortable between her thighs. His hands went to her pumping hips to steady them as he guided her down the length of him.

Sharae released a whispered moan as his dick seemed to melt inside her moist softness in one long, thoughtful stroke. His hands went beneath her behind to support her weight as he slowly administered deep strokes, causing Sharae's breath to get trapped in her throat. He was encouraged as she wrapped her arms around his neck and shoulders for her own support as her body met the demands of his.

"I love you," he told her on an up stroke.

She let her response be her moans of pleasure as he demonstrated that love stroke after long, slow stroke. After three minutes, James quickened his pace and his strokes became more frantic. Sharae's labored breaths were short and fast as she bobbed up and down on his dick. She attempted to hold her breath as she felt the build-up of her orgasm begin to tickle up her back. She closed her eyes tight, praying that he'd last long enough for her to achieve the earth- shattering orgasm she'd had her mind set on since he slid into her.

That prayer died, unfulfilled on her lips as he grunted his release and leaned into her, letting his forehead touch hers. He kissed her lips and murmured again, "I love you."

She had to keep her eyes closed in fear that she'd roll them, and when she wanted to scream about her own unreleased joy, Sharae murmured, "I love you too."

Chapter Three

*M*arital *unions between young African* Americans always made Sharae's heart swell. Celena and Anthony made it official as they accepted one another as husband and wife in front of all their family, friends, and God. Their union supported the fact that there were still good black men who wanted to marry good black women, and it brought a smile to her face. She'd found that a man would string you along as long as you'd let him, and there was no guarantee that he'd pick you in the end. Their ceremony had been wonderful and sentimental enough to bring light tears to the corner of Sharae's eyes. The reading of 1 Corinthians 13 was cliché but so fitting for them. Celena was a romantic like herself and had been in love with the verses since both she and Sharae had proclaimed them as their favorite and motto to live by.

Sharae believed and lived the words so much so, that she'd had the lines Love is Patient, Love is Kind, Love Never Fails tattooed in the shape of a large heart on the upper left side of her back and shoulder. She figured once she and James were married, she'd get James inked inside the heart.

Love is patient, she reminded herself.

Too damn patient if you ask me... The thought had her tracing her thumb over her own promise ring. Not one of her friends or family members understood why she wore it, and in the back of her mind, neither did she. Yet, Sharae wore the band without fail, regardless of the fact that James did not wear one. At least she had until doubt pertaining to his fidelity had made an appearance into her everyday thoughts. She desperately wished that the intimate evening in she had planned would give them an opportunity to reconnect.

Though she didn't believe any of the news reports forecasting possible destruction to the Tri-State area, she'd purchased candles and stocked up on perishables from the local Walmart in hopes of being hurricane bound with her boo.

The shreds of doubt had briefly replaced the smile with a confused pout. The sight of the pelting rain discouraged Sharae and increased her lonely mood. She prayed to God that she didn't carry that mood back into the reception with her. The last thing she wanted to do was put a damper on King's or Ava's wedding experiences. On second thought, she doubted that she could. They were both four shots into their drinking and past the point of being affected by anything going on around them.

Sharae took a deep breath, looked into the mirror, and began to retouch her lips with her MAC gloss applicator. She puckered her lips, blew herself a kiss, and was reaching for the exit when Celena stepped into the bathroom, shut the door quickly, and leaned up against it. Sharae smiled. "Hey, honey. You tired?"

Celena dramatically put her hand to her forehead. "Girl, it's so freakin' hot up in here," she said, fanning her clearly-flushed face. Her light-skinned cheeks were rosy and blushed-filled.

"It's a good, hot thought, right?" Sharae questioned. Despite the flushed cheeks, Celena's eyes were bright with love.

"I's married now," Celena creaked out the famous Color Purple line, causing them both to laugh.

"You're crazy. But you look beautiful and extremely happy."

"I am extremely happy. Now, when you and James gettin' married? Or are you still Mrs. Career woman and married to them jobs?"

Sharae had to bite her tongue to keep herself from cursing. It got under her skin that the majority of her family members saw her career as second-rate to their marriages and families. She was the only one on both sides of her families to have a doctorate degree and was constantly judged because of it. All of her cousins in her age range were either married and/or had babies. They all presumptuously believed that she was too busy with her career to want either. She could cry at the thought of how far off they all were.

"When the time is right, I'll put on the white dress and all the extras."

Celena turned her lips and nose up. "White? Girl, you trippin'. Your hoe ass ain't even 'bout to be up in nobody's white dress," she laughed.

Sharae held her stomach as she doubled over in laughter. "Oh, Please! Don't front, heffa, we did hang out together. I know your secrets." Their college years had been memorable.

"Well, as long as you don't let Anthony know any of them, we good. You know he thinks I've always been a good girl. That's why he married me," she said in an innocent voice as she stepped away from the door and stood in the mirror.

"I'm sure that's why he married you," Sharae responded.

"I'm rocking the shit out of this dress," Celena admired herself in the mirror. She straightened her gown, cupped her hands under the sweetheart bodice, and squared her shoulders.

It gave Sharae an opportunity to study her before she agreed. Celena's hair was classically waved and swept up to the side and pinned with a sparkling diamond flower hair clip. The off-white lace bodice was molded to her curves as it gleamed with flecks of platinum and diamond accents as it flared out into yards of organza. The princess ball gown worked for her, Sharae concluded. "You do look very beautiful, Lena. I'm glad all this rain didn't put a damper on your day."

"Well, at first I was devastated, but we barely got wet and fuck it, it's about us and our family; who cares about the weather?"

"That is a beautiful attitude to have—" Her cell began to ring. The assigned ringtone of *Give Me You* let her know that it was James. "I'll be right back," she told Celena as she made a move to exit the bathroom. "Hey, Babe, wassup?" she answered.

"Nothing. These dickheads on the fourth floor left their windows open, and it was leaking from up there down into the studio. So I had to go upstairs to close the windows and shit."

"That's messed up; why didn't the landlord come down there?"

"I don't have time to be waitin' on them. The rain was damaging the equipment," he told her.

"Oh, well I know that's right," she agreed.

"How's the wedding? I know you look good. Take a pic and send it to me," he told her.
Sharae smiled. "Aww, it was beautiful, Babe. Absolutely beautiful. And I do look good. Gonna look even better later on," she responded with a hopeful invitation.

"I can't wait to see that. I'm definitely gonna try to get back home to you before it gets any worse. I have to make sure that everybody straight down here. I'm in Fresh Grocer grabbing them some food now."

Try. Sharae leaned up against the wall as his words registered. "That's nice of you to make sure that they all are alright, but it's supposed to get bad out there, and you know you hate driving in the rain."

"Don't worry, Babe; nothing could keep me from you. Go ahead back to the party. I'll see you when I get home. Love you."

She doubted that she would but still said, "I love you too." James had said *"try"* which told her that there was a chance that he would not make it home.

Another excuse, she murmured to herself. Sharae wanted to believe that he'd make it home to her. She'd travel through a hurricane to be with the one she loved. There would be nothing that would keep her from being with her family. If reports were accurate, devastation of homes was to be expected.

He's gonna make it home, she settled on the thought.

Sharae frowned but wasn't able to indulge in a pity party after spotting Ava headed her way. "What are you holed up in the hallway for?" Ava questioned as she approached. "You, a'ight?" she asked as she caught the sadness in Sharae's eyes.

Sharae shook her head. "Umm-hmm. I'm good. Where's King?"

Ava rolled her eyes. "In there shaking his dick all over these thirsty-ass old hoes," she said with an attitude. She made no secret of her crush on King. Sharae had stopped that short as King was flirtatious but didn't think of Ava as a grown or available woman beyond that of his own younger siblings.

"Girl, please. King ain't even messing with you, so get a damn grip and stop mooning over his womanizing ass. Anyway, he's like a big brother to you." Sharae informed her baby sister.

Ava folded her arms over her chest. King was anything other than brotherly. She knew better, Ava reasoned. She knew things that Sharae did not. She was inclined to scratch his surface to see if there was anything beneath it. There had been. "Oh, I'm damn sure gonna get him. Now stop blockin'."

"Really? How much did you drink?" Sharae glanced at her through slit eyelids.

Ava sucked her teeth and rolled her eyes again. "Whatever, Rae."

Sharae shook her head at her sister's nonsense, put her arm through Ava's, and said, "Come on sweet child." She pulled Ava towards the ballroom.

The ballroom was illuminated by a soft glow of lights and candles. Flowing white and violet fabrics were draped from the high ceilings, creating alcoves for lounging areas furnished with white ottomans, chaises, and sofas in each corner of the massive ballroom.

Sharae immediately spotted King lounging on one of the sofas with a young lady. She sat crossed-leg beside him, looking as if she was dying to hear every word that left his lips. She could see King put a hand on the woman's knee and had leaned in to whisper in her ear. The brown-skinned woman laughed and patted King's hand, which caused Ava to walk over to where they were.

"Oh, no that bitch didn't!" was all Sharae heard as she stared at her sister's back making strides to cut across the dance floor to reach King and the woman. She coughed as she followed, hopeful that in her drunken state, Ava would remember where she was.

"Ava," she whispered in a hushed voice as she continued to close the distance between them. Sharae was unsure what brought on Ava's renewed interest in King. She could see it ending disastrously if she didn't nip in the bud.

She could have slapped Ava when she saw her remove King's hand from the woman's leg and pull him up to stand.

The female said, "Damn, excuse me. I know you see that we talking, right?"

Ava had been staring at King and frowned her face as she looked down at the woman. The woman stood up just as Sharae stepped up to them.

"Excuse us," she said to the woman. She turned her attention to King. "We have to tell you something."

She grabbed Ava's arm, King's hand, and flashed the woman a smile. She pulled them away but not fast enough for Ava to hear the woman say, "Bitch,"

"What?!" Ava immediately responded, stopping dead in her tracks.

Sharae shook her head and dug her fingers into Ava skin. "If you don't act right," she warned her.

"I got her," King volunteered and held a hand up at Sharae. He could see that she would soon explode on Ava and didn't want to draw any more attention to either of them. Quickly, King took Ava's hand and pulled her onto the dance floor.

"What is wrong with you?" he questioned as his hands went to her slender waist. It irritated him that he could almost taste the signature semi-sweet scent that she wore.

Ava defiantly looked up into his face. "What is wrong with you? Feeling all over her in my damn face?" she responded. She could feel his fingers — tense as they were holding her waist securely as she began to sway them into a dance.

King could see that the effects of the alcohol she'd consumed glassed over in her eyes. "Ava, calm down and stop it before Rae think that something is up."

"There is something up," she pouted.

The first chords of *'I'll Be'* by Edwin McCain pumped from the speakers as she continued to sulk, waiting for his response and admission of the same gut-wrenching feelings she felt for him. The crowd of people on the dance floor began to thin out as Edwin's trail of promises wrapped around the people open and dreamy enough to enjoy it.

"It didn't mean anything to you, then?" she demanded.

That one perfect night six months ago when he'd crossed the line and kissed his best friend's younger sister was still a very vivid memory. The stolen hushed kisses and flirtations between them had been special and something he cherished.

At the time, he'd wanted to blame it on the Mo' or anything other than the swirling need that he'd began to feel when she aimed those sultry hazel eyes his way. It made him uncomfortable to know that she had feelings for him and that if she'd been anybody else, he'd be able to reciprocate those feelings.

Shit, King cursed himself as she continued to stare into his eyes. Ava, as beautiful and well put together as she was— was only twenty-three years old and not available to him.

Sharae would kill him.

"Ava, we can't get together or anything like that," he explained. It broke his heart to see the disappointment begin to swim into her eyes. It infuriated him that he continued to be attracted to her when she was off limits forever to him.

The thick layer of haze that the liquor had created did nothing to protect her from his words. She knew he had urges, wants, and desires. She could feel the heat of it in his stare.

Yes, she resigned that King was rejecting her with his words, but his eyes and his body told a different story. She didn't care that he was *sometimes* with Kyrie. It didn't matter to her that he was her sister's best friend. It only mattered to her that when King kissed her, everything around her disappeared. That everything inside her felt alive. That her heart sang a new tune filled with love and optimism. None of the men she'd dated made her feel that way.

Ava knew King wanted to argue that their ages made a difference. To her, it did not. They weren't even ten years apart. She understood that King assumed it would affect his relationship with Sharae but was determined not to let it.

Sharae would have to get over it, Ava concluded.

Distance would be good, King decided. He'd transfer all of Ava's training sessions to his assistant.

"The only one judging you— is you," she told him.

He laughed. It was rich with self-pity. King was sure that God was laughing at him. He'd never known what it was like to have limitations when it came to women he wanted. "You'll find some young boah to treat you nice and give you what you deserve."

"Could you picture me with some young boah? Him doing all those things to me that I know you want to?" Ava breathed, her lips close to his.

King shook his head to clear it. He wouldn't allow her to see him sweat. Shit— he would not allow himself to sweat. If he did, he was sure both Ava and Sharae would know it. "Nawl, I'm good. Now, behave yourself before you mess up your cousin's wedding."

Ava frowned as she pulled away from him, arched both her brows and aimed a steely gaze at him. "We'll see," she told him. She turned and walked away, leaving him on the dance floor, ears full of the same promises made by crooner Edwin McCain.

Chapter Four

*W*ith her skin still warm from the steaming hot shower, Sharae scraped off all the rain and crud and crept into her bedroom, convinced that tonight would be a good night. The wedding had put her in a romantic mood and nothing— absolutely nothing— would change that feeling.

She peeked out her windows to check the current weather condition. It didn't seem that bad; she'd seen worst.

Sharae laughed to herself when she noticed that none of the neighbors' cars were in their driveways. They'd all taken heed to the media's hype regarding estimated damages. She did have to admit that she'd done the same, parking Brooke, her jaguar, in the shelter of their garage instead of her normal space in the driveway.

"Hmph, it rained harder last week," she murmured to herself as she pulled the curtains closed to block out the sounds and sights of the storm.

Satisfied with the soft glow of the candles she'd lit around the room, she sniffed the air and smiled at the thought of having a cozy night at home.

Sharae made a fresh batch of chocolate chip cookies and steeped a pot of tea with a hint of peppermint to have ready for when James walked through the door. He'd need something to warm him after coming in from the rain. She'd prepared his pajamas and robe and left them folded at the foot of their bed.

So far, the ambiance for a cozy romantic evening was set. James would be the last and final piece to show up to make it complete. It made her glance at her cell phone to check the time. Just then, it rang James's tune and a picture of him displayed on her screen.

"Hey," she answered.

"Hey, I'm just calling to say I'm about to leave down here, and that I'll be home in less than an hour."

Sharae climbed into her bed and made herself comfortable beneath the handmade quilt and duvet. "Ooh. Okay. Be careful though because they're supposed to be putting out an alert that only emergency vehicles can be on the roads," she informed him. She reached for the television remote and pressed the button to get an update on the storm.

"I know. You know I hate driving in the rain," James replied.

Hadn't she said the exact same thing this afternoon? "That's why I'm saying that you should hurry up and get here," Sharae explained.

"I am. What you doin'?" he inquired.

"Nothing. Getting ready for you," she told him.

James smiled. "What that mean?"

"That I'll be just the way you like me when you get here," she said, her voice low and sultry with promise.

"You how I like you, right now?" he indulged in the play.

"Wet, warm, and waiting, Daddy," she stated.

"Won't you touch her for me and tell her I'm on my way," James persuaded.

Sharae smiled as she thought about it. If they took out time for phone sex, it'd take longer for the real sex to go down. "I'ma keep her warm for you while we wait, and you can tell her about it when you get here."

"Damn, you gonna do me like that? You think you want some vanilla ice cream?"

Sharae licked her lips as if she could already taste it. "It's my favorite," she responded to their private joke with a laugh.

She made him smile, despite what he had going on. She could always make him smile, he reasoned. "I'll be there," James told her.

"Alright, see you in a bit. Drive safe," She laid the cell phone beside her as she began to watch the news.

ABC News had full coverage of the hurricane. She could see her favorite channel's meteorology team shine together as a unit for once. She turned the volume up to listen to the reports.

Sharae was surprised to see that Atlantic City and County were evacuating people in buses. She had to admit, the rain there appeared to be getting out of control. They were sandbagging all the buildings in attempts to avoid flooding. The water seemed to be raging against the docks. The wind, furious as it all but blew the reporter down the boardwalk, mocked those who attempted to document it.

People did what they had to for their jobs, she knew. Just as she understood that she'd never make it in the world of meteorology. They were always chasing storms, tracking heat streaks, and cold fronts. Sharae shook her head, and even though she was watching it unfold on TV, she wasn't entirely sold but was happy that she was inside the comfort of her home as opposed to being out in that mess of a storm.

She texted Tamika to check on her and waited on her response before she called Ava.

"You didn't call when you got home," Sharae immediately accused when Ava answered.

Ava shrugged although she knew Sharae couldn't see her. "Thanks for checking up on me, mother, but I'm safe," she said, instead of letting her sister know that she had yet to arrive to her apartment.

"So, you have water, flashlight, batteries, candles?" Sharae inquired.

Distracted, Ava looked out her car window and zeroed in on the door to the brownstone through the pouring rain.

"Ava?"

"Yea... Yeah. I'm prepared. You bought all the stuff, Rae. You know that I have them."

"You sound preoccupied; just make sure you use them. I love you and will call to check on you in the morning." Sharae smacked her lips in an air kiss.

"I love you too, Sis," Ava replied and disconnected the call.

Sharae glanced at her laptop and decided to log into Facepage to check on how all the people she knew were faring through the hurricane. She laughed at peoples' comments about satellite cable not working. She reviewed and made random comments on her friend's post and took the time to post that she couldn't wait for her honey to get home to keep her company.

Just as she was logging out, she saw a status post by the girl Daneen appear, stating that she was happy that her boo Semaj had decided to rent a suite at the Hilton. She'd uploaded a picture of herself sprawled across the hotel bed. One of her guy friends was quick to jump on her status, saying how bad he wished he was her dude.

Sharae frowned and rolled her eyes. *These nuccas stay hyping up these busted-ass broads.* Because her attitude came too close to hating for her taste, she spared the girl one more glance and decided aloud, "Hope she have fun; everybody should be cuddled with the one they love."

Her cell phone beeped with a text message from King.

Just checking to see if you're cool, the text read.

I'm good. Just waiting for James. What you doin'? Sharae responded quickly.

Lounging was his response

Alone? she inquired

Yes, Alone. I ain't feel like being bothered by any company.

Sharae wrinkled her nose. King never wanted to be alone if he had a reason to be cuddled with some willing female.

She wondered at the tone of his text. ***What's wrong with you? Kyrie made you mad?***

No, I made her mad. She wanna chill and I'm not feeling it. I have a lot of shit on my mind. It's not even raining that hard. Just don't think it's that serious.

King was a complicated and extremely moody man. There could be a million things going on in his mind, Sharae reasoned. God had spared her the heartache of ever having him as a lover. Instead, He'd given him to her as a best friend. The way she saw things, she'd been lucky all around. His past could tell the tale of a string of women with broken hearts. Poor Kyrie's heart seemed destined for the same.

LOL, me neither, but I'm ready to take advantage of the hurricane and cuddle up.

Well, you need it. Pussy is the last thing on my mind.

Whatever; it's always on your mind. I can see you're brooding. I'll call you to make sure you weren't washed away in the storm.

Not likely. Holla at you later, he texted.

She swears she funny, he thought to himself. And he wasn't brooding, King concluded. He was assessing.

Kyrie had gotten on his nerves as she insisted on coming to his house to chill. Up until the point he'd seen Ava at the wedding, he had every intention of being with Kyrie. Now that Ava was on his mind, Kyrie wouldn't come close to compensating for Ava's absence.

To his dismay and annoyance, Ava caused unwarranted feelings when they were together. The ball of anxiety at the pit of his stomach expanded every time she was within his reach. The thought of it made him sick. She was just as young as his youngest sister and certainly off limits, King tried to convince himself.

The plan to play a quick game of Call of Duty: Black OPS was quickly replaced by his need to stew. King dragged his hands over his face before he plopped down onto the oversized, chocolate brown leather recliner that was tucked in a darkened corner of the room. He grabbed his remote that controlled everything, including the lights, heating system, television, and stereo to dim the lights and turn on his stereo.

Pandora's live stream of music played rhythm and blues group Silk's, *'Let's Make Love'.* He sipped on his hot tea and tried to figure out how he'd gone from wanting to shoot off his gun in Call of Duty to listening to a song that he'd used to seduce a number of willing women onto their backs during his college years. He laughed at that thought.

Aaliyah's, *'Can I Come Over'* began to drift from the speakers as a brisk knock at his door diverted his attention. He got to his feet and contemplated not answering, sure that Kyrie would be pissed enough to break the door down if he didn't. King knew she could hear the music.

King padded barefoot across the gleaming hardwood floor to the front door. Attitude and curses ripe on his lips died when he saw Ava standing there. Seconds passed as he stood shocked that she'd been on his mind, and now she was here, standing at his door, dressed in five-inch heels and a short, trench overcoat in the pouring rain. She carried an enormous purse on her shoulder and held an oversized umbrella to protect her delicate body from the angry showers.

Ava spoke first. "I'm getting wet. Aren't you gonna invite me in?"
If steam could have come out of his ears, it would have. King moved to the side to allow her access but asked, "Ava, what the fuck are you doing here?"

Ava rolled her eyes and stepped inside and handed him the umbrella to fold down. She left him at the door, removed her coat, simply letting it slid to the floor where she stood. She put her hands on her hips and posed in the middle of his living room.

King remained at the door, submitting a brief prayer for patience. He knew that Ava was stubborn but had no idea that she'd do something as reckless to show up at his house uninvited. Had she been any other female, he would have quickly shut the door in their face. She wasn't leaving him with much choice or respecting his request for her to stop pursuing him.

Boundaries were about to be crossed, King thought as he closed the door and turned. Then every coherent thought disappeared from his mind. She'd removed the coat and now stood clad only in thigh-high stockings and a matching black lace panties and bra set.

None of the illicit fantasies he'd had about her ever had Ava showing up at his door in her underwear. Not just any underwear, he corrected, but the, *I'm-getting-fucked-tonight* heels, bra, and panties. Need coiled throughout his insides, tying his muscles together in a tight ball. He shook his head to clear it. When that didn't work, King attempted to open his mouth to object, but his throat was entirely too dry to form any words.

They were past the point of conversation, he decided, when he felt the king begin to rise. He'd always enjoyed the slow journey to arousal but couldn't deny the quick punch of lust and straight to the point hardness he now felt.

King stalked towards to her and could see Ava's smile begin to form.

Death would become me if he denies me this simple pleasure, she thought.

"Yes?" she questioned right before he pulled her into his arms and had his lips on hers.

"Hell, yes," he breathed between the nips he took at her lips. The heat of her mouth as he delved his tongue in was like an answer to his silent prayers. Gently, her soft lips played with his as his fingers massaged the small of her back.

Hungrily, King took the kiss deeper. The urgency of his attraction had him devouring her mouth. They kissed for what felt like an eternity.

"You sure?" he demanded of her, tearing his mouth from hers. Months ago, she'd informed him that he would be her first. Knowing Ava, nothing had changed.

Ava let out a nervous laugh. "Of course, I'm sure. Are you?"

King didn't speak when he linked his fingers through Ava's and began leading her towards the stairs. There were no sounds coming from Ava's mouth, only the heavy breathing escaping from her lungs as she followed him up the stairs. She smiled to herself in victory.

The King had finally been checked.

The midnight blue walls of his bedroom gave her a jolt. She'd always suspected that he was a man who preferred muted tones and neutral shades, which she believed was a perfect match for his personality. They were adorned with wall shelves and a massive entertainment system, complete with a stereo, flat screen TV, and an Xbox.

Her thoughts of room décor soon became a distant memory as she was visually treated to the most inviting-looking California king bed she'd ever seen in her life. No one privileged enough to be allowed in his bedroom would ever be confused as to what the focal point of this room was.

Ava chuckled. There was no doubt that she'd be testing it out. She crawled onto the middle of the bed and leaned back seductively on her palms.

"You think you ready for me?" he inquired with a sleek grin, taking pleasure in her silent approval. King climbed onto the bed and hovered over her.

Ava could feel his breath tickle the fine hairs along the side of her face as she extended her neck to expose naked skin to his lips. King explored the bare plains, dusting kisses along her collarbone in a trail to her shoulders and up her neck to her ear.

Ava shivered as the promise of him filling her caused an indescribable anxiety.

Ava licked her lips as her hands went to the hem of his shirt. "I'm waiting," she returned, inching the hem of his undershirt up toward his stomach.

"I'm not who you think I am," King warned her as the shirt came off.

Ava shook her head and pecked at his lips. "This won't be what you think."

King's lips masterfully covered hers, demanding more than she gave. Her sweetness poured into him as Ava flicked her tongue over his before capturing it to suck on it. King's hands slid beneath her body, gathering her closer to him. Sharing his warmth, Ava gyrated her hips as she laid her back onto the bed, willing him to cover her.

Ava welcomed the feel of his weight as King settled between her thighs. She stroked his face as he kissed her in every place she'd ever dreamed of. She giggled as he made his way down her stomach, dipping his tongue in her navel. Ava breathed deeply as King gently traced an imaginary line to the moistness of her center as he tattooed his name into her silky folds.

No other woman had ever been so sweet, so open, so his.

King made his way back to her lips and nibbled at her mouth to sate a hunger he wasn't sure could be quenched by just having her. Ava blinked in response to the sensations she felt. Her heart beat rapidly as King linked their fingers together. He kissed alongside her neck, his breath tickling the hairs and making them stand on end. "Hmmm," Ava moaned.

"Hmm is right," King agreed. "This gon' be so right," he murmured into her ear as he slowly entered and began to sink into her. King opened his eyes when he was met with resistance and shot Ava an accusing look as if he had to reassess the situation. He'd known she was a virgin, but somehow the reality that he had to actually break that barrier left King hesitant. He held himself still as he searched her face. "Fuck, Ava, I can't," he resigned but didn't move as she unashamedly wrapped her thighs tighter and hugged him closer as not to break their connection.

"Yes, you can," Ava murmured, untangling their limbs. She framed his face in her hands said, "I am for you," and kissed away his doubts.

It took all his self-control to fight against the urge to push past the barrier with one swift thrust. She felt like heaven, spread open wide before him and offering him her most precious gift. And she'd chosen him.

She chose *him*, so like the stairway to heaven paved with good deeds, he took care on his journey there. King kissed her full on the lips and murmured the sincerest of apologies as he gave one hard thrust. Ava's body, quivering beneath his, tightened as she enclosed him into a fevered embrace. Her thighs slightly shook as he thrust again, and she whimpered in discomfort as another stroke parted her velvety warmth and melted around him.

Yes... She felt like paradise, just like he imagined heaven to be.

"You okay?" King asked, holding himself above her.

Ava bit her bottom lip and nodded her head, wondering if all women who lost their virginity felt so—so glorious inside, so beautifully content with the man filling them. "I'm fine," she quietly replied. A moment later, those passion-filled eyes rolled in the back in her head as King tested the depths of their union.

"Aaaah," she breathed as her hips began to slowly move in an attempt to control some of what she felt.

Ava smiled at what she could only describe as the heated deliciousness of hot chocolate, warmed to perfection, spread throughout her body.

Yes, you are for me, King thought as he lost himself in the pleasurable sensations they created with each other. Stroke after stroke her hips rose to meet him; they mated, curled around one another, intertwining the fires of their burning need. King lingered inside the warmth of her, attempting to make sense of the position he found himself in. There was no sense. It wasn't illogical that the first time with a woman was at best a testing of sorts to see if they were sexually

39

compatible. This was completely out of his scope of what was considered normal. Ava passed the test with flying colors. She was his. Signed, sealed, and delivered in the rarest of packages.

Ava's lips curved into a smile. She wasn't sure if it was the time for the whispering of sweet nothings or if pleasurable moans were enough to describe what he made her feel. When she opened her mouth to speak, King's lips expertly covered hers. The sensation building as he withdrew and re-entered her with deliberate slowness peaked as he nipped at her mouth. There was a lightening spark deep inside her as King hit her jackpot. "Ooooh. Right there... Right there," she moaned, curling around him as she reached her first orgasm, honey seeping.

The warmth of Ava wrapped around him kept him deep inside her as the familiar coil of heat began unraveling in what would be the most climatic release of his life. Spent, King collapsed on top of her and breathed her in.

"Ummm. Don't fall asleep on me," Ava said, happily thinking that he could stay where he was for an eternity.

Chapter Five

*G*roggily, *Sharae squeezed her* eyes tight as she fought off the sleepiness she felt. With her eyes still closed, Sharae extended her arm and brushed it across the empty space beside her. She slowly opened her eyes until they were just slits to be greeted by the darkened room. The early morning light crept along the curtain's borders, but the darkness still couldn't hide the fact that James had not come home.

Sharae frowned as she sat up. She wiped her eyes and shook her head to clear it, laughing to herself as she realized that she was alone in her bed. *Always alone.*

Her eyes shot to the clock. It was six a.m. She scanned the room for any traces of him. The pajamas that she'd set out the night before were still in the same space she'd left them. She'd fallen asleep while watching *Something Borrowed* as she waited for him.

A rush of worry came over her and had her reaching for her cell phone. Mind racing, close to raging, she dialed his number. It went directly to voicemail.

She called again, same outcome. Out of habit, she turned on the news to catch reports of any accidents and mishaps from the night before. She attempted to call him again.

Annoyed when she heard his voicemail recording, Sharae began to leave a message asking him to call her back as soon as possible.

The worry quickly turned to outrage when she noticed he'd sent her a text message at twelve a.m. saying that he couldn't get on the expressway because there were roadblocks and asking if she was okay. He'd texted her twenty minutes after that demanding her to answer. There was also a missed call from him.

She rolled her eyes. "Ahhhhh!" she let out a frustrated sigh. "I can't believe this shit! I told his ass," she murmured as she felt her eyes begin to water.

She'd weathered the history-making Hurricane Irene alone, and he wasn't answering the damn phone.

Sharae got out of her bed began to pace the floor as she rationalized his reasons for not being there. She called the studio, listened to the line ring. "James, call me back when you get this message. Your phone is going to voicemail and I'm worried," *only half worried.* She thought. The other half was fighting to be concerned because she wasn't entirely convinced that his absence had anything to do with the rain. "You better fuckin' be hurt. I'm serious," she added, ending the call and tossed the phone onto her bed.

Thoughts raced a mile a minute through her brain. If their roles were reversed, there would have been nothing that would have kept her from making it home to him especially during a storm that promised all kinds of destruction. She would have driven through hell and back to be with him, she reasoned. And he let some nut-ass rain and wind keep him from being there for her.

Why didn't he do the same? her conscience demanded of her.

There had to be a better reason than just road blocks. She'd spoken to him before the roads were closed and had even urged him to hurry in fear that he would not make it home.

Sharae sank down onto the edge of her bed and dragged her hands down her face. She shook her head as she felt the rush of emotion come to the surface. Her attempt to ward off the pain was futile as she bent over and let the tears flow. There were small pangs of hurt stabbing at her heart. How could he not come home to protect and keep her safe from the unknown?

She wrapped her arms around herself in consolation as her shoulders shook violently and the tears continued to pour. An hour passed, each minute was filled with a manifestation of her pain reflected through her tears.

Sharae collapsed onto the bed and took a few minutes to stare up at the ceiling. Her cell phone beeped and vibrated, alerting her of a new text.

Baby, my phone is close to dying, lost electricity for a while so couldn't charge it but I'ma be home as soon as possible. I love you.
She didn't want to be cliché but found herself thinking about that line in the movie *Boomerang* when Halle told Eddie, *Love should've brought your ass home last night*. She curled up onto her side and responded to the text.

Whatever, Jay…

The scent of his cologne seemed to permeate from his pillows as she let her face sink, soft cheeks into the fluffy mounds. She clenched her fist at her sides, brought them up to her eyes as her heart tightened, rolled over painfully in her chest. Aching, she buried her face into one of his pillows to muffle a low pitched scream and smother her fresh streams of tears.

Her heart stopped when she heard his ring tone. She ignored it.

It rang again, Mary J. Blige pleading, *"Give me yoooou… Give me you… Give me all your love…"* Sharae finally answered as she put the phone up to her free ear.

43

"What the fuck you mean whatever?!" James's voice thundered through the receiver.

Sharae sighed heavily. "Just what I said. You weren't here. The whole fuckin' house could have blown away, and you weren't here," she responded calmly.

She heard him suck his teeth. "What was I supposed to do? Drive through the damn roadblocks?" he shouted.

"You were supposed to be here!" she shouted back. She waited for his response, and when silence continued, Sharae added, "What don't you understand about that? All these days and nights, you been missing. But last night is a night you should have been here, and you were not."

Sharae was devastated that he hadn't come home. That he didn't see the need to be here. And that he had the nerve to respond negatively to her reaction.

In her mind, Sharae assumed that James didn't care and that whatever and whomever he was preoccupied with at the studio was more important than being with her. She shook her head as she realized that he didn't get it, no matter what she said or how she said it. He would never get it.

Sharae's throat was so raw that it hurt to swallow.

"I'm tired, Jay. I'll see you when you get home."

"Rae? Sharae?"

She disconnected the call.

The voices from the television were covering the reported destruction that Hurricane Irene had caused. A house in North Philadelphia section of the city had been completely destroyed. She tried to dismiss the fact that it was located only three blocks from the studio.

Sharae bit her lip as remorse ate at her for being snappy at him. Then she rolled her eyes. She didn't give a damn if North Philly had gotten swallowed up in its entirety. It did not justify his reasoning for not making it home. Nothing would.

He gets on my nerves.

He'd spend the rest of his week making up for it, she decided as she slipped back into a welcomed sleep.

Chapter Six

*N*ow, how am I going to explain showing up at her house unannounced like some nut-ass, lovesick puppy? King wondered as he hesitated to press the call button to Ava's apartment.

He imagined Ava would be thrilled at his presence and would not turn him away, but he struggled for clarity. There was no justified reason for him committing an act that he himself despised. It had been a week since Ava had shown up at his house wearing nothing more than a trench coat and her underwear, offering herself as a sacrifice. In that moment, she'd gifted him with something she'd never trusted another man with.

Her innocence.

Now a week later, with the vivid flashbacks of their seductive encounter, King was annoyed that she treated the matter as if it were nothing. She was acting as if they didn't have mind-blowing sex for more than a day and a half. And ever since, he'd been ducking Kyrie's calls, aggressive advances, and a pop-up visit, all because he couldn't get Ava out his mind. The young woman had him open, he admitted to himself for lack of a better term.

King shook his head; it was more than sex. It had to be more than sex for both of them. It irritated him that he'd hoped to see her during their training sessions, but Ava hadn't showed up. She'd texted him some bullshit-ass excuse about a last minute group project meeting.

And fuck— He'd actually warned her not to have stars in her eyes about their relationship, but could now see stars of his own begin to form. Why else would he be at her doorstep like a lovesick fool?

Hadn't he talked himself out of any doubt he was feeling about being with her and came to the conclusion that he had to see her again? King sighed heavily. If he were honest, he would acknowledge that he was afraid of hurting her as he'd been known to do, afraid of loving her and having her hurt him.

Shit, how the hell did he get here? Frowning as if his thoughts disturbed him, he turned around to walk out the foyer and stood beneath the entryway. And that was how Ava found him as she walked toward the building after getting out of her car.

Ava smiled victoriously.

He was there. The King had come to her, though he seemed to be having second thoughts Ava noticed as she heard him swear and go back into the building.

Feeling triumphant, but without saying a word, Ava let him go into the building and watched as he pounded numbers into the intercom. Ava could see his temper flare in his eyes as he looked up when the call went unanswered. She felt a trickle of power seep through her veins as she allowed King to repeat the action without announcing her presence. Thrilled, Ava almost laughed out loud when she heard him say, "Fuck" after the voicemail picked up, informing him that she wasn't home.

Overjoyed with emotions of love and triumph, Ava wiped the smug expression from her face and planned to act surprised when she "bumped" into him. She purposely turned the volume of her phone to the max level and began to sing along with 112 as the group belted out, *'Nowhere'* as she stepped into the foyer. She instantly began rummaging through her huge black Gucci purse in search of her keys while pretending not to notice him.

Ava was clearly consumed in her music that she didn't even have her keys out ready to have instant access to get inside of the building. She paid absolutely no attention to her surroundings, King noted. The music was so loud he could hear the buzz of sound pumping from her earbuds. Not one care if there was a burglar behind her. Hell, she didn't even notice him standing there. He made a step toward the door at the same time she stepped up to put the key into the lock, startling her and finally getting her attention.

The welcoming smile doused the fire building within him.

"Hey," she said, removing one earbud from her ear. "You here to see me?"

King cleared his throat. "Umm, you should definitely pay more attention to your surroundings. And I don't know anyone else in the building. I didn't mean to just show up, but from our last text, I thought you were going to be home already."

King cursed himself. He hated having her think that he was clocking her time.

Ava held out her arms to display Fresh Grocer bags. "Stopped at the market for snacks."

"Oh, so you 'bout to cook?" he asked, relieving her of the two shopping bags. If she wasn't going to fuss over him being there uninvited, neither would he.

Ava laughed and shook her head. "I said snacks, but I'll let you try to talk me into making you a meal," she told him coyly as she let them into the lobby.

They made small talk about their day as they made their way up to her third-floor apartment. King didn't wait for an official tour as he walked around the two-bedroom apartment while Ava quickly put away her groceries. The apartment was neat and organized. Her bedroom

48

was painted a shade of buff— he had no idea why he knew what buff was, King reasoned as he took in the warm borders of tawny browns, the four poster canopy bed was draped with what looked like sheer orange fabric. The bed itself was topped with mountains of burnt orange, and tan pillows and small accent pieces sitting on top of a huge duvet cover. An unbidden image of her sprawled invitingly naked across that bed whipped through his mind. He closed the door as if the image would disappear, all the while biting back the urge to just pluck her from the kitchen and have his way with her.

She'd turned the second bedroom into a walk-in closet. It reminded him of his own second bedroom.

Common ground, King thought. They shared a love of clothing and nice shelving. There was a wall lined with cedar oak shelves that held columns of jeans and pants. He imagined the one large chest of drawers held lace panties, bras, fishnet stockings and other undergarments. Shirts, dresses, vests, sweaters, and coats hung from several showroom-like garment racks on one side of the room. Another wall held boxes of shoes, sneakers, and boots. If he had to guess, there were at least twenty boxes of designer shoes stacked neatly. And he couldn't even begin to count the number of bags in their protective sacks. There were large ones and small ones, color-coded and hanging from hooks. He noted Gucci, Louis Vuitton, and YSL immediately but didn't have the patience to find out who the other designers were. Based on her appreciation of the finer and more expensive things in life, King figured his pockets were going to be empty if and when he took this to the next level.

When had he decided that he wanted to spoil her with luxury handbags?

King shook his head and he peeked into the bathroom. It was clean, and it smelled lavender fresh. *Huge points for that alone*, he thought, although he couldn't imagine Ava having any hygiene issues. He made his way back into the large living and dining room areas. There was a computer desk and chair with a small file cabinet in one corner near a window. He could imagine her sitting there blogging or professional social media-ing, he meant networking. He laughed at the chalkboard wall covering over the desk. There was a To-Do List written in hot pink. At the top of the list were the words *Graduate in 3 months!* It was underlined four times in four different colors.

"Well, looks like you gave yourself the tour," Ava interrupted.

"I like your style. That closet is crazy," King told her.

Ava shrugged unembarrassed. She made no habit of making excuses for what she liked, just as she made no mistake in choosing him to be hers.

"What?" he asked, catching sight of her smile.

Honesty rushed out. "I've imagined you here. A lot."

"I'm here. I really apologize for not calling first. But I had..." he held his arms out to summon her because no more words were needed.

Comfortable with her newfound power, Ava followed up by saying, "I know. You just had to see me."

King nodded. She deserved to hear the words, though. Despite her innocence, Ava had to know that her absence that week had driven him completely mad. "I *needed* to see you. I think you tryna treat me like a young boah, and I'm not having it."

Ava tilted her head and squinted at him. "No, I'm not."

King was unsure if his presence informed her that she was all he could think of, yet... Ava *was* all he could think of. "What are your plans for the evening?" he asked.

Ava shrugged, sending a regretful glance at her computer desk. She had to type a review and post it on her blog, revise a paper, answer questions from inboxes and check her email.

"Nothing."

"Would you like to go to dinner with me?"

"Like a date?"

"Yes, like a date. I want more than you showing up at my house in your trench coat."

As much as she wanted to accept his invitation, duty called. There would be no way she could get all that done and go out to dinner with him. "Actually, I'm lying. I'm working on a deadline. I have a review, a paper, a post, and some emails to respond to before I do another thing. If you don't mind hanging out, I can whip you something up."

"How about I cook and you do your work?" King offered.

Ava eyed him. "You can cook?"

"Hell yea, I can cook." Hadn't his momma taught him? He also had a degree in food and nutrition to compliment his kinesiology degree.

Ava laughed, closing the distance between them. "Sounds great to me." She flung her arms around his neck and reached up on her tiptoes to peck his lips. She had meant for the kiss to be soft and playful but it quickly turned into an intensely passionate one as King banded his arms around her, molding Ava's body to his.

King took all of what he felt for her and gave it back in his kiss. Barely audible, he murmured, "Missed you," as he put considerable effort into devouring her mouth.

Ava had one arm crooked around his neck while the other crept up to hold his head as he continued to hungrily kiss her, removing any thoughts, except of him.

She hummed in appreciation. To hell with whatever work needed to be done. "All that can wait."

King stopped kissing her. "Nawl, get your work done. This is going to take all night," he whispered in her ear.

His dangerous tone sent rippling waves of heat over her skin. Ava smiled as he touched a kiss to her nose and pointed her in the direction of her computer.

~ ~

Sharae

The delivery of two dozens of red and yellow roses to her office was enough of a hint to her coworkers and friends that James was in the dog house. Three workers had already stopped in her office to chat and see what the special occasion was. Sharae had learned to brush off the annoyance of inter-office nosiness. She even found herself laughing about it during lunch with Tamika, one of her closest friends.

They celebrated that the sun was shining high in the sky and used that as an excuse to walk down Walnut St. to check out the shops and to have an extended lunch at one of the sidewalk Bistros.

Sharae ordered a grilled chicken salad, staying close as possible to her meal plan. Tamika, on the other hand, took the opportunity to indulge in a salmon burger and fries.

"Samantha was all like, 'Umm, it must be nice'," Sharae told Tamika as she nibbled on her lettuce. "I smiled and said, 'You don't even know the half of it.'"

Tamika laughed. "I bet she smiled and was waiting for you to tell her more."

Sharae's bottom lip dropped to mimic the stunned "O" that Samantha had displayed.

"Too funny. You know better than to tell these hoes your business up in there. They'll all be talking 'bout your ass like you the latest unfit mother or father."

Sharae nodded in agreement. "Don't I know it?"

"Umm, and you know half these hoes be having they eye on him when he be up in the office."

"Girl, all that fineness hiding his sneakiness. I think he's been lying," she confessed to her friend.

There was no surprised smirk on Tamika's lips or confused look in her eyes, Sharae realized. Tamika was her female version of King and knew her inside out. They'd become fast friends during their training program with the department and had been the closest of friends ever since. Sharae was her maid of honor at her wedding and was also godmother to Tamika's brand new baby girl, Camille. Tamika's husband Stephen was friends with James, and Tamika had introduced the two.

"I keep telling you that you're too predictable. You need to pop up on his ass to make sure he is where he says he is when he says he is. You ain't crazy enough, though," Tamika told her. Her eyes rolled to emphasize her advice.

"I'm not into that."

Tamika sucked her teeth and gave her a head-on look. "Well, you better get into it. You know how many girls be hanging around studios? He fine, got major swagger, and he own a studio. Steve ass cain't even go down there. You know there are plenty hoes on his ass."

Sharae swallowed the lump in her throat. "I know that. I've been down there. All the regular people know who I am—"

Tamika held up her fork to make her point. "Girl, ain't no groupie bitches worried about you, and if he there more than he's at home, you don't know what he saying to them." She dipped her fries in Sharae's extra salad dressing.

It was just like Tamika to breathe life into her fears. That's why she loved her. Tamika never shied away from telling her the truth or what she thought her opinion of the truth was.

"Sometimes, things are not as they seem, and I don't like jumping to conclusions without any proof."
Tamika's hand reached out to grab hold of hers, causing their eyes to meet. "There is nothing wrong with paying attention to that feeling in your gut that says something is out of place. Pay attention; God gave us intuition for a reason."

"I wanted to think that it was the strain of both of us having such demanding jobs. I was so busy with the contract for the state last year, we barely spent any time together. Then he was spending all his time working and making the studio happen. I thought it would ease up when he took the leave of absence. Instead, he now spends even more time there."

"Tell him how you feel. Stop thinking these nuccas are smarter than they really are. Sometimes they don't know something is wrong until we tell them. On the other hand, sometimes they're being sneaky and dumb, thinking we won't find out."

"There's always an argument when I say that we not spending enough time with one another. He just keeps asking me to be patient and reminds me how patient he was with me and all my stuff."

Tamika sighed and figured that James probably was cheating. His behavior did fit the profile of a cheater. "These niggas want they cake and wanna eat it too."

Sharae sucked her teeth and laughed as she thought of King. He always made it a point to argue that; of course, men wanted their cake and wanted to be able to eat it too. Who wouldn't? "The problem comes when he wants her cake, and hers, and that extra piece in the freezer." Sharae dramatically put her hand to her forehead. "Oh my God, I think I'm the piece in the freezer."

Tamika shrugged and rolled her eyes. "Is that what you think? That he having all the cake in the world?"

Sharae closed her eyes and said, "There has to be someone else. He doesn't call me like he used to. The 'just because' text messages are damn near nonexistent. When he is at home, we're rarely intimate. He says he's preoccupied. I say he's fucking someone else."

"You know your man better than he does. If you ready to go digging, are you going to be ready for what you find?" She could already hear her husband Stephen's booming voice telling her to 'mind her own damn business.'

Sharae shrugged in response. She was tired of the uncertainty and possible lies. "It's the only one way to find out."
Her cell phone began to ring. Tamika laughed. "He must can feel when you're talking shit about him."
Sharae laughed as she answered, "Hey, Babe, wassup?"

~ ~

When she returned to her office an hour later, the six case record folders she'd requested from Samantha were stacked on her desk. Sharae rolled her eyes at Samantha's timing. She'd expected to stroll into her office and then stroll right back out an hour later with no work in between. The salad she'd eaten threatened to send her off into la la land as she was aching to close her eyes and lay her head down on the desk.

Just for a moment, she promised herself as she let her cheek rest on the desk. After a second, her eyes snapped opened just as it registered the name she'd caught sight of before closing her eyes. *Daneen Roberts.*

Sharae frowned to herself. Where had she seen that name?

The girl from Facepage she acknowledged. An eerie feeling came over her. Why the hell was this girl suddenly popping up all over her life? "Stupid heffa on Facepage chilling all day and her kids in DHS custody," she murmured aloud.

Sharae pulled out her cell phone, logged into her Facepage account, and tried to pull Daneen up in her friend search. Nothing came up. It struck her as odd that she was no longer the girl's friend. Obviously, Daneen had deleted her. She searched her by her name and was not surprised when the girl profile came up and the last comment from an hour before was about her chilling.

These young girls never learn, Sharae judged. She scrolled down, reading more of Daneen's feed. Someone Daneen knew asked if she rapped. The girl responded no with an "lol" and explained that her dude owned the studio and that was why she was there so much. Sharae imagined the girl's voice was as ghetto as the pictures she displayed.

A sick feeling began to rise into her throat. Sharae could feel her stomach clench, and her heart begin to pound heavily in her chest. She could feel her temperature rise as she hurriedly scanned all the feeds.

None of them specifically named James as her boyfriend; in fact, hadn't she said something about a Semaj the day of the hurricane?

No damn way she talking 'bout my man. I know this nigga ain't fuckin' with this dusty heffa. The urge to scream was won over by her need to move. She stood up and began pacing. She held the phone in her hand and continued to read through all the feeds.

The usually frigid room suddenly became stuffy and humid. Sharae came out of the sunshine yellow linen blazer she wore and let it fall in a pile on her desk. Her adrenaline was pumping as she read her posts line for line. The day of the hurricane when she'd spoken to James and he was in Fresh Grocer, Daneen also made a post referencing how crowded the market was.

Sharae laughed to keep from crying.

No jumping to conclusions, she instructed as fire raged in her heart and began to spike through her veins.

Jump all over conclusions, girl...

Black spots began to appear in her vision, the pounding in her head felt like a ball threatening to bounce right out of her temple. Cursing the spots, Sharae squeezed her eyes shut, then opened them, hoping they'd disappear. She put her hand to her head and rushed to her seat. Dropping the phone onto her desk, she opened the case file and began to read over the girl's case.

A hoarse, strangled sounding scream erupted from her mouth before she could stop it. She dropped the file onto the floor in front of her and just stared at it in total disbelief.

James's old address stared boldly back at her. There was no fucking way that the address on this girl's case was correct. She logged into the system to check. And there it was for sure.

Has to be some crazy type of coincidence, she rationalized. He'd moved from that address two years before when he'd bought their house. He had not been displaying signs of cheating then. Or maybe he was more careful about it.

"Are you okay?" a hesitant voice belonging to the office clerk questioned from her opened doorway. She looked up and saw at least seven people huddled in her doorway.

A rush of emotion promised to overtake her when she caught sight of Tamika walking up to squeeze through the crowd.

Concern was apparent in Tamika's eyes as she stood beside Sharae and questioned her friend, "Rae, you okay?"

When Sharae failed to respond, Tamika turned to the onlookers and said, "Excuse me" to the person blocking the door, before closing it in all their faces. "Nosy asses," she murmured absently, turning back to Sharae who still sat quietly staring at the file on the floor.

Fuck weird coincidences and conclusions.

She couldn't speak.

All she could do was think. Eyes closed, Sharae mentally scanned every deed and action of James's that made her reevaluate things over the past two years. All those weird feelings, all the notions, all the signs were building up to this moment.

He wouldn't do this to me. Not with some chickenhead with three fuckin' kids that she isn't even taking care of.

Even with the reassuring thoughts battling the ones that felt more like common sense, Sharae still found herself decidedly sure that he was. This couldn't be a mistake; there was no way that all of this was pure coincidence. They're always in the same place, at the same time.

She wasn't sure if the stabbing pains in her chest were real or a figment of her imagination. Everyone had always accused her of being overly dramatic.

So, this is what real heartbreak feels like? Every heartbeat felt like spiking shards of glass, tightening like a clenched fist inside her chest repeatedly shattering it to pieces. She could feel the tears wreaking havoc on her senses as she forced her tear ducts to hold them in. There was no way that she was going to have an emotional breakdown in front of Tamika and the rest of her office. She damn well would wait until she got in her car, so the tears would have to hold out until then.

"Rae, what's wrong?" Tamika asked again, this time touching her arm.

Sharae grunted out another frustrated scream as she stood up. She did not care that the entire office would be talking about this tomorrow.

She grabbed her blazer and yellow Elly Clay tote bag. "I have to go. I'm cool. I will call you later." She started to walk away but went back to grab the folder from the floor. Without a second thought, she left the room. She ignored people's questions regarding her well-being and walked straight to the elevators.

Sharae punched at the elevator button impatiently as she noticed people lingering around to watch her. Filled with anxious fury, she burst through the exit and started down the five-story flight of stairs in a hurry. Adrenaline pumping, Sharae ran down the last flight, cursing herself for wearing four-inch heels to work.

Chapter Seven

Thoughts of murder bounced around in her mind as Sharae raced her car northbound on Broad Street going towards Dauphin Street, speeding through most red traffic lights. Sharae nervously bit her bottom lip as she pulled up in front of the massive building that housed Horizon Studios. She parked her car directly behind James's Audi Q7 SUV.

Sharae shook her head to clear her thoughts and pulled down her mirror to take in a quick assessment of her appearance.

She felt as if she was going crazy. Sharae could feel pulse point at her left temple throb as it begged to be massaged away. Tears made their way down her cheeks, even as she wiped them away. She took in a deep breath and opened her purse to search for the emergency pack of Motrin she kept there. She cursed herself for not carrying the prescription- strength ones. She picked up the bottle of water from the console beside her and downed the water and the two small round pills in one gulp. She closed her eyes as she swallowed and prayed that she would find relief from the pounding ache.

Sharae was certain it wouldn't matter as the headache was bound to grow after the confrontation she was imagining. She could already see it playing out. There was no doubt in her mind that James would deny it and be angry and defensive that she had the nerve to approach him on the subject. He'd probably shout and try to dismiss her claims as her own self- depreciating insecurities. Their future as a couple depended on his actions, and he damn well was going to provide some answers.

The thought that he was putting some skanky broad up in his old apartment tormented her. He was cheating on her with a jobless woman who had three children with different fathers.

All those inklings and uncertain feelings now had reason. *How could he do this to me?* Humiliation flooded her heart. She could testify that she felt its long fingers wrapping themselves around her throat to suffocate her. It mirrored itself in her reflection. She ran her fingers beneath her eyes to even out the puffs underneath them. When she realized that the tale of her tears would still show she placed a pair of sunglasses over her tear-stained eyes.

Sharae swallowed her nerves and got out of the car. She stopped at the door to request admittance into the building by saying that she had a scheduled session with one of the engineers. She made her way up to the third floor by way of the three warehouse-sized flights of stairs without losing her breath or courage. She did cough as the layers of dust inflamed her allergies.

She took notice of the art studio's collages and sculptures as she rounded the corner with the worn wooden floorboard creaking beneath her shoes. She stopped at the first door on her left and stuck her head inside the office. The computer screen was still active, and the chair behind the desk was pushed back from the desk. She stood where she was for a second, contemplating if she should wait inside the office or just go back to the recording rooms.

Impatiently, she walked down the hall to the two recording rooms. She peeked through the small square which exposed the booth. James could be seen sitting behind the engineering desk speaking to his cousin Taron who co-owned the studio with him.

They both turned their attention to her when the door opened and she stepped through it. James was up and walking toward her before she reached him. Sharae could see the clear confusion of her unannounced visit as he caught her around the waist.

"Babe, what you doing here?" he inquired, his voice brisk with authority.

Sharae freed herself from his grasp. "Who the fuck is Daneen?" she demanded.

Immediately, his lips twisted into a frown, distorting the truth that could be read in his handsome face. "Who?"

Sharae removed her sunglasses, tilted her neck to the side, put her hands on her hips, and questioned him again. "Some bitch named Daneen. Why the fuck is she living at your old address, and why the hell is she hanging around here saying that you are her goddamn boyfriend?"

Taron coughed to let them know that he was still present in the room. Sharae's eyes darted to Taron's. "I know you know what the fuck I'm talking about, so don't stand here and try to deny it!" she screamed at James.

James made a motion to grab her arm, which she avoided by sidestepping him. The glare in his eyes expressed the anger that he would not allow his temper to display. His exterior was controlled. "Rae, I'm recording somebody. Don't come in here with no stupid bullshit!" he told her.

"Stupid shit?" she repeated to herself. "You think this stupid? That this bitch is openly stating that you her dude?"

"I'on know what the fuck you think you saw, but I don't mess with nobody named Daneen, and it be a whole bunch of bitches in here wishing they my girl."

"Won't y'all take that into the office before y'all have everybody coming in here," Taron suggested when the artist being recorded came out of the sound-proof booth to see the action.

Sharae rolled her eyes. Taron was right. She turned around and walked out the door.

"What the fuck is up with that?" Taron asked James.

James cleared his throat and then shook his head. "Man, I don't know what she found."

"Who the hell she talkin' 'bout?"

"Fuckin' Goldie," James answered.

Taron sucked his teeth. "Damn, told you that fuckin' girl was nothing but trouble. She ain't here is she?" Taron knew that she could be found at the studio day in and day out while James recorded. It had become a regular hangout for her and her other girlfriends who skipped the welfare to work programs.

Taron shook his head in disgust at his cousin. Sharae was a good girl. She was beautiful, independent, and just as bad as James claimed his jumpoff, Goldie, to be. He inwardly hoped that James would be able to get himself out of the mess he'd created. As James made his exit, Taron also hoped for all their sakes that Daneen did not show up while Sharae was still in the building.

Sharae was not in the hall when James finally left the recording room. He narrowed his eyes as he made his way down the hall. How the hell had she found out about Daneen? Not once had she mentioned this girl's name. He huffed as he prepared himself for Sharae's onslaught of accusations and rampant emotions.

When he reached the door, he found one of the recording artists standing against the door frame speaking to Sharae. "Hey, Jones what's up?" he asked the dark-skinned round guy.

"I was waitin' to see if you could record me later on, and I was tryna see if shawty needed any help. I need an hour," Jones told James.

Annoyed and territorial, James stepped inside the room and stood behind Sharae. "Jones, this is my wife, Rae," he informed him.

Sharae observed the man as his eyes widened and his mouth dropped open an inch in surprise. It was replaced quickly by a firm-set face, but she'd seen the uncertainty in his eyes. Jones's response was enough to tell her that James had been in the studio pretending like he was single. Jones cleared his throat and said, "My apologies. Nice to meet you, Rae."

Sharae nodded in acknowledgment but didn't speak. She was not in the mood to exchange pleasantries with anyone.

"Jones, I got you in like an hour after I'm done recording with Rell," James told the guy.

Jones spared one last glance at Sharae then dipped his head and coughed before he left the room. Sharae turned to face James as he closed the door to ensure privacy. She hoped for his sake that the office was soundproof.

"I don't know—"

"And before you start lying, I'm asking you to tell me the truth." James rolled his eyes and shrugged his shoulders. "Babe, I don't even know what you're talkin' 'bout. There is no girl in here thinkin' she my girl," he told her, making a step to grab her forearms in an attempt to have her look him in the eyes.

Sharae dragged her hands down her face as she fought to release herself from his grasp. Her emotions were so raw that tears began to escape from her eyes. "Get off of me!" she shouted at him. Her throat ached as she swallowed.

James held her tight despite her attempts to free herself. "Rae, look at me. I ain't fuckin' with nobody. I'm here to work. Period!. I don't have time to be fuckin' with none of these hoodrat bitches that be up in here."

Sharae knew better than to believe what he was saying. "So again, why is this hoe living at your old address? And up in here talkin' bout her dude own it?"

James let out an aggravated sigh. "Where did you even get this from? I don't even know a fuckin' Daneen."

63

"You know her. Y'all call her Goldie; her boyfriend's name is Semaj, and he owns this studio. That is James spelled backward, Nigga."

"So the girl be in here, but she ain't fuckin' with me!"

"She requested me as her Facepage friend a while ago."
James sucked his teeth and finally let Sharae's arms go. His eyes turned hard and serious. "You in here on some stupid ass Facepage shit? I have a lot to do, and I don't have time for this bullshit," he told her.

Suspiciously, she eyed him. This was the start of his making her feel like this was nothing. Like she was jumping to conclusions. She already knew it, but she could feel her courage begin to wane under his steely gaze. "I don't care what you talking 'bout. You fuckin' her, *and* you putting this bitch up?" she shouted as she approached him. She pushed him.

The unexpected physical contact threw him off his balance. "Rae, I'm being patient—"

She poked at his forehead with her finger. "You being patient? Don't make me fuck you up in here, James. You lying!"

He grabbed her hands before she was able to mug him in the forehead again. "Rae, stop fuckin' playing with me," James warned before continuing. "And the girl that you're talking 'bout mess with my man Maj who lives upstairs from the old apartment. And as far as she saying she fuck with the owner, it's fuckin' Fakepage. Bitches be on there lying all day long. So again, if you're done with this stupid shit, can I get back to work?"

Sharae searched her memory for the name Semaj. Was that the guy's name who lived upstairs? She wondered. She did not recall them being friendly with one another. She could only remember speaking to him in passing. On the other hand, she contemplated James was a very social person and could have had a friendlier relationship with his neighbor than what she was aware of.

How could this possibly make any sense? She was certain that she was correct. Sharae began to add her evidence together: Daneen's friend request, them being in Fresh Grocer at the same time, the apartment. It didn't add up to him cheating with Daneen. At least not with the information he'd supplied back to her. Anything was possible.

Sharae wanted to slap the smug look off his face. He was successful at making her feel small. The headache grew more. "I'm going home to lay down. I'll see you later," she told James.

James smiled and folded his arms over his chest. "You was tryna fuck me up in here, huh? Babe, don't worry, I would never jeopardize what I have with you for none of these nut-ass broads." James ignored her protests and wrapped his arms around her waist. "I love you. And I forgive you for wilding out in here. Just remember that you can't believe everything that you read on Facepage." James gave a dismissive shrug. "I'm not even on Facepage."

Chapter Eight

*S*haraes's head was still pounding a half hour later when she decided that she would meet King at the gym to discuss the situation with him. She knew that he would give her his honest opinion from a man's point of view. He promised to do as much when she'd phone him briefly to ensure that he'd be available to see her.

She hopelessly gave up sitting outside the studio, hoping to catch Daneen entering the building as she checked her watch and mentally calculated the amount of time it would take to get to City Line Ave from where she was. She'd go straight up York Street, over the Strawberry Mansion Bridge, and be there in less than twenty minutes.

King could lay it out for her point blank. She contemplated going to the apartment and knocking on the door. She figured it would prove pointless; she already knew that Daneen resided there, so it would be no surprise at the woman answering the door. She would have difficulties proving that James was there as well.

Unless...

Unless, she pushed the woman aside and raided Daneen's space while she searched for signs of her cheating boyfriend.

No, I can't do that, Sharae decided as she navigated Brooke through the ragged streets of North Philadelphia.

Still, the idea nagged her.

It would be an absolute no— no. And completely inappropriate, given her ties to DHS, not to mention beneath her own code of ethics. It barely registered on her moral compass. Yet, she felt the need to act swiftly and aggressively.

The woman would probably call the police. From what she'd seen of her, she'd better be in for a fight. "Kee Kee" a name she'd sarcastically given side chicks everywhere looked like she was the rowdy type.

It was okay, she resolved quietly. Things done in the dark always came to the light. She figured that James could lie in this present moment but was certain that his lies would be uncovered, and not by his own actions but from those of another.

Yea, she was going to keep a close eye on Ms. Daneen's Facepage postings.

It had always been her personal opinion that men did not know how to handle their business when it came to being with other women while involved in committed relationships. Didn't she have King and her closest male cousins as examples of men falsely believing that they were smarter than women? Even her father had slipped a time or two, and while her mother seemed to have been either too blind or too naïve to notice the signs until, she was not. She couldn't quite understand why the need for lies was so necessary for them.

Stupid nucca is going mess up and his little girlfriend will tell it all. They constantly making these bitches feel more important than they really are. Sharae smiled at the thought of catching him red-handed but felt her heart turn over painfully in her chest. Damn, if the outcome wasn't destined to hurt.

With her mind convinced that James was lying and that Daneen was his side piece of ass, Sharae shook her head. *Why would he ever mess with other women when he has me?* she wondered.
They were polar opposites.

Whereas Sharae was childless, Daneen had three children by three different men and was apparently or proven to be an unfit mother because they had all been taken away by DHS, the very agency that Sharae worked for.

Sharae was sophisticated, cultured, and educated as evidenced by her multiple degrees Daneen had barely graduated from a high school as a result of a troubled and unruly youth.

The woman appeared short and petite from her pictures, whereas Sharae herself was taller. The one thing they did have in common were wide hips and a large backside. She had to admit that Daneen was shaped like a brick house, a shorter and much thinner version of her own body, Sharae figured, once she'd lost all the weight she'd gained.

As a nervous habit, she bit the inside of her cheek. Even with the thought of her weight being a contributing factor to his cheating, the woman in the Facepage pictures and the one she'd conjured in her mind were busted. The tacky golden weaves, drugged and glassed over eyes, and barely-clothed body may have excited the tons of men who viewed her profile, but that look did nothing for her. In her opinion, no matter how tight the girl's body was, it didn't hold a candle to her naturally beautiful looks or her overall physical package.

For the remainder of the ride to City Line Ave, in Bala Cynwyd, PA, Sharae listened to a mixed genre playlist of slow songs. She cautiously eyed the parking lot before deciding to go into the Sunoco gas station beside it. As much as she enjoyed working out there, she hated the parking. It seemed like everyone in the city of Philadelphia worked out at what she liked to call Club L.A Fitness and was there every day after work. The gym had very flexible hours, she suspected, so they could meet the demanding schedule of its clientele. King was using the location to meet his clients until he was able to afford enough space to open a small gym of his own.

She really didn't feel like it—smiling, presenting a happy façade for all the other gym members' benefits.
At this point, it was either the gym and a Motrin or an Ambien and home.
Going home was still a ways away; it was rush hour, and since she was already there, it made absolutely no sense not to go in.

She pulled up behind the freshly washed and waxed silver Range Rover with a familiar license plate. Her heart sped up as she anticipated seeing the owner whom she'd affectionately named Mr. Fine. She exited the car, making quick work of swiping her bank card to pay for her gas.

Mr. Fine, her certified eye candy. For the moment, he'd act as her painkiller. The sight of him was enough to make the jumbled mess with James sit on her back burner. Daydreaming and damn-near stalking him with her eyes during her daily workouts had served as motivation to get Sharae through plenty of dull moments on the treadmill and revolving staircases. She weaved a wicked scene, starring him aggressively ripping at her top to release her breast into his awaiting mouth as she bounced up and down on him in the passenger seat of his Range Rover. Those very same thoughts had her ogling him as he emerged from the gas station folding a receipt into his wallet.

She had no idea who he was, what part of the city he lived in, or what he did for a living. She'd seen him leave a couple times in a three-piece suit, it had to have been tailored because it fit him too nicely to have been off the rack of some store. So she imaged him as banker or lawyer, something white collar that went with the suit and car. All six feet plus of his golden-toned body and his undeniably handsome face. From their usual distance, she figured his eyes were an almond brown. Not as light as her own, but if the sun shined in them, she was sure they would be a shade brighter. The dark, curly hair was cut into a modern day frohawk. She remembered seeing the same haircut on Usher.

Sharae bit her bottom lip as she took in the sight of him. She'd never thought a neatly trimmed beard could be so sexy until seeing one on him. His athletically-toned body displayed the results from daily weight-lifting and bench pressing though he wasn't overly bulky like a bodybuilder but still managed to fill out his suits and shirts. His sculpted forearms were sleeved with tattoos she'd never been close enough to see what the intricate body art actually was. If she admitted it, Sharae felt like a stalker but didn't care either way. What good was eye candy if you couldn't admire it, imagine how wonderfully delicious it would taste.

The way he walked exuded that he was a man confident with his position in this world. His aura demanded attention. She was but helpless to give in to the urge of the silent command and pay him the attention he so deserved. His entire being made her mouth water. His presence, when in close enough proximity, had the ability to send her into a nervous, adolescent-like fit. It wasn't as if she'd ever actually have the nerve to act on her attraction and speak to him. The polite smiles and nods were enough.

Sharae swallowed as she assumed the sweat ring around the collar of his gray shirt and under his armpits meant that he'd already worked out.

A ball of lust tightened in the pit of her stomach as she stalked him with her eyes. Mr. Fine climbed into his car and sent her a wave of acknowledgment before pulling off. She was appreciative that the sunglasses covered the desire in her eyes.

The growing cloud of lust deflated in a puff, leaving imaginary remnants swirling in front of her eyes the minute her phone began to ring with James's ringtone.

Sharae rolled her eyes even as she answered the call, "What?"

"What are you doing?" James inquired. His level tone did not indicate any of the earlier friction between the two of them.

"Nothing; came to meet King at the gym for some kickboxing," she told him.

He cleared his throat. "I guess you gonna imagine kicking my ass then?"

"There's no point for that, right? She's Semaj's girl and doesn't have anything to do with us," she countered.

"Rae, if you're going to be tripping over some broad that I'm not even fuckin', then you need to let me know. I'm chasing this money right now, and I don't have time for the stupid shit."

Sharae frowned as she started the engine to her car. She made a quick right and another right into the parking lot of LA Fitness. She made a quiet survey of the lot and prayed that one of the people exiting the gym would pull out of one of the spaces closer to the front. She figured from the looks of it, she'd have to park on the other side. As she caught sight of a thin woman walking in front of her car, she tuned out her conversation with James.

Within five minutes, they'd come to the same conclusion as they had when she'd departed the studio.

Nothing.

Sharae pitifully shook her head and backed Brooke into the empty space the woman vacated.

Sharae climbed out of her car, secured her emergency workout bag she kept in her trunk and went into the gym. She half-smiled at the check-in counter as the receptionist scanned her key card. Her eyes roamed over the gym and zeroed in on King coaching someone through some reps on the free weight squat machine. She winced as she noticed Ava alongside the woman. Her heart sank to her feet along with her hopes of speaking privately with King regarding her issues. She didn't want Ava to know the issues in her relationship with James.

King smiled to acknowledge her presence. Ava smiled and sent her a wave, "Hey, Sis," she said. "What are you doing off work early?" she asked.

"Bout to kick King's ass. What are you doing here?"

"Well, I set my friend up with King, so I came along to make sure that he don't put too much of a hurting on her," Ava responded. Sharae caught the lingering smile in Ava's eyes that mirrored hero worship as she spoke of King. She pushed the thought away and hoped that King would not take advantage of Ava's recent fixation on him. She was too exhausted to kick his ass.

"Will you be able to squeeze me in?" Sharae asked King.

King nodded in response. "Just go do some cardio for like fifteen-twenty minutes."

"Alright," she said, as she turned away from him.

Close to ten minutes later, she emerged from the locker area ready to burn off some steam and some calories. Her pulse jumped at the sound of Dirty Money's, *"Your Love"* as she climbed the revolving staircase.

Fifteen more minutes of this torture is bound to keep my mind off this BS, she encouraged herself after five minutes. Her heart pumped fiercely, determined to remain in the zone. The sweat beads, already formed at her temples, made their way in slick streams down her face.

The deep ache in her heart caused her to press the stop button. Sharae closed her eyes, took a deep breath, and slouched over the rails, murmuring motivational quotes to keep herself in the workout zone. The sixty-second rest time ticked away in slow seconds as she held a mental conversation with herself.

I don't feel like this, her thoughts betrayed her heart, chipping away at her resolve.

I can't take it, her heart gave in.

Thirty seconds left, she noticed, still contemplating the failure of her relationship. She let the stairs drift to the bottom and waited for the machine to beep, sounding her official "surrender".

Sharae let out a pitiful laugh of defeat and shook her head to erase the black specs that had begun to appear before her eyes. She fanned herself with her hands to cool down.

Eyes closed, she sensed a shadow over her. Sharae looked up at the figure belonging to the shadow and let go of a deep, ragged, and embarrassed breath. Tapping into her reserve stash of strength, Sharae began to climb the stairs to reset the training program just in time for

Mr. Fine to flash her with a blinding smile as he climbed onto the stairs of the machine beside her.

"I thought you were done," his smooth, velvety voice spoke directly to her for the first time.

Mouth dry, Sharae shook her head and a nervous laugh emerged. "Uh," she murmured, as one of her earbuds dropped from her ears. "I thought it had gotten the best of me," she added as she programmed the stairs to revolve for another ten minutes. "But I'm not a quitter."

Mr. Fine licked his lips and nodded in agreement. "I can tell."

Completely surprised at his presence and his attention, Sharae prayed that she wouldn't end up embarrassing herself by reducing the ten minutes to five.

Now I have to show off for this nucca.

She scanned the room for King, silently praying that he would bail her out of her self-imposed torture.

He did not. She spent the next nine minutes of hell climbing the never-ending staircase. Sharae reset the machine, not completing the cool down. She could feel beads of sweat slide in streams down her face, neck, before settling on her chest and soaking into the fabric of her T-shirt. As her heart threatened to jump from her chest, Sharae stood still and let her head fall back. She closed her eyes as deep breaths emerged from the tightness in her chest and restraints of her lungs.

When she finally opened them, she found the intense set of dark eyes belonging to Mr. Fine's locked on hers. His gaze transfixed her as she tried to focus on anything other than him. His eyes were shades darker than she'd imagined.

Why the hell he staring at me? A nervous smile circled her lips. Too tired to be cute or embarrassed, Sharae folded over, resting her hands on her knees as she struggled to breathe.

"These stairs are definitely a killer," Mr. Fine's voice cut through the haze.

Without straightening up, she murmured, "They damn sure killed me." When she felt him move to assist her, Sharae held up a hand to ward him off as she stood up. "You'll have to excuse me until I can breathe again."

"It's cool. Don't sweat it. I've seen it get the best of people every day," he responded with a chuckle. It was the laughter that made her look at him. Sharae tilted her head to the side, cursing the sweat dripping into her eyes and disrupting her view. She quickly wiped her face in her shirt. "Eeeww, I hate doing that."

"You built up a good sweat there," he told her. Disappointment danced in her eyes as the realization that he was a personal trainer sank in. She couldn't pinpoint ever seeing him train anyone, but the words he spoke to her read "Personal trainer for hire". The trainers there did what they had to do to make their money and their sales. It was as if they'd target the vulnerable-looking big girls, the athletic-looking white girls, and the underdressed, *"I'm too cute to actually be working out",* black girls. It was sad, now that she thought about it. The excitement from him speaking to her had brought a small ray of light in a space in her heart that had become darkened because of the day's events.

To think all those slow smiles and long stares her way were to drum up possible business.

I apparently know nothing about men. Shit, I don't even know the one I have.

"I'm not interested in a personal trainer," she let him know.

Mr. Fine laughed as he shook his head. "Nawl, I'm not a personal trainer."

Yes! "Oh. Okay, 'cause they be on you in here."

He shrugged and chuckled. "Yea, I know. Everybody has a hustle, though."

Sharae noted that he absently licked his bottom lip as he spoke. If her heart wasn't already skipping beats, it would have tripped all over itself. The man had to know that he was attractive beyond words. It boosted her spirits that he'd even acknowledged her.

"I guess you would be correct."

"You cool now? You still look a lil' bit flushed."

"I'm getting there. Thank you," she responded.

He was definitely serving a purpose. The unsolicited attention made her smile.

He could almost make her headache disappear.

Almost— but not quite.

Beneath the edges of her upturned smiling lips lurked a waiting monster. Its ugly claws were already sinking its razor-sharp tips into her temples, dragging her back into the depths of despair that had brought her to the gym in the first place.

"Are you sure you're okay? I can grab you some water and get a chair for you."

Squinting against the pain, Sharae declined his offer, "I have a killer headache. Thought that coming to workout would make it go away."

"Exercise doesn't solve everything," he murmured.

His tone suggested more, but she didn't give time for interpretation and she mournfully announced, "You're so right. I'll have to catch you some other time."

Chapter Nine

Movie *night was a success if King* took Ava's eagerness to eat dinner at a little diner next to the movie theater as evidence.

"When was the last time you and Rae hung out?" King asked Ava as they sat down at their table.

Ava shrugged her shoulders as she thought about it. "I talked to her yesterday. We haven't been out to the mall in a while or dinner for that matter. Why? Wassup? She's seemed a little edgy like she needs space and that I'm annoying her, so I kind of just give it to her."

When King sat beside her in the booth instead of across from her, Ava smiled.

King frowned. "You're right. She seemed a lil' distant the last couple sessions. I guess she'll tell me when she's ready. I was thinking about telling her about us." He put his arm around her shoulder and coughed in his hand.

Ava tilted her face to his. "Oh, I got you," she laughed.

If she could click her heels in her seat, she would've. He was ready to announce to her sister that they were seeing one another.

"Whatever."

"I don't?" She leaned in and placed a playful kiss to his lips.

The last month had seemed to pass in a blur. A blur in which she could document all the details if it were possible. Ava couldn't imagine that she would feel like Cinderella. Although she'd know him since she'd become a teenager, King never seemed like the type who would pamper her into utter contentment.

"Nawl, you definitely have me," he affirmed. "We're exclusive."

Exclusive. He hadn't spoken those words to a woman in more than five years. Ava had slipped past his defenses. *Well, pushed past my defenses would be a more accurate description*, he reasoned.

Ava clapped. "I know that's right. Mine."

King laughed at her reaction. He couldn't explain that her youthfulness was different from the overly stuffy persona Kyrie possessed. Being with her felt easy. She felt right.

They had differences of opinions on several issues due to their personal experiences. Ava still partied some, and he was a homebody. The partying had tapered off, though, since they'd started dating. Though she currently did not have a full-time job, she ran a heavily-trafficked lifestyle blog highlighting fashion, health, fitness, and cuisine.

The discovery of its popularity had surprised him. She had used her passion for documenting her love of life as a billboard for effectively utilizing her marketing and sales degree. Her blog had a huge following, and she produced a sizeable monthly income through advertisements and promotions for other sites.

The newfound knowledge of this altered his perception of seeing her through the tinted eyes of Sharae, who had always painted her as the spoiled rotten princess. Ava had layers that he had been guilty of never taking the time to explore because he, too, had seen her as the spoiled and pampered, everything-gets-laid-at-my-feet Ava.

Discovering the "adult" Ava who worked for what she wanted only added to his newfound hopelessness for her.

How was it possible to become more tangled up in a person you had no business being tangled up with in the first place?

The fact that she was humble about it made him smile. Ava's fresh eyes had swept over his social media profiles and marketing campaigns, which he'd been handling himself, and had given him her professional critique. Since implementing her suggestions, inquiries from prospective clients had begun to pour in. After checking her resume, King considered hiring Ava to become his media and marketing manager. For right now, he was content with her just being his woman.

"You want dessert?"

"I guess I'll let you have some of mine," she murmured.

King kissed the space behind her ear and murmured, "Or you could just be mine."

"Sounds delicious," she responded as her cheeks deepened to rosy hue.

The stars in her eyes still sparkled when she thought of him. Every moment spent in his presence was like finding her other half. Discovering what she assumed love was, she figured this was how her mother had described her love for her father. Filling her up until there was only him. Thoughts of loving him. He wouldn't understand, though. Not this early, Ava figured.

As quickly as stars rose, they also fell, Ava realized as King quietly and almost successfully declined Kyrie's call as his phone vibrated on the table. He missed Ava's quick glance.

King cleared his throat and went in for another kiss.

Ava let out a long sigh and put her hand to his chest. "So, what does Kyrie think of you being unavailable?"

"Here we go."

Ava laughed. "Yes, here we go. You should've answered your phone," she advised him.

"I could have, but Kyrie and I don't have anything else to say to one another," King said confidently. He'd made his intentions to break it off with her pretty clear to Kyrie the last time they'd spoken. Kyrie had in her impulsive nature shown up at the gym to confront him about not responding to her calls. And up until that moment King didn't have the foggiest idea as to how he was going to handle the situation. He had rules against lying to women but just this once, he had wanted to break them if it meant cushioning the blow to Kyrie's heart. *He had been testing the theory of just explaining that he was going to focus on his career and chill out on dating but there she was before he could find the right words, and up against her anger his attitude and ego had taken over.*

"I'm confused," Kyrie had said, arms folded over her sports bra covered breast, hip cocked to so side. She'd come dressed to work out in capri tights, Nike running sneakers and a halter top sports bra., King had observed knowing that by the end of the conversation she'd be disappointed. "Hold up," King grunted to her.

Kyrie sucked her teeth and didn't move from where she was standing. She flicked her hand over her hair and then shook it out, the long length of it falling down her back, between her shoulder blades in what King figured was her battle prep.

More annoyed with himself than with her, King sighed heavily as he instructed his client; a burly man who looked to be in his fifties to run through a five minute HIIT routine while he took care of Kyrie. King excused himself and went over to Kyrie, directed her to the smoothie bar and motioned for her to take a seat. Kyrie pulled away from him, her eyes never leaving his, leaned against the bar. "Like I said, I'm confused. What the hell is going on with you?" She inquired shooting daggers of anger from her eyes.

"I'm in a session. You tripping!" he told her. "I don't know what would possess you to come here without shooting me a text or a

call first," King continued. If she'd shown up only seven minutes earlier, she would have seen him kissing Ava goodbye. And understanding both women, the outcome of that would not have been good.

Kyrie rolled her neck and pointed her finger at him accusingly, "The reason I had to just show up here is because you're not answering my calls or text messages."

Listen to her feelings. You should've called her, he reminded himself silently. "I'm sorry. I should've called you but I've been crazy busy—" King started but was interrupted by Kyrie sucking her teeth.

"Too damn busy to answer your fuckin' phone, though?" Kyrie questioned stepping closer to him. "Save that for them other hoes. All I know is that a man pulls three—" she demonstrated by putting up three fingers, "no call no shows on the job he gets fired." Kyrie added her lips tight as she looked him directly in his eyes.

And because the tone of her voice increased an octave about what he thought appropriate, and the fact that the bar worker was paying more attention to their conversation than she was to making her smoothies, King made a motion to grab Kyrie's arm as he asked, "Would you like to go outside?"

Frown still in place, Kyrie declined with the shake of her head. "Outside for what? You're obviously not interested in having anything with me."

She was a good woman, she deserved respect, he thought as his temper began to spark. "It's not like that at all, Kyrie."

One perfectly arched eyebrow shot up as Kyrie shifted her weight from one hip to the other. "You're always talking about how honest you are. How you different," she laughed mockingly at him. "And you just like all other men. Lying. And for no damn reason."

The worker at the smoothie bar cleared her throat to remind them of her presence and diverted her eyes when King shot an angry glare her way. Hadn't she just served him and Ava a smoothie and witnessed their heated kiss? King shook his head. He was beyond annoyed. He glanced over at his client who was huffing through a set of burpees.

"Now hold up—"

Kyrie put her hand up to stop him. "No, you hold up. We were having a good time and if that has run its course, you should say that then. Be the man you sold me," She said to him. "Tell the truth."

The truth. Kyrie's words hit home. He had to admire her directness. King cleared his throat. "It's not you, it's me."

Kyrie was shaking her head, annoyance sparkling in her dark brown eyes. "Nooo. Don't say that. Please don't say that! Bullshit ass, "it's not you, it's me". I'm all the way good, King."

There was no way to handle this delicately, King reasoned. It didn't matter what he'd said at that moment, she wouldn't have taken it easily. "You are a wonderful woman with a lot going for herself. A million dudes would love to be with you."

Kyrie frowned. "But not you? Right? So who is she?"

King took a step back from her, squinted his eyes. There was hurt there but she was shielding it well. "Who is who, Kyrie?"

Kyrie laughed in response. "Do I look stupid to you? Who is the bitch that you choosing over me?"

Shaking his head, King declined to answer. "Nawl, we not doing that. But it is what it is, though," he murmured.

King could tell that her anger was controlled when he saw her flex her hands into fist and he wanted to end the situation before it escalated into something more. He imagined Kyrie screaming at him at the top of her lungs right where they stood and everyone in the gym turning to look at them. In quick flashes, he even saw her taking a swing at him.

Kyrie flagged him. "It is what it is? That's how we're going to leave it?"

There was a mixture of guilt and arrogance battling beneath the surface. When cornered he attacked whether he was in the right or completely in the wrong. King had to remind himself that she was a

81

good woman when he spoke his last words to her. "I'm sorry but I have to get back to my client." And with that said, King had left her standing there staring after him. Kyrie would hate his guts for a while until she found another man to set her sights and intentions upon. Now as he thought of it, King figured he had emerged from the confrontation unscathed as Ava's voice brought him back to the present.

"Exactly what does that mean?"

"It means that I already took care of that situation."

Ava tried not to be affected but was not able to pull it off. "She don't look like she knows it," Ava returned as his phone vibrated again displaying Kyrie's name.

King tilted his head and talked himself into checking his instant attitude. Explanations came with exclusivity, he reasoned.

"I already told her that we're over. She keeps calling; she'll get tired."

"You want me to tell her?" Ava offered quickly.

"Nawl, settle down. She's a good woman, and even though we were not an official couple, we dated for six months. She needs time to adjust. Be respectful."

Ava rolled her eyes. He was right, of course, and had also managed to make her feel small. "You're right."

King tugged on a loose strand of hair. "Don't be acting stank all night now. You mine, she's not."

"I'm not acting stank. As long as you know what's what."

King frowned. "And what's what?"

"That you lucky," Ava answered.

As frown lines on his handsome face disappeared, King kissed the tip of her nose and tilted her head up so that the fiery spark in her eyes met his calmer ones. After nodding in agreement, he laughed. "I'm lucky as hell!"

The kiss started off as a promise and then lingered until the waitress interrupted them by clearing her throat.

Chapter Ten

O
h, *how she loved to watch the* sunset in the fall. Sharae stretched her arms over her head letting the final glimpses of light touch her fingertips. She could smell the scent of her neighbor's freshly cut grass drift in the wind as a breeze blew by. She wrapped her arms around herself and then rubbed her hands up and down them as if to ward off the chill. The seasons passed so quickly, it seemed like it had just been ninety-degree weather. Now the temperature was dipping into the low seventies, high sixties. Just last week they'd drained and covered their pool with the specialty flooring so for her that marked the onset of winter. No matter that she still had to make it through the fall.

Shit, she was hoping that she made it through the dinner party she was hosting for James to woo a new artist into signing a contract. Everything was done, all she had to do was take a shower and get dressed, plaster a, "I'm-your-hostess-with-the-mostest", smile on her face and be whatever James needed her to be for the next five to six hours.

Sharae sighed. But first, she wanted to watch the sunset. The melting sun and the sky held no pretenses. They exposed secrets while the darkness, for which she awaited, covered them up.

A sense of tranquility stilled her spirit, seeping into her veins as she witnessed the tinting of the sky. The sun sank into a horizon of pink and purple-hued clouds. This single vision had inspired many postcards and letters to her parents. The picturesque scenery displayed tonight was no different.

If she closed her eyes, Sharae was confident that the vision would be etched on the inside of her eyelids to bring her peace. She'd take this vision of the fleeting light of day in her backyard over dark basements any day.

At one point, she'd imagined their backyard venue to an intimate wedding beneath the sunset with a faceless groom. Sharae dismissed the thought. She was no closer to a wedding than she was to having a million dollars. She'd whispered many of her dreams into the wind, perhaps waiting for them to return back to her before she fulfilled them.

James always accused her of living in romance novel. After all she'd been through, a romance novel? No. A survivor's tale was more like it. He'd almost convinced her that love was supposed to hurt. But she knew better, and perhaps that was his truth. If she didn't have more sense, she'd be balled up in a corner somewhere afraid of her own shadow.

It was a theory that she'd never breathe life into. Love only hurt when a person didn't realize its potential to heal. Didn't she display that to him in her everyday actions? Admittedly, she knew that falling in love was so much easier than staying that way. The everyday challenges of their regular lives seemed to be enough to tear them apart. It was time to recalibrate her life's desires. She wasn't as wholeheartedly convinced anymore that they wanted the same things. The studio was pulling him in one direction. The women there were pulling him even further away and, he was so damn stupid, he failed to see it. It was a path that she could see and almost predict the ending.

Nothing had ever come of her spying on the girl Daneen. James's routine had basically remained the same. In the first two weeks after their confrontation, he'd been more attentive to her wants. He made sure to make time for their relationship. They'd done the "couple" things she'd desired—the quiet, nothing time when long looks and fire-scorching glances created passion-filled evenings. And for the first time in a very long time, he'd made her feel special, for a moment she'd felt like a priority. It was in those moments that she remembered why she loved him.

The gifts were also a plus. She loved jewelry and adored the Tiffany bracelet and diamond earrings he'd added to her collection but privately acknowledged that they were just hush gifts. She'd sensed it was the honeymoon period but also noticed when it was nearing its end.

The actions were so textbook as he'd slid back into his normal pattern of behavior. The unmistakable air of arrogance returned. That was followed by the unending dedication to making music, which included multiple days of the week of sleeping at the studio.

Sharae felt it happening, all the unspoken things widening the distance between them. Something as simple as touring complicated the stability of the relationship. He'd mentioned taking his artist on tour for two months down south in November. It was said only in passing, but she realized that when he made the move, he'd remind her that they'd previously discussed the trip and tour in vivid detail.

She wanted to fight for their relationship but couldn't muster up the hope needed to make it survive. They were in that place: the unspoken; just let it ride place. Half-assed efforts apparently were the new keys for relationship success. Maybe she'd let him half-ass until he'd finally just walk away. It was easier to go along with the flow and let him walk away than it was to muster up the courage to do it herself.

Her mouth twisted in thought as she shook her head and dismissed the nonsensical theory that she'd just allow him to simply walk away from her.

It would get better. It simply had to. Every relationship had to weather the storm to remain standing. At its core, they were strong enough to withstand anything that fate threw at it.

Were they really? A resounding fear nagged.

But in the meantime she needed— no required something for her that took her mind off their relationship. She couldn't tell whether the depression from having been fired from the state lingered or if the nightmares were finally getting to her. The whirlwind of events with James had taken the edge off the sting of both. The warmth of his arms around her fought off the memories of the ones that held her prisoner fifteen years before. Sharae agonized over the dissipation of his interest in her and their relationship, and with that agony came the uncertainty of her inadequacies. The thought of being alone haunted her and left her vulnerable to thoughts of her darkest days. It gave room for the man who was now awaiting a parole hearing an opening to consume her thoughts.

Sharae shrugged. She couldn't think of Matthew being out in the world. Free. Walking the streets, lurking behind corners, somewhere; wanting her. Sharae shivered. She didn't want to think of him at all. She promised herself that she'd never give another moment of her life to a man who tried to take away everything that she was with a selfish act that had left her irrevocably broken.

"I hope you don't plan on keeping this moping shit up all night," James told her, intruding on her solitude. He'd come out to the yard to see what she was doing. James frowned because he couldn't gauge her mood these days. He figured she was still upset over what she thought she knew was going on between him and a woman from the studio. The two weeks of pampering and spoiling failed to yield the results he'd expected. He'd wanted her malleable and agreeable and susceptible to his suggestions but could see her falling back into her old ways where she was none of those things.

He needed a cigarette but couldn't indulge in the urge to calm his nerves because she had no idea that he'd picked up that habit. It was his fault that she was out of sorts, James figured. She wanted marriage and babies to go with their huge home and he was still playing around not ready to commit to anything larger than their mortgage.

"I'm not moping," she corrected, partially happy that he'd broken through her troubling thoughts.

Sharae smiled at him despite the negative energy he'd brought along with him. "I was watching the sun set. Wanna sit with me for a minute?" she invited, patting the lounge chair beside her.

"Nawl, I'm cool." His decline was quick and cut like a knife. "You've been acting weird the last couple days. Are you pregnant?"

Sharae fought off annoyance. "No." Sharae sucked her teeth. "Where did that come from?"

James ran his hand over his waved head. "I'm just asking."

"Don't worry. If you gon' be a daddy, it won't be because of me," she told him.

Sharae stood up, yawned, and stretched her arms over her head.

James frowned. "What the fuck is that supposed to mean?"

Sharae laughed. "Whatever you want it to mean." She turned and almost made a clean getaway before he caught her arm.

"Look, tonight you're a hostess, and nobody wants to be around that sad shit. So smile and be nice," he instructed.

"James, I'm fine."

"Look, I don't want to fight," he told her.

Within less than a moment's time, she noticed the annoyance in his gaze dissipate only to be replaced by lust as she stared at him. It was confirmed when he kissed her palm.

Resisting the urge to roll her eyes, Sharae pulled her hand from his and stepped away from him. "I'm not trying to fight with you," she admitted.

Victory swirled with the raw desire that shined in his eyes as he stared at her. "Why make war when we can make love?"

He was a man in a desert, desperate for water.

"Nawl, I'm cool," Sharae fed his words right back to him.

He'd die of thirst. She deftly freed herself from his grasp and walked the short distance back to the house, leaving him standing in the yard; annoyance and anger all over his face.

His temper, quick to flare, erupted. "That's what the fuck I'm talking about! If I had a hood bitch, and daddy say it's time to get at this dick, she on it! You better get your mind right!"

James was right. Sharae paused at the glass double doors before entering into the house. She coached herself to be calm before she turned to him.

"We have a while before any people get here. Come show me what else hood bitches do." She entered the house without as much as a backward glance.

Clearly surprised and even more intrigued by her invitation, James rubbed his hands together and ran inside to join her.

There was no concise moment when she remembered making the decision to handle the situation differently. Her choice could be contributed to the subtle warning he'd given her only seconds before. The old adage 'what you won't do, someone else will' floated through the air unspoken. He basically insinuated that there was a plethora of hood bitches lined up to do just that.

In reality, she couldn't fathom the thought of another woman having him. The very possibility of him seeking from another woman what she wouldn't allow herself to give him didn't sit well with her. This was her opportunity to show him that she could be spontaneous. That she could be aggressive and provocative.

James knew her well and made those comments to provoke her. Sharae despised that he had the audacity to challenge her.

She detested herself more for entertaining his calculated threat as she turned the lights down to a low, flickering glimmer. Sharae finally stopped lying to herself as she stepped out of her four-inch platform leopard print shoes at the base of the stairs. She shook off the chill as her bare feet touched the hardwood floor.

Sharae wanted him. James was an arrogant asshole, but she wanted him. The unadulterated need for him mystified her. As smart as she was, she'd always allowed herself to become prisoner for her sexual desire, which he could quickly stir with a mere glance.

Sharae started up the steps. She next removed the off-the-shoulder shirt seductively over her head and left it on one of the steps. She continued up the staircase. She caught sight of him when she reached the landing at the top.

She smiled; James had both of her shoes in his hands.

Sharae waited until he lifted his gaze before she licked her lips. With her eyes locked on his, she could feel her pulse beating extremely fast as she shimmied out of her black tights. She waited until James picked up her shirt and inhaled her scent before turning toward their bedroom. Her lace and satin bra only made it halfway down the hall. Once she reached the bedroom door, Sharae looked over her shoulder at him, opened the door, stood in the middle of the doorway and removed the matching panties of the bra he now held in his hands. Sharae stepped inside the room and stood naked as she awaited his approach.

Each methodical footstep that he took toward her was in sync with her pulsating womanhood. She watched, trapped in a haze, as James kissed the fabric that moments ago cradled her most intimate parts. He dropped all of her belongings in a pile at the door. The anticipation of having him buried deep inside created an immediate need, and she rushed to meet him. James accepted the weight of her body as she pressed up against him.

He licked his lips as he managed to shut their bedroom door without breaking their connection. He continued to kiss her as he backed up against the door. His hands traveled up and down her spine. He promised himself that he'd kiss it later. Now that she'd lost all the weight she'd gained after they first got together, he could see and feel the dip between her back and ass.

Sharae closed her eyes in pleasure as his hand cupped her bare bottom. She let out a pleasurable sigh as he took her nipple into his mouth. He sucked on it like a starving newborn as he caressed and kneaded her firm posterior. He palmed both cheeks, making them shake. She giggled as he alternated between shaking and slapping her newly firm globes from all the time she put in at the gym. She rubbed his head of waves as she held him to her.

James let the nipple pop out his mouth. "Put your shoes back on," he ordered huskily into her ear as he nipped her earlobe. Sharae pulled away long enough to step into the sexy heels.

Sharae was stopped in her tracks when she attempted to kiss his lips to resume the sensual play. "Nawl, suck my dick right now," he instructed, grappling with his belt. Defiance danced in her eyes when her gaze shot up to meet his. "You wanna do it like these hoodrat bitches, right?" he asked when he noticed her reluctance to do as she was told.

Fire spiked as her desire for him heightened. Sharae sank to her knees and took over freeing Mr. Penis from James's boxer briefs. As she eyed James's eight-inch member, Sharae licked her lips. The familiar tingle of desire tickled her insides like flutters of butterfly wings as the thickness of him pulsated in her palm. Tilting her head to the side, Sharae admired the size of him and decided the best way to express her what was going on inside her was to get right to the task at hand. She hummed in appreciation and without a word his thick dick was inside her mouth before James could even utter a word. Still on her knees, Sharae pressed him up against the wall. She let her hands roam beneath his shirt. James assisted her by taking the shirt off. She let her hands travel freely over the planes of his six pack abs. She bobbed her head up and down as he'd taught her how to pleasure him orally. Repeatedly, she let his manhood slide in and out of her mouth. She gave extra attention to the head, licking at the engorged tip like a lollipop before drawing as much of his dick into her mouth as it slid its way to the back of her throat. She looked up at his face to find his head pressed into the door, tilted up to the ceiling. He must have felt her eyes penetrating him.

James smiled down at her before letting out a satisfied groan. He traced the pad of his thumb over her eyebrow and let his hand go wild in her hair. His fingers sank deeper as he grasped her hair to thrust his dick deeper down her throat. Sharae closed her eyes and let him have this moment.

"Spit on it," he instructed. She followed orders and began to put in work. Her saliva trailed from her mouth as she pulled him all the way out and slapped it up against her lips. She cupped his balls in one hand as she kissed the underside of his penis. She then drew them into her mouth and gently sucked as she watched James's eyes roll to the back of his head. She reveled in the power she wielded over him with a few expert licks and sucks. She turned her attention back to sucking his dick. Her own fingers soon traveled to touch her sweet spot. She let her fingers roam, brushing her clit briefly as she caressed her silken folds.

"That pussy wet?" he questioned, pulling her mouth away and holding her steady by her hair.

Sharae moaned. "So wet, Daddy," she purred. "Oooh," she moaned again. Her hips wined to the beat she'd put together in her head.

James pulled her up. "Stand up and turn over," he growled. His hands traced the curve of her back. "Spread your legs and grab your ankles," he instructed as she bent over.

Sharae complied, stretching her legs as far apart as she could and grabbed her ankles. She laughed to herself, excited that all those body sculpting classes allowed this moment to be possible. Sharae gyrated her hips and licked her lips when James smacked her ass.

The slap tickled down her spine with tip-toeing anticipation. It radiated down her thighs, sending waves of pleasure that made her inner walls pulsate and tighten. Flashes of him taking her from behind caused her to strain towards him.

James teased her by grasping her hips and double-pumping without entering her. He ground himself against her, used his open palm to slap her ass.

Sweat began to form at James's brow as he swiped traces of it away with his arm.

"I want you," Sharae begged. The slapping sound was erotic music to her ears. "Please," she whispered.

Her submission was music to his ears. James sank to his knees behind her and continued to slap and spread her cheeks apart, making them jiggle. James bit her right cheek hard, leaving an imprint of his teeth and slapped it again when she moaned.

Sharae closed her eyes to relish the sensations flowing through her body. It wasn't until she felt him spread her cheeks again and his tongue began to caress her silken folds that she thought her knees were going to buckle.

James held her in place with a hand on her thigh and the other at the base of her back.

"Aaahhhh…" she moaned as James licked her sweetness from behind.

"This pussy taste so good," he told her, lapping at her clit.

Sharae closed her eyes as the beginnings of her orgasm began to clap her vaginal walls together like thunder, every lap pulling at her heart strings.

She hated that he could make her feel so complete in the throes of pleasure, that on the crest of her orgasmic peak she could feel her heart swell with nothing less than adoration. Words of love battled to escape from her lips as her orgasm crashed, scrambling her senses.

"I love you," she uttered as she twerked her backside against his continued assault. Her thighs began to shake in final surrender and buckled beneath her. James was swift and managed to capture her before she collapsed languidly to the floor.

He carried her to their bed, murmuring promises of never-ending orgasms. Sharae opened her eyes as James slid into her. She allowed him to pin her arms above her head. She lifted her gaze to meet his.

"This my pussy and you my woman, right?" he demanded as he continued to administer deep strokes. He laughed smugly when her felt her muscles tighten and flutter around his shaft.

"Oh, yes," she moaned. She'd agree to whatever he wanted as long as he gave her what she needed. "Oh yes," she purred as she nibbled on his earlobe. "This my dick, right?" she countered. There were no words she could use to describe what he stirred inside her.

"You know it is," he whispered. The heat of his breath traced a slick line down her exposed throat and across her collarbone that he followed up with actual kisses.

He used one of his hands to ride the silken curves of her body, letting it roam the length of her leg until he reached the tip of her big toe. He kissed the instep of her foot before licking her toes. He lifted her leg and held it at the knee as he continued to dance inside her.

Sharae added to the sexual two-step as she swirled her hips, pulled him deeper inside her with desperation as her hand kneaded his strong muscled backside.

"I love you, Rae."

Heart pounding, Sharae surrendered to the ache at the center of it. She whispered, "I love you too." Each practiced stroke brought her closer to climax. She rode the wave of the building ecstasy. The familiar spark spread like fire through Sharae's veins, scorching the cry of pleasure as it left her throat. Sharae's thighs tightened around James's hips as she locked her legs around his waist.

"I— aaaah. I'm coming. I'm coming…" she moaned as she exploded, pulling his mouth to her for his kisses. Sharae needed the final connection to make it real. To make it about love instead of some crazed challenge. She let his lips devour hers, tongues intertwined as they feasted on each other's mouths.

Not yet depleted, she mustered enough strength to match him stroke for stroke. Her third visit to the heavens exploded at the same time as James. He collapsed on top of her, his body weight pressing her into the mattress. Carefully, he rolled them over allowing her to lay over him.

"Whew!" he exclaimed. The toe curling orgasm left him limp. He stretched his body, arms and legs straining in opposite directions. "You're lucky we're having company," he murmured over a yawn.

Despite his exhaustion, James's heart was racing. The discovery that Sharae had in her all along what he'd spent the last year trying to compensate for with different women shocked him to his core. He smiled to himself as he stared down at her. It'd still take a while to teach her everything he wanted sexually. He knew she had inhibitions with good reason, but if this evening was any indication, she'd been holding back on him. He'd be sure to explore the rest of her offerings after the dinner party. James could feel his manhood rise at the promising thoughts.

Sharae had to appreciate that James had given her the privacy to recuperate and refresh after their intense loving making session and was even more appreciative of his absence because she was so sore, she literally had to crawl out of the bed just to reach the door. She was not altogether clear on who had showed who what.

That single round of sexual healing had temporarily put a bandage on her wounded heart. She chided herself for falling under the spell of a sexual haze. It had the power to rob a person blind of all common sense. Hadn't he already dickmatized her several times before? The "good" dick had the power of replacing lingering doubts with votes of confidence.

Sharae rolled her eyes at the smug, "I just drank the canary cream" look that stared back at her in the form of her reflection and shook her head. She felt too sated and so open that she had to remind herself that sex meant nothing. "It was good dick. I'll just leave it at that," she murmured as she glided MAC Rebel lipstick over her pouty lips. Sharae puckered up, smoothed the lipstick out, and applied a coat of lip gloss over them.

Sharae shrugged off the urge to obsess over her uncharacteristic behavior. She'd surprised him. By all accounts, James enjoyed it. Shit, she'd enjoyed it. He'd even promised her a repeat performance later that night after the very last guest walked out the door. That notion made her smile. Sharae spared the mirror one last glance, smirked in wicked approval, and blew a kiss to herself. All she had to do was maintain this current high, and she'd make it through the evening.

~ ~

It was already easier said than done. Sharae had to roll her eyes at the sound of the chiming doorbell. After surveying the living room, she realized that the intimate party of six had become a much larger party of ten and counting. Their guests were an eclectic bunch: Taron and whomever he was dating now, the gritty thug-looking rapper, the fast-talking A&R Rep, and the slick looking music executive with their bougie-acting, modelesque, arm-candy dates. Sharae was thankful that she was in the kitchen and out of their presence. She took a deep breath and let out a tired sigh. Lifting the tray of assorted treats from the counter, she took another deep breath, plastered her face with a smile, and walked back into the living room.

The potent smell of marijuana assaulted her nostrils, and with that, she made a point to shoot a warning glance over at James who was now walking up to her with their new guest in tow. She set the tray down just in time to have James lean in to take her hand. Before she had an opportunity to say anything, James said, "Babe, this is my man Aaron, the producer I was telling you about." James stepped aside, and if he had not been watching her, Sharae would have swallowed her tongue whole, and her eyes would have rolled to the back of her head.

Aaron, her mind rolled the name over. The face that had inspired a few sweaty rounds of self-love smiled handsomely at her now had a name.

Aaron. The voices practiced his name.

"This is my wife Rae," James introduced her.

Wife? Sharae's eyes darted to James. Brows creased in deep thought. Sharae smiled, despite the fact that she came to the conclusion that fate had to be laughing at her, allowing her male fantasy to be acquaintances with her boyfriend.

Aaron cleared his throat. "It's a pleasure to officially meet you, Rae." He reached to grasp her hands in his for a handshake.

Sharae smiled nervously, "It's nice to put a name to the face," she politely responded, allowing their handshake to linger for an acceptable time before nervously taking her hands back. "He also works out at LA Fitness," she hurriedly explained to James who was now paying more attention to their obvious connection.

"Oh. Everybody go there," James said, mentally noting that he'd have to add a weekly gym workout to his schedule.

"Babe, can you grab me and A a drink?"

Sharae smiled at the quick dismissal but turned to Aaron. "Sure. Red, white, Hennessy, or Corona?" she asked of her guest.

"The Corona is cool," he responded, his voice heated with tones that made her feel anything but *'cool'*.

There was a jolt of electricity floating through the air as she let her gaze linger in the welcoming warmth of his. They both grew bolder, and the gaze morphed into something darker, dangerous, and more inviting. His quick smile only added to the ball of lust she was carefully attempting to reign in just as ferociously as it was trying to jump out of her and all over him. Sharae swallowed hard, hoping to wet her suddenly desert-dry throat. "Let me get those drinks," she murmured, turning away from them.

"Thanks." James met her before she could cross the room to them, intercepted the drinks, and planted a kiss full on her lips. "Go keep the ladies occupied. We 'bout to go talk a 'lil business," he added.

"Sure will," she agreed, but not before she and Aaron traded one last parting glance.

Sharae spent what was left of her evening pretending not to be interested in the business between James and Aaron. It took every practiced ounce of self-control not to stare at Aaron after having been caught. He was laughing, and she was transfixed on how bright and beautiful his smile was when his eyes caught hers staring at him. The instant their eyes met, the challenge was issued. Not quite prepared to accept it, she quickly turned her attention back to the women and their idle chatter.

Sharae had absolutely no interest in the debate over who they thought was the hottest new rapper. She tuned in to laugh on queue when she heard the others ladies giggle. Then there was the part where they discussed the realness of Nikki's ass, which lead into the discussion on pole dancing and to her own dismay, the idea did pique her interest. That was how she'd learned that one of the women was a stripper, the other a professional escort, Taron's date was a waitress at Perkins diner, and the other was a girlfriend to the young rap artist being wooed by James.

Once her intrigue over the art of mastering the pole faded, Sharae was annoyed that with the exception of the rapper and Taron, these seemingly influential men had brought their paid acquaintances into her home to eat at her wholesome table.

Unbeknownst to her, she was hosting a party where it was acceptable to bring your side piece of ass. She excused herself, positive the discovery of that alone made her want to swallow her entire bottle of Motrin to soothe the instant headache it brought on. She rushed into the kitchen, thinking it was the only safe place she could retreat to without catching James's attention.

97

"You think I can get another Corona?" Aaron asked, disrupting the quiet. He had been watching her all evening and had almost thanked God for the opportunity to speak to her alone. James was so distracted at the possibility of signing the young rapper that he'd encouraged Aaron to ask Rae for a new drink instead of offering to get it for him. As sure as he was that this wasn't the place or the time, Aaron couldn't fathom going another second without declaring his interest or his intentions toward Sharae.

But she was a wife— to another man. There were no rings on Sharae's or James's fingers, so Aaron assumed that they used the "wifey" term figuratively. *An entire year. A year and six months to be exact*, he asserted. He still remembered the first time he'd seen her. She'd been a good fifty pounds heavier then but still beautiful. Stop you in your tracks beautiful when she smiled. She'd been frowning at her trainer and apparently defying whatever it was that the trainer was instructing her to do. He'd watched her in the gym and had even changed his schedule to the same early hours that she had. And when his schedule permitted, he made sure he was there to watch her.

Sharae smiled before turning to him. "You most certainly can."

"You look tired," Aaron observed. He fought off the urge to wrap his arms around her, to shoulder some of whatever weight she carried that caused the sadness in her eyes.

She let out a shaky laugh. "I don't think I was all the way prepared for entertaining. I know that sounds crazy considering that I've planned this down to every single detail except—"

She broke off when she realized that he was staring at her. "What?"

"I wasn't prepared for tonight either," he confessed. And now that she was off limits and someone else's, there was no point for him to even pretend.

She smiled away the thoughts of how the intimacy of his words wrapped a blanket of warmth around her. "I imagine you come to these types of things all the time, being in the music business."

Sharae turned away from him to get the beer from the refrigerator. She used those few seconds to calm and coach her shattered nerves. The hairs on the back of her neck stood to attention the moment she sensed him move closer. Sharae quickly pulled the beer out and handed it to him.

The sexual tension was unmistakably ripe in the air. Being alone with him made her feel uncomfortable. A quick vision of her ripping off his clothes and allowing him to have his way with her on the very same counter she'd served James's breakfast on played out in vivid detail.

Aaron was uncomfortably yet deliciously close when he unabashedly declared, "It's not every day that you're officially introduced to the woman you've planned to be your future wife by an associate who is her current husband." His words only added to the tension between them, then he abruptly left her standing there alone with her thoughts.

What the fuck...

With that said, Sharae spent the rest of her evening as far away from him as possible.

Chapter Eleven

*A*va *had been willing to compromise* to accommodate him. That had surprised King about her. He had preconceived notions about Ava being the spotlight of everyone's attention, having to be seen, to be noticed, to be someone— Shit, knowing her, she wanted to be seen by everyone.

Chilling, dinner, and movies represented the simplicity of his life. At the heart of who he was, King was a homebody, so she had compromised and seemed content only to be seen by him. Tonight they had settled on dinner and a DVD at the house. A slow smiled had appeared when he'd pulled out the wicker basket with a blanket and had announced that they were going for a walk along the banks of the Schuylkill River to watch the sunset. He had rolled his eyes and realized that he enjoyed her immensely more when she'd inquired with much spice about how many hoes he'd actually spread that blanket for. He'd laughed and kindly ignored her.

With a picnic basket in one hand, the other clasped Ava's smaller more delicate one, and they strolled the trail, searching for a semi-private spot with a bench. He couldn't wait to see her eyes shine as the sun melted beneath the trees and the water sparkled as the fading light shone against it.

There was idle chat of their reviews on *Limitless*, the movie they'd watched before coming to the park. Of course, they'd had a difference of opinion. "So you're saying that there's no way you would take a mind-enhancing drug that would make you smarter than everyone else and damn near a millionaire? Get the hell out of here!" King howled.

Ava frowned. "That's the problem with men. There's always a price. What's wrong with focusing and tapping into your maximum potential on your own?"

He reassessed the cost and came up with the same conclusion. "Give me the pill," he laughed. "Shidddd. I'd sell it to people and then work on a cure to decrease the side effects too."

Ava shook her head. "There's no point to selling it. No one's brainpower is technically limitless. And when everyone is the same, there's nothing special about you." She took their joined hands and pressed them against his heart. And with a shrug, she added, "Then you're just average or mediocre at best. Now, if you wanted to hide it all for yourself, you could make money, but it's always trouble. And the maintenance on that would take work and take away from the joy of having it."

King looked down at her. "Everything worth having requires a lil' work, babe. And maintenance on the upkeep," King advised, coming to a halt when he spotted a lonely bench beneath a weeping willow tree halfway between the East Falls Bridge and Boathouse Row. King pulled Ava from the path and into the grass.

She laughed as the cool and moist grass tickled the tops and sides of her feet. She pulled her hand from his and ran in tip-toe fashion across the semi grass-covered distance so that her slipper-covered feet didn't get wet.

Ava held up her hands when King joined her. "I didn't want my feet to get wet." She hadn't been prepared to walk the trail but couldn't fathom turning him down when he'd made such a romantic gesture for a sunset walk, which to date, would be her first. She sighed at the fact that King had absolutely no idea how far gone she was over him.

King shrugged, imagining how cold her feet were, and sympathetically swept her up and sat her down on the bench. Pulling the blanket from the basket, he joined her and spread the warm fleece blanket over them. He pulled her closer to him and pointed out toward the river as the reflection of the descending sun danced in the waves. Ava sighed and snuggled closer to him. "More reason," she murmured.

"More reason for what?" he asked.

"Sunset strolls on the drive, dinners, movies, you fine, all muscled and such. You're all dark and brooding. Your moody ass attitude is like a magnet and a challenge to women."

"Sometimes, I have absolutely no idea what you're talking about." But he loved it, King mused, kissing the top of her head.

"Of course, you do," Ava murmured. "But it's ok. Dinner was delicious, and I don't care nothing about them other hoes," she added with a yawn.

King shook his head, dismissing her comments. "What are we doing on Sunday?" King inquired.

Ava shrugged. She had a long list of items to complete for her blog. She had two freelance marketing projects to work on. She'd started an anonymous piece called, A Table for Two, which detailed the highlights of her evenings with King. She also spotlighted submitted pieces from her followers and had to go through them to select one for this week's entry. And then there was a trip to City Hall to review the PCA's Senior Citizen Art Exhibit with her Aunt Eliza, her grandmother's twin on her father's side. The woman was a feisty seventy-five-year-old with a penchant for fashion and flair, and Ava enjoyed spending her time with her once a month for lunch, dinner, or whatever the elderly woman wanted to do. "I'm hanging with my Aunt Liza on Sunday for brunch, and then we're going to an exhibit showcasing her artwork," she informed him.

"That's your gram's twin, right?"

Ava nodded. "Yup, she's funny. Why wassup? You cooking?"

"Well, my mom invited us over for dinner."

Her heart stilled, the beauty of the river could not compare to the simple invitation to Sunday dinner with his family. "As in you told your mom about us?" She turned to face him, the blanket falling from around them.

He caressed her cheek with his palm. "I did."

Ava placed her hand over his, drowned in the sea of his gaze. She graciously allowed the warmth of his hands and his eyes to speak volumes of what his lips and mind were not ready to commit to. She'd take that and be content with it.

"She was a lil' bit excited. I think last year at Christmas dinner, she caught me giving you the look."

She recalled that dinner in which she'd given several provoking signals for him to follow up, but of course, at the time, he had not. "So Aasiyah, Maryam, and your dad are going to be there?" She wanted to know asking about his sisters.

"Nawl, Aas isn't coming," King told her.

He'd told his entire family about their relationship. They were accepting her as his girlfriend at Sunday dinner. That meant a lot to her. And while she felt great that he'd shared with his family, he had not shared it with Sharae, and until he did, she was not free to announce to her world that he was hers. They were a secret. Secrets were meant to be hidden away. "You need you to tell Rae."

King nodded. Accepted that. It wouldn't be easy when you felt that you committed the ultimate offense against your best friend. But it hit home that he was doing more damage to Ava by not saying anything to Sharae.

King reached up, cupped the nape of her neck with his hands, let one hand creep into her mass of curls, and murmured, "We will, Babe. I promise." And because he would have said anything to have her look at him with her heart in her eyes, King realized that he meant it.

Stunned at the news, Ava leaned in to kiss him. King held her off, captured her face in his hands, and stared into her eyes. He became lost in her hazel gaze. The autumn evening chill wrapped around them as they became intertwined in one another. King didn't know where she ended and where he began as he took all the pent up feelings for her and channeled them into a kiss.

Hungrily, King pulled Ava onto his lap. "You make me happy," King murmured in between nips at her lips.

"You make me happy," Ava breathed back as she made an impatient motion to unbuckle his belt.

Lost in his feelings for her, King did not object as Ava freed his over- stimulated member from his boxers. Ava pulled the blanket around them both and quickly hiked her skirt up around her waist. King groaned as he strained upward to make contact. Unaware of anything and everything around them, King ripped her stockings at the crotch to discover that she wasn't wearing panties.

"Shit," he hissed as he pulled her down onto him. The heat of her tender flesh yielding to his scorched all reason from his mind.

Ava settled on top of him, her legs bent on either side of his. Eyes focused on his and hands on shoulders, she rose up until their physical connection was just a millisecond from being broken and stayed there. King lifted his hips to coach her slick body back down onto him. She didn't budge but dropped her forehead to his and kissed his lips.

"You make me happy," Ava sighed as she encased him in her warmth.

Mesmerized, King counted the rise and fall of each climb as she bowed back. Ava, too flushed with desire to feel the crisp coldness of the air, was engrossed in making them both reach their ultimate goal. She rode the waves his body elicited to fulfill their need, and as his vision blurred, the sight of her merged with the beauty of the moon shining on the water. King grunted as Ava shuddered and shook his head to clear it from the thick fog of lust clouding it. He then took in his surroundings. There was no one walking or driving for as far as his eyes could see in either direction, and the cars zipping along the drive wouldn't see that little space he planned on laying her back onto and having his way with her. It would have to be quick, his mind assessed, as the coils of need that bound him irrevocably to her began to unravel.

The move was so quick that Ava didn't have time to protest. Not that she would've, King concluded, as he braced himself above her and primed to bury himself inside her until he was lost.

Chapter Twelve

till, she thought of him. Aaron's words haunted her and managed to creep unbidden into her daydreams, which were now set far off from the steamy, lust- and sex-filled ones she'd become accustomed to. Now she dreamed of him being that faceless man in her yard waiting for her as she walked down the aisle to meet him.

It irritated her that she'd avoided going to the gym for more than two weeks. When Sharae reached the point that she felt unhealthy, she'd caved in and went to a different location. She sucked her teeth because it seemed so cowardly to inconveniently adjust her schedule to avoid any conflict bumping into Aaron would cause. He was dangerous. Thoughts of him were dangerous and were consuming her.

The nerve of him to make a life-altering statement like that and then walk out as if he'd simply said goodbye as nicely as he'd asked for the Corona. He'd even thanked her for her amazing hospitality and had kissed her hand when he finally left that night. Then nothing. She even contemplated telling James but didn't want to cause any problems regarding the deal they were making.

The knowledge that the man she'd spent a considerable amount of her time fantasizing about was actually attracted to her as well did considerably more than stroke her ego. In the time she'd been going to the gym, not one guy had ever tried to come on to her. She wasn't sure if her face read, 'Please don't F with me,' or if she just wasn't their types. She'd always automatically assumed it was the latter, not because she lacked self-esteem, but simply because no one had ever attempted to do anything more than assist her with information on how to use the machines.

Her mouth would still form a small unbelievable "O" when she thought of it. It even served to boost her confidence that he'd been fantasizing about her in the same state of undress as she had done about him.

Sharae shook her head at the absurdity of the situation. Indulging in the simple pleasure of allowing it to make her smile made her uneasy. She wasn't a woman who openly prided herself on desiring her significant other's business associate. She couldn't believe that she'd allow herself to dwell on him when sex with James over the past few weeks took her to heights she'd never experienced. Despite the fact that multiple orgasms had become a regular occurrence and James had his ass home damn near every night on time, thoughts of Aaron tip- toed around the edges of every single one. Clear visions of his face had appeared as she peaked, his name had drummed in her ears, begging for a whispered release.

The unwanted fire burning beneath her skin made her feel— feel like— she couldn't quite grasp what she felt. Her desire for the stranger was stronger now that he was no longer the ominous *Mr. Fine*. She'd considered looking him up on Google as well as other social media outlets but had talked herself out of it. Then she even contemplated going back to her regular gym just to get a glimpse of him. When she feared that she had become obsessed with the idea of him, she'd discussed it during her session with Dr. Trainor who assured her that it was natural to fantasize about a person when you found out more about them. She also assured her that it was natural to feel guilty because her moral code couldn't fathom cheating on James. And that would require more couch time with Dr. Trainor who had her own thoughts where James was concerned, and as far as she could tell, they were not favorable.

Sharae couldn't explain why, and although she vowed she wouldn't feed her obsession with Aaron, she found herself logged on Facepage and typed his name in the search box. Not to mention, she'd had to go on James's page to find him tagged in a picture to discover his full name. Sharae laughed to herself as she pushed away from her desk and shrugged her shoulders, giving in.

She erased his name and then typed Horizon Studios first. She scanned their page for posts. She found one about them being at the radio station and smiled and then typed a shout out to James. So, with girlfriend obligation completed, she contemplated another second. With a sigh, she typed in Aaron's name in the search and waited for a list of matches.

As she waited a message box appeared at the bottom of her screen.

The smile faded.

Finally, there it was. It wasn't as subtle as expected. Nor did it come to her in clues she had to piece together but something much more direct in the form of a chat message.

Look, you don't know me, and I don't know you, but the only thing we have in common is that my dude used to be your dude. So fall back before there is a problem.

There was the dance of nervous butterflies as she contemplated in disgust the sheer audacity of that broke nobody who was more concerned with the placement of her dude rather than that of her own children. The tingles of anger quickly pricked through her veins like wildfire. Before she could talk herself out of it, she punched in, *From what I see, you'd be correct. We have absolutely nothing in common, so please refrain from ever messaging me again,* she replied.

Sharae pushed away from her computer screen and glanced down at her watch. She still had enough time to speak with James before his radio interview. She pressed a button, opted for speaker, and paced the floor as she waited for him to answer. Out of habit, she tried him again, and then again when he didn't answer for the third time.

Sharae chewed the inside of her cheek as she tapped her phone against her palm.

Was it possible to feel numb and still be enraged? Was it at all possible that this was the coincidence of all coincidences, and that they both were wrong?

No, that didn't make sense as Daneen had no reason to ever have contacted her or to follow her if she did not have something to do with James.

She needed a drink. Vodka would have to do, Sharae reasoned as she stomped off to the kitchen to rummage through their alcohol selection. Her telephone beeped with receipt of a text message.

Babe, the interview 'bout to start in two minutes. Me and the guys gonna get a drink afterward, so I'll be home late. Love you. Make sure you listen.

You need to call me as soon as you get done.

Something wrong, you cool?

Just call me when you get done she responded with swift taps to her screen.

The Facepage notification that she usually felt was annoying alerted her that she had a new message. She hesitated before taking a deep breath and opened the message.

As long as you know what it is. I won't have to contact you or anything along those lines.

Bitches are bold on social media, Sharae thought. She wanted to ignore it and told herself that she shouldn't even entertain it but couldn't let it go.

Let's first be clear on who we're speaking of. Who's your dude and why would you ever think that a man I'm associated with would be associated with you? You should fall back honey, I'm certain you have better use of your time.

The reply came back in under a minute.

You know who I'm talking about. Maj, my dude, your name on his car insurance so I'm tryna figga out what's what?

Evidence, her inner thoughts screamed. Sharae shook her head in disbelief as her heart shattered into a million pieces.

Shoulders hunched in defeat, Sharae leaned back on the counter for support. She let her head fall down, allowing her chin to rest on her chest. She took a minute to massage the ache of her beating heart as a single tear slid from her eye. She poured the liquor into the shot glass and threw it back, wincing when the burn of the velvety smooth liquor hit the back of her throat. She squeezed her eyes tight, mentally envisioning that in doing so, it would snap all sound into silence.

She poured another shot and drank it.

Tears freely flowed.

Not exactly sure who Maj is honey. But please don't ever contact me again.

She poured yet another shot and hesitated before swallowing it. *This is so beneath you,* she chastised as she downed another one.

It was demeaning to have a chat message blood match with a woman who apparently had some connection to James based on her having access to his car but not enough to have his full name.

The nerve of bitches.

Fuck that! The nerve of these niggas...

With that, she started calling his phone. Continuously, ten times in a row with no success. Only the sound of his voice, declining availability.

Sharae paced the floor quickly as mental flashes of Daneen's pictures completed a photo slide show to torment her. Sharae dragged her hands over her face, hoping to wipe the images clear.

She failed miserably.

Impatiently, she crossed her arms and paced the floor some more.

Sharae checked her messages once more and found at least three more with additional info linking James's and Semaj's identity as one and the same. The last one indicated that she'd be having a conversation with him as soon as he got home.

Tell your dude to call me when he arrives "home" so we can all discuss it, she typed.

Sharae stalked to the living room and threw herself onto the couch where she shed her tears until slipping into a tear-induced sleep.

At two a.m. Sharae found herself looking at the front door, primed to attack as soon as James walked through it. Not one of her calls had been returned, and now his phone was off.

She'd even taken an Ambien to help relax her and put her back to sleep, but it had yet to kick in. There was an indescribable ferocity clawing at her heart. Fire seeped out her pores.

Deep breaths, deep breaths, she coached.

She wasn't entirely sure if she was breathing at all, though.

Past the point of disappointment, and on the brink of insanity, Sharae gave in to the urge to check Daneen's status, and right there in the comments was something posted about her man being home right where he belonged.

Impulsively, Sharae jumped from the couch to stand up, stumbling slightly. She shook her head to clear it as the remnants of an alcohol and pill-induced haze reared its ugly head. Decision made, despite her current physical state, she stumbled to where her gym sneakers were and slipped on a pair, grabbed her purse, and was out the door.

It took a record twenty-six minutes to reach James's old apartment on Roosevelt Boulevard.

"Get out the car. Don't get scared now! You drove all the way here," her mind, sick and twisted with pure anger, persuaded and taunted her as deftly as the serpent did Eve.

She quickly assessed the area, looking for his car but didn't see it.

"That don't mean shit," the slick voice countered.

Pure adrenaline had gotten her to this point, but rage took over and gave her the courage she needed to walk up to the house. Goosebumps formed and the hairs on her body all stood up in attention at the same time as the brisk cold air, reminding her that it was the end of October.

Sharae stopped in front of the converted duplex and stood there. She closed her eyes as nerves and common sense battled with anxiety and rage. Fear had her slithering back toward the direction of her car, but the spikes of anxiety turned her around had her in front of the door and banging without precaution.

The banging on the screen door was loud enough to wake the entire building. She persisted until the small light above the door illuminated. Sharae stepped back, waiting for the door to open but continued banging when no one appeared. The lights in the first-floor apartment cut through the blinds to show that there was indeed someone who was peeking. Taking it a step further, Sharae went to the window itself and began beating directly on it.

It did occur to her that it was close to three a.m. and that she could be arrested for disturbing the peace, but she threw the cautionary thought out the window. At this point, she didn't expect for James to come out even if he was there. That still wasn't enough to make her leave.

Sharae stood back, detached from reality as she watched the shadow of a woman observe her from the other side of the blinds. The shadow was soon joined by another one. It was unmistakably James's silhouette. Reserved energy spiked a new resolve, and she frantically tapped at the window until the blinds finally slid up. Then the window opened and out popped a bonnet-covered head with strands of blond hair escaping it.

The same unattractive face that graced her social media profile stared at her. Lips pursed in disdain as she began speaking, "Now why the fuck you banging on my window at 3:00 a.m.?"

This was the reason you showed up, right! To confront this bitch and James's no good ass? Sharae tapered down the sense of urgency to pull Daneen from the window and stomp her into the ground. Instead, her words were very calm.

"I'm sorry, but is James here?" she asked politely as if it were three in the afternoon. "I couldn't help but to read your post where you stated that the two of you are snuggled up. So, I thought I would show up to confirm."

She struggled with focusing on the girl's face. Now was a hell of a time for the pills to kick in.

Daneen's head went back into the window. Her screaming voice could clearly be heard telling the man with her to "go handle that bitch outside."

"Yes, James, come handle this bitch outside!" Sharae repeated.

Was that crazy sounding calm voice hers? Excitement bubbled over as fear continued taking a back seat to her rage.

"Yes!!!! Come the fuck outside! I know you're in there. You have the nerve to embarrass me with this— this trick?!" Sharae ranted. "How dare you?" She paced outside the landing. Clearly, void of all reason, she peered into the open window and saw Daneen's back displayed with hand gestures to the person she spoke to behind a wall. The apartment, she noted, still had a couple of the same pictures from when James still lived there. Telephone in hand, Daneen issued the man an ultimatum, "You either go the fuck outside, or I'm calling the cops on her ass."

"James, I know you can hear me. Come the fuuuck outside!" Sharae yelled into the open window.

James appeared fully dressed from the other side of the wall. And within less than two seconds, the world crumbled beneath her feet.

His face was blank; there were no traces of emotional regret; only anger peered through those soulless eyes.

Sharae could feel the hatred in his glare, the heat of it scorching her skin as if it were fire. She looked over her shoulder and clapped her hands as he came to the front door of the apartment.

No the fuck this negro didn't just come out this bitch house.

She needed several minutes to compose herself.

Fate did not allow for that.

Sharae tasted the salt of her tears as they streamed down her face. She couldn't muster enough dignity to not be embarrassed. She could imagine the neighbors with scarf-covered heads peering out their windows and guys with their hands stuck in their boxers looking out their doors.

There was complete silence; her thoughts ceased. There was nothing. The overwhelming sense of calmness stilled the air and blocked away the noise. Then she snapped.

Sharae was up the steps pushing him back into the entry way of the house. Both hands striking out, making direct contact with his face. She continued to scream and shout obscenities at him with each blow.

"Are you fucking crazy?! You messing with this nothing-ass trick!"

Slap! It could have been seconds or minutes before she was able to tune into the voices other than the ones in her head.

"But he was here with me, though, bitch." It was the mocking laughter in Daneen's tone that had her turn her attention to the woman.

The laughter was quickly replaced with fear as Sharae's fingers tightened the circle she formed around her neck. The rage heightened in anticipation as the feel of Daneen's pulse frantically beat beneath her very own hands. Daneen's sculpted nails raked at Sharae's hands.

"Rae, what the fuck are you doing?" James choked out.

At the sound of his voice, Sharae used all her strength to push Daneen by the throat into the wall behind her. Without a second thought, Sharae hurled herself at James, hands up, nails primed for facial contact. James blocked his face but managed to grip her hands.

"Yo, you need to fuckin' chill," James choked out as he attempted to get his bearings. He had completely underestimated Sharae's reaction, he realized, as he finally had got enough leverage to literally throw her over his shoulder.

"I'ma kill this bitch," Daneen yelled as she made an attempt to pull Sharae away from James.

"Let me go, James, so I can fuckin' kill this bitch," Sharae countered. In response, James held a hand up at Daneen, warning her silently to back off. As Daneen made another move towards them, James sidestepped her.

"I hate you, James! I fucking hate you!" Sharae yelled and screamed as James began exiting the hallway. She pushed at him as he carried her towards the side street where he knew she parked her car.

"You stay in your home with that ugly bitch and make her fucking happy," Sharae shouted as he dropped her down at her car door. She lunged at him and was able to mug him in the face.

Dry tear streaks marked her flushed cheeks. Sharae shook her head. "Don't come near me. Don't ever come near me again." Tears welled in her eyes, threatening to start a full on flood.

"Rae, baby. I'ma need you to listen to me."

"Go call that dusty bitch you was just laid up with *baby*!" she shouted at him. She started to feel the pain as the cold air surrounded her.

"Get in your car, and I'll follow you home," James ordered.

"That's right, bitch. Get ya ass in that car and go home before the cops get here to arrest ya dumb ass. I'll send him to you when I'm done," Daneen yelled from where she stood on the corner.

Don't put your hands on this bitch. You're too good for this, the optimistic angel advised.

Fuck him and her up right now... her ride or die devil interrupted.

Sharae took a deep breath as she contemplated rushing to the corner and blacking out and doing whatever it was that crazy people did when they lost it.

She laughed at what her desperation for this man had led her to. "You know what?" She blocked out the images of her physically taking her frustrations out on their faces. "You're right. I'm going to leave. I'll make arrangements to separate all of our affairs so that you may never contact me again."

There was nothing dignified about her situation, but she managed to hold her head high as she turned to get in her car but realized she didn't have her keys. Daneen laughed and hurled them across the street into a grassy, tree-filled lot. "Yea, bitch. Catch that."

Did this hoe just throw my keys in that fucking lot?

"Yo, D, go over there and get her fuckin' keys!" James shouted at the woman.

He quickly reached in his pockets pulling out the remote start and unlocked the doors for Sharae with his copy of her keys. Without a word, Sharae ducked under James arms and ran over to where Daneen stood.

The woman was still making crude remarks when Sharae punched her directly in the mouth and then followed up with more punches. Daneen was fighting back at this point. Sharae could feel James pulling her off of the woman by picking her up and placing himself between the two women.

She tasted the salty twinge of blood on her lips as her tongue licked at the fresh bruise.

"Rae, you gotta get out of here. Someone called the cops."

Faintly, she heard police sirens in the distance.

"I called the cops on this crazy bitch," Daneen offered, jumping closer to Sharae. James blocked her. "You betta take ya ass home 'fore you get locked up and dey have to three-oh-two ya ass!" she shouted out at Sharae.

"Come on now, Daneen," James warned.

"You said she see a doctor and take medication, which means she's fuckin' crazy," Daneen added.

Sharae's heart shattered, a million shards of glass pounding painfully in her chest as she realized he'd shared the most intimate part of her with this woman.

I gave him everything I had to give, but I won't give him this.

Shoulder slumped in defeat she took a step back. Tears slipped down her cheeks, carelessly unaware that they were unwanted as she turned quietly and got in her car.

Chapter Thirteen

reams, she claimed... *Dreams...*

No reality would ever be so harsh as to reach into your body and take hold of your heart, only to rip it from your chest. But beneath the layer of hope, Sharae knew that life could be much crueler. She'd experienced the cruelties of reality times ten.

The pain beneath her eyelids killed the hope. Her unfocused mind attempted to reason and rob truth directly from her memory. Eyes still tight, Sharae rolled over onto her side. Flashes of the night before played out. The tighter she squeezed her eyes, the more vivid the images became. She rolled over to the other side and then onto her back.

"I know you kicking his ass out, right?" Tamika's voice cut through the quiet.

Hope did not spring eternal nor was it going to save her.

At the sound of her friend's voice, Sharae's heart clenched. Eyes still closed, Sharae laughed a husky, hurt laugh. She remembered calling Tamika and unloading everything she had inside her as she drove home. She remembered pulling into her driveway and her friend being there. And then she didn't remember anything at all.

Tamika crawled up beside Sharae and snuggled in, wrapping her arms protectively around Sharae's waist. "When you get up, we're going to burn all his shit like Angela Bassett did in *Waiting to Exhale*," Tamika suggested with a hug. "I know you hurt in ways I can't imagine right now, and I know that you don't think so, but everything is going to be fine."

Is it?

Sharae didn't trust her voice and was convinced that it would break if she attempted to speak.

So, for a while, she didn't say anything.

Later, it was the sound of Tamika's laughter that made Sharae smile as she made her way to the kitchen. Some of the pressure had lifted from her temples. Those few hours of sleep did not require the assistance of sleep aids or any other prescription medication and left her mind feeling clearer than it had hours before. She wished her heart the same fate, the same sense of clearness. She prayed for anything over the pain she felt— that ache that seemed to never leave. Sharae leaned in the doorway of the kitchen as she watched her friend efficiently flip chicken breasts, stir sauce, and open the oven, all while having a conversation on the phone.

"Ummmm. Cookies?" Sharae asked, sniffing the air as the aroma of chocolate chip cookies danced into her nostrils. "You know how to put a band-aid on a fat girl's heart!"

Tamika smiled and searched Sharae's face for traces of distress. "Rae is awake. I'm going to call you back, babe," Tamika said into her phone. "Thought I'd make you some thangs to hold you over for a couple days so you don't have to cook since I know how much you love it."

"Thank you," Sharae said plainly. "For everything," she added as she slid into the seat on the opposite side of the counter.

"No worries. You want a plate?" Tamika questioned as she moved from stove to sink to strain the water off the pasta.

Sharae rubbed her hands over her face and ran her fingers under her eyes to soothe out the puffs. "Of course, I want some," she laughed, although her appetite declined to send signals of hunger. Tamika made quick work of making them both plates and setting the cookies out to cool and pouring them some water.

"The locksmith came a 'lil while ago. He replaced the tumblers," she informed Sharae as she slid into the seat beside her. "It was so loud. I'm surprised you slept through it," Tamika continued.

"I called you out, pretending I was you. Rana thought it was me but I coughed a lil' bit and assured her I was you. Then I had to call back twenty minutes later for myself."

Sharae showed a half smile. "I'm sorry. I was rocked. It doesn't seem real you know?" Sharae said with a shrug. "I'm stupid. All the signs were there. I was damn-near done, and then he started fucking me extraordinarily good and treated my heart so tender that it didn't have that painful I-know-you-don't-love-me-like-you-should ache." She rubbed the ache she spoke of and looked down at her plate. She scooped a heap of noodles, tilted her head to the side, and brought it to her mouth as thoughts tumbled into one another. "And she's nothing. Her ass don't know me. She don't owe me shit. But..." She placed the uneaten forkful back onto her plate. "She some stupid welfare broad who doesn't even take care of her kids. DHS file this thick." She made an example with her fingers.

Tamika sighed as she felt the pain. Sharae rolled her eyes with a shrug of her shoulders.

"I don't want to make it about her when it's all his doing. He don't give a shit about her not having nothing. He probably like it. Rowdy-ass ratchet chick. Need him financially..."

Sharae pulled her shattered iPhone from her pocket. She'd thrown it against her bedroom wall in a fit of rage before she fell asleep, realizing that James hadn't even called her.

She looked at the blackened glass-shattered screen and sucked her teeth as she dropped the phone in front of her plate.

"Fucked my phone up. He told that hoe I take medication, and that bitch called me crazy. That shit hurts. He let her call me crazy. I hate him." Hated that he didn't protect her, if that made any sense given the circumstances.

This time, with the ache as real as if it were her own heart, Tamika said, "Awwww, Rae."

"I'll be okay," Sharae murmured.

"I just don't want him to hurt you anymore."

Sharae shook her head. "I'll be okay. I am okay."

The simple untrue statement gave her the strength she needed to make it through the next two hours of Tamika's company. Just as Tamika was leaving, Sharae didn't think she would make it through the rest of the night. She hugged Tamika close and absorbed her strength.

"I've been through so much worse. You think I would be fine."

"Heartbreak, honey, is different. I'm going to call you when I get home on your house phone. I love you," Tamika said as she brushed her lips across Sharae cheek and then got into her car.

"Love you too."

Sharae stood in the driveway and waved to Tamika as her friend backed out onto the street and down the block.

When the lights on the back of the car disappeared around the winding bend, Sharae lifted her face towards the sky and let out a piercing scream. "*Aaaaahhhh!*"

She yearned for sleep and prayed that a nice, long bath with bubbles and wine would bring that about. She wished that she could erase the ache of the overwhelming sense of loneliness. It was an ache she was familiar with, and no matter how many times she'd experienced it, the results were the same. It was like being consumed in total darkness without one ray of light. And even worse, not an ounce of hope existed to muster the courage to seek any.

She'd felt this before. She wouldn't allow those same demons to get her, though, Sharae thought as she turned back to her house, a house they'd bought with a two-hundred-thousand-dollar mortgage loan.

Everything they owned was tied up together. The cars, the house, and one joint bank account with a bulk of the savings for household maintenance and vacations. She couldn't fathom the technicalities of their break up when she couldn't get past the feeling of her shattered heart.

"Rae, hold up," the voice acted as referee to her thoughts. She turned to see James standing on the edge of their driveway. His hands were in his pockets, and he was standing as if he had the indisputable right to be there.

Emotions be damned. She stared him directly in the eyes. "You have the nerve to show up here?"

"This is my house too," he stated as a matter of fact. He stayed where he was.

Sharae rushed quickly to close the distance between where she stood and the house. The sound of his brisk movements up the paved walkway could be heard behind her. She was joyously relieved that he wasn't fast enough as she slammed the door in his face.

The first knock was brisk and sharp. "Alright, Rae, open the damn door."

"Nawl. I'ma bring your shit to the door," Sharae said to him. She could hear the jingle of his keys.

"What the fuck?" he yelled with a bang of his fist against the door. "You changed the Gotdamn locks?"

Sharae could image him looking down at his own keys in shock that they did not fit into the locks. "Sure the hell did. You can use those keys to gain access to your other house."

"Yo, open up the damn door!" he shouted; this time, there was a kick.

"No, I'm not going to open the door, and if you don't get away from my house, I'm going to call the police."

"Rae, can you open the door so I can at least get some of my shit?!" he yelled again.

Moments of silence passed. She wanted it over.

Sharae unlocked the door, opened it enough to stick her head through the crack. "I'm only letting you in long enough to collect some of your stuff. When I leave for work tomorrow, you can come and collect whatever else you need until we can make other arrangements." She widened the door and stepped aside to allow him entry.

James saw the sadness in her eyes that her nonchalant attitude attempted to mask. He was again sorry that he had put it there. "Nawl don't worry about it. Can I at least explain?" he asked after locking the door behind him.

Sharae shook her head to herself and walked out of the room without a word.

James stayed where he was until he heard their bedroom door close.

Fuck, he thought realizing that it was too late. There were no words that he could give to her that would make sense.

Chapter Fourteen

*T*wenty-five minutes later, when he found himself sitting outside their bedroom, back pressed against the door, hands on his knees, and head tilted back, James wished he had the courage to actually knock. The sound of her muffled sobs pounded like sledgehammer on his usually impenetrable heart.

The entire situation had spiraled out of control. It was never supposed to spill over to his home life and endanger what he was building with Sharae, yet unforeseen circumstances had brought them to this point. He was at a crossroads. Sharae was the type of woman every man wanted as his partner. She was intelligent, beautiful, sexy, funny, independent, driven, and ambitious without being cold or calculated. With her, he knew it wasn't about his money or his status in the music industry. His innate sense of self-confidence and arrogance had not been a turn off for her, and she constantly called him on his shit. When he first met her, he was just a Septa engineer who spent his free time rapping and recording other artists. And she'd become his biggest supporter, cheerleader, friend, and partner instantly, fitting seamlessly into his life.

He half-smiled at the thought of her quirky, motivational text messages: "POM POMS", meaning she was always cheering for him.

Physically, it had been love at first sight when he'd seen her walk through the station break room with Tamika, who was meeting her husband and his railroad partner and friend, Stephen. Her thick frame, clothed in all white with silver stilettos, demanded the attention of every man in the room. Her hair was a mass of natural curls, free tendrils framing her heart- shaped face. The moment she smiled, he knew she was the one. He still remembered the quick flash of disapproval in her hazel eyes at the sight of his filthy work clothes when Stephen had introduced them. He'd spent a week talking Tamika into hooking them up on a date. And they'd been together ever since.

Five years, a house, a promise ring, and two messy indiscretions later, James was on the verge of losing everything he'd worked tirelessly for. And he couldn't explain why. He wasn't secure enough to admit that the fear of her being too good for him turned him to the arms of other women. Aside from his idiotic belief that his penis would not allow him to be faithful, James drew a blank. Everything boiled down to both his physical and emotional needs not being met. Given the current situation, it would be insensitive to tell her that he cheated because she wasn't there for him. Or the fact he feared that one day she would wake up and see him for the true asshole he was and would walk away.

"Babe, I never meant for any of this to happen," James finally spoke. "I don't know what the fuck is wrong with me. You're perfect. I'm messed up. I mean, I know I fucked up." He continued when he was greeted with only silence. "I just kept thinking about how I was going to leave her alone for good and marry you."

Sharae's body mirrored his on the other side of the door. "You are such a liar," she creaked out. "I spent my night Facepage-beefin' with some bitch that can't come close to me in real life. I mean, aside from fucking my dude. I was calling your ass all fucking night long, and I get there and you actually with her."

Because Sharae wanted to see his face when she poured out her heart, she stood up and opened the door. "There is nothing you can say or do that can get me to take you back. I deserve more than this. The moment you were not happy, you should've said something. We could've fixed this." She shook her head when he stood up and reached for her.

Hadn't she voiced her displeasure?

Considering that she was speaking calmly to him, James leaned against the wall, figuring he was in for at least another hour of lecturing before he could coax her into seeing his side of things.

"And you care enough about her to try and make me nothing?! You told her that I was crazy! I trusted you!"

"No the fuck I didn't. I told her that you suffer from anxiety," he corrected. But he wouldn't allow her to believe that. It was something he, himself battled with. "Rae, she just some stupid mistake I made."

"Mistake?' The word tasted as ridiculous as his usage of it. "Do I look stupid to you?" she asked, shaking her head. "This nut-ass broad living in your shit, same furniture, everything. You were supposed to get rid of that shit years ago."

"First off, I'm not putting her up in shit. She moved there after I moved out, and instead of paying for storage, I let shortie cop the furniture too."

Sharae took a deep breath. "I hate that you're gonna stand in my face and lie. Ain't no point to talk or none of that. You think I'm stupid as hell."

James scratched his head at her agitation. She wanted the truth. He wasn't overly convinced that she could handle it. "I said she a fucking mistake. Of course, I'm stupid. I'm a fucking man. Shortie been tryna fuck since she moved there—"

It was pathetic but she had to know. "Do you love her? Tonight, you went home to her. So do you love her?"

James pounded one of his fist into the other. "Rae, everything is not about love. I went there first because she said that she was going to show up here." His face twisted in automatic disdain. "I wasn't having that shit. So I went there. Point is, she do whatever I say. She at the studio all day long at my beck and call. If I wanna fuck, she fuckin'. When I say suck my dick, she down on it. Right in the booth if I want. When I'm riding, she in the passenger seat. She was there when you was too busy working, or at the fucking gym, or the damn mall, instead of taking care of your man."

Sharae laughed even as tears flowed. Typical of a man to ultimately blame the woman for his shortcomings. "Well, go be with her then. Don't worry about me—"

"I love you. You always gon' be my first priority. You not hungry, out on the street, walking, or none of that shit."

Later, she would smack her own face to have stayed quiet. She knew that he wasn't really saying that she was fed, clothed, and had a home and a car because of him. She had all of those things because of her hard work, not because of him. Sharae shook her head. "You don't know nothin' about love!" she shouted.

"I know you the only person I've ever loved, no matter what bitches I fuck, what we go through, or get into. You are mine as I am yours."

"Do you even hear yourself right now?" Sharae questioned. This display of arrogance was far beyond any she'd ever been witness to. "Just leave."

"This my shit. Our damn house, and I'm not going anywhere until you hear me out."

Sharae nodded at his brazen attempt at dominance. "You're right, of course. I'm going to leave instead." She went back into her bedroom.

127

"You ain't going nowhere. I'ma need you to listen." James followed closely on her heels. He touched her arm to turn her to face him.

Sharae snatched her arm from his grasp and pushed him so that he rocked back on his heels. "I'm through listening to you!" she raved. "I cannot. Absolutely will not be with someone—, she affirmed, pointing at him, "be with you, and you literally fucking out there disrespecting me." Sharae flagged her hand instead of using it to slap his face as she wanted to. "Are you out of your damn mind?!"

"Rae, I'm sorry." The apology was completely out of character for him and surprised her. It momentarily caused her heart to tremble and her mind to question her anger, but she tuned him out. His apology was granted its desired effect. Share shook her head. How was it that she now felt guilty for being upset?

"Stand firm!" Share challenged herself. *"Don't fall for this bullshit!"* her mind screamed.

"I'm sorry that I hurt you. You gotta give me another chance, though. I don't know what I would do without you in my life."

Heart overflowing to the brim with hurt, she finally said, "No, I can't. Not right now. I need time. I need space." Eyes closed, Sharae pushed at the air with her hands.

James clasped her hands in his and ignored her resistance when she attempted to pull away. "Babe, I swear," he said, lifting her chin up so that she could look at him. "Do you hear me? I swear to you that I will never do anything to hurt you ever again." He dropped to his knees before her, encircled her waist his in arms, and pressed his face into her stomach. Trapped in his embrace, all she could do was listen to his muffled apologies.

Mind raging, Sharae managed to break free. She had to express her feelings. She wanted him to listen and understand that irreparable pain that he had caused her. The urge to inflict that same pain upon him physically battled with her urge to wound mentally and emotionally;

however, calm and controlled actions beat erratic and frantic ones every time.

He would hate it, the detached sense of emotion.

"Just shut up!" she shouted, freeing herself from his stifling embrace. Sharae stepped back and stared down at him. "Know that in this moment, I hate you for breaking my heart so selfishly."

"You can hate me, but don't let me go."

She wondered if he possessed the emotional capacity it took to understand the gravity of what he was asking. "This entire situation is too much. If you didn't want to be with me, you could have said that. If it were me, you would—"

"If the situation was flipped, I would be in jail right now," James asserted and shrugged at her frown. "That's me being honest. I know you mad. I know you hurt, but I want you to know that she don't mean anything to me."

"So you risked everything that we have for nothing? I'm good. I keep telling you what I need. You don't want to or can't be that man, then that is cool. No pressure. We good."

"We not good if we not going to be together. You think I'm 'bout to allow some other boah to have you. Nawl; you my everything," he told her.

Sharae started to remove clothes from her dresser as she spoke. "It's funny you here saying that I'm everything but lil' Ms. Goldie thought I was nothing." She tossed some bras, panties, stockings, and socks onto their bed then went into their closet and came out with her Louis Vuitton duffle bag. She stopped and looked up at him. "You made me nothing to you to please someone else, so let me be nothing to you then."

Because having her look down on him made him feel uncomfortable, James stood up. "Rae."

Sharae sucked her teeth. "I know. She nothing now too, right?"

"I know you need and deserve space and time. But I need for you to not give up on us. To not give up on me," James pleaded as he stepped to her. "We have so much going for us, and I don't want to lose it. I want babies with you. I want to wake up every day—"

"But the truth is that you don't want those things," Sharae interrupted. "At least not with me. If you truly wanted them with me, you never would have been with someone else. I'm always saying talk to me. I'm always open."

Sharae calmly packed her bag. She continued when he remained silent. "I've asked you a million times, and you walking around trying to make it like I'm acting crazy, *and* that you ain't doing the exact same shit I'm accusing you of. All of the arguments and anger. We can just let it go today. Go our own separate ways. My life has revolved around you from the jump, yet you're putting it on hold so you can be with someone else."

Just let go… Breathe and let go…

Sharae continued, "I'm saying that's fine. I want you to be happy. I want to be happy." She looked down at her promise ring. It no longer held any promise for her. It was a circle of infinite lies. A band that kept her heart tied to his.

"We all make decisions that we have to live with forever. The next ones I make will be for me." Sharae removed the ring from her finger and stepped to him. She placed the ring into his opened palm and covered his hand with hers. Sharae closed her eyes and squeezed his hand one last time before letting go.

James pulled her into a hug and tucked her head beneath his chin and held on. "I'll go," he murmured before turning around to leave.

The embrace felt like forever. Her arms were hesitant to let go long after his arms fell from her body. The room was empty once he'd left, but Sharae didn't mind empty, considering that was exactly how she felt.

Chapter Fifteen

*S*harae sent a sideways glance at Dr. Trainor for the first time in forty minutes since she lay down on the long leather sofa. Much like the glasses perched on the tip of her nose, Marcella Trainor was no nonsense. The sassy, short bob hairstyle and perfectly-arched eyebrows always gave Sharae the impression that Dr. Trainor was perfect. Always impeccably styled and coiffed and expertly dissecting every moment Sharae shared, Dr. Trainor took notes as the pen she wrote with glided across her lilac-colored pad in quick strokes.

Though she knew it was necessary, Sharae hated the note-taking. It was Dr. Trainor's style to listen and take notes and then overwhelm her with questions that she assumed Sharae could make sense out of.

Dr. Trainor had smiled when she'd arrived and had even given Sharae a compassionate embrace. But her heart rumbled over in her chest for the pain Sharae felt. She'd just come to hope that Sharae had moved to a better place in her life where she would no longer require her services as a doctor but would accept them as a friend.

Personal feelings aside, duty called. "So, let's get this straight, you drove from Conshohocken to Northeast Philadelphia under the heavy influence of Ambien *and* alcohol? At any time, did you even register the danger of that act alone?" Dr. Trainor questioned.

Sharae sat up, placed her feet flat on the floor, and looked her in the eyes. "When you say it with that disapproving look, it sounds very irrational," Sharae responded.

"Did you think that you could have hurt yourself or others? Did you think at all?" She followed up.

Sharae jumped to her feet. She needed to move. "No, I didn't think. I took the pills. I cried myself to sleep, and when I woke up, he still wasn't home. I couldn't think of anything expect him being there with her. I felt a lil' bit disoriented at first, but I shook it off, and I was fine."

"You were mercifully fortunate, but the action itself was very reckless. You placed your life in danger as well as that of everyone else on the road because you couldn't think."

Sharae let out a frustrated sigh. "Yes, but... No. I can't explain the anxiety pumping through my veins at the moment." She began to pace. "And the meds weren't stopping me, so I just went. And when I got there, my whole world fell apart. There was a part of me like "this nigga not gonna walk out this house while I'm standing here even though I know it's him in there." But there he was."

"Yes! There he was. He's out of the house. You canceled the car insurance and took half of the money. So, what's next?"

"Hmp." Sharae folded her arms over her chest. "I don't know what's next. I couldn't think past the moment. I still can't think. I don't feel anything. The only reason I know my heart is beating is because I'm standing here. The nightmares are back."

She saw Dr. Trainor eyebrows raise at the news. "Oh, it's possible because of everything that's going on."

There was a question behind that. Sharae answered before she could ask. "Sometimes, they're so real that I can feel his touch burning on my skin."

"Mr. Hall's parole hearing is coming up soon. How have you been dealing with that?"

Sharae's fears came forward. "I have decided that I'm not going but am deathly afraid that this combo of fucked-up-ness will kick off some chemical imbalance, and I'll be on antipsychotics and in my pajamas for the next six months."

Dr. Trainor placed her pad aside. "Have you thought about harming yourself? Are you having any disturbing thoughts?"

Sharae shook her head. "No suicidal thoughts, if that's what you mean. But the battling voices of my emotions seem louder than ever. I want quiet and can't get it because mind is always racing with thoughts. In my weakest moment, I yearn for a deep sleep that I'm not sure I will awaken from. I know the only way to get that kind of sleep is through death, so it's not an option."

"No. It is not an option for you. I've watched you grow emotionally in these last couple years. I've seen you deal with an array of life-changing events and still manage to stand tall. You are stronger than that helpless fourteen-year-old child inexcusably hurt and more than a slew of heartbroken voice. You have to believe that you are."

"I know that I am. It's just..." she closed her eyes as she searched for that quiet place inside of herself. "Sometimes, when there is nothing except the quiet that I seek, then it gets too quiet. I have all this space filled with memories, and I thought that if I fill that space up with James, there would be less room for Matthew. I've spent so many years trying to prove that I'm enough because he took everything."

"He took what you were then. Don't give him any power over you now. You are Dr. Sharae Jones. No one can take that away from you. The battle of your emotions is natural. It's natural for you to want to silence them when it becomes too overwhelming. We're here so that you can learn to handle that correctly."

133

Hurricane

Nerves calmer, Sharae took her seat, and they continued with the session.

~ ~

Twenty minutes later than scheduled, Sharae arrived at her office with her written doctor's note, in hand, to cover her absences.

She sucked her teeth at the pile of files on her desk, annoyed that her alternate never completed any of her reviews while she was out. Sharae placed her black Cabas-monogrammed YSL leather bag atop her desk, shrugged out of her short, hot pink Victoria Secret leather coat, hung it up, and settled at her desk to get to work.

Three reports in, Sharae's manager called her to meet her in the conference room. Assuming it was to discuss her absence and sick leave approval, Sharae grabbed her letter from Dr. Trainor and took a quick glance at her reflection. She smoothed out the skin around her eyes, unconsciously ran her tongue over her teeth, checked her smile, and hoped that the meeting would be quick. Sharae figured once the meeting was over, she'd eat her lunch at her desk and catch up on her missed work.

She walked the hall in a hurry as if she was five minutes late for a three-minute meeting. Sharae walked into the open door conference room but made a motion to back out when she saw that it was occupied. She checked the room number and frowned.

"Dr. Jones?" one of the men sitting at the huge conference table asked. He made his way over to her.

Sharae entered the room, "Yes. Am I in the right room? Carol is supposed to be meeting me in here."

Mr. Black Suit nodded. "She'll be joining us shortly. I'm Thomas Jenkins." He stuck his hand out for an informal handshake. "I wasn't able to reach you prior to this conference but was sent to represent you—"

She took his outstretched hand into hers and shook it even as she interrupted him. "What conference? I'm sorry. I don't understand. Why would I require representation for this meeting?"

"I am the union Rep." He motioned for her have a seat on the large conference table. The other male left them alone in the room.

"This makes no sense," she murmured aloud as she took the seat beside Mr. Jenkins. In her head, she made up all viable scenarios. Discipline for absence would require an abuse of time, which she was not guilty of.

The obvious confusion marked on her face made Mr. Jenkins feel uneasy. He cleared his throat as he prepared to take notes for her response. "The city has been really tight-lipped about this issue. I only received the request to come just yesterday. Do you have any idea what it could be?" he asked of her.

Sharae held up her hands. "I've been out sick all week. Is this about someone in my unit or me?" she inquired.

I don't have time for this shit.

"From what I know, it is a matter dealing with you directly," he filled her in.

Speechless, Sharae stared at the man. He twisted a little under the heat of her glare. "I mean. I've never done anything wrong or anything like that so I'm not really worried. But still. I have no idea what it could be."

It was very rare that the agency requested a conference for an employee without giving the heads up or a rundown of the issues to the union representative. He was only told that it was a direct follow-up as a result of a report from Harrisburg. The young woman before him seemed as clueless to the reason she was here as he was.

"This is how we're going to play it. If you don't know what they are speaking of, just let them know that you need more time to review it. Never admit to anything. Most of the time they are really fishing for information, and we give them the rope to hang us with."

135

Sharae stared him in the eye. "Shit, I thought she was trying to see my doctor's note. I can't get written up for using my FMLA time, can I?"

He frowned. "They'd have to prove that you were abusing it. So unless you're going to tell me you were a no-call, no-show for four days, then yes.

"It's nothing like that. I always have a doctor's note and any other verification they request. I know you hear this all the time, but I seriously doubt that I did anything wrong. We may as well just get this over with. This is very unnerving; I have a headache. I'm going to need a damn Mortin."

Mr. Jenkins nodded. "So, go get your Motrin, and I'll let Carol and the HR Rep know that you're ready."

Sharae stepped out the office to find some co-workers standing around the area of the door. She instantly rolled her eyes at the nosey women and stormed off to her office.

Her thoughts began to throw a wild party within her already-fragile psyche.

Calm down; listen to what they have to say.

You already know that you haven't done anything wrong.

I hope no kids died that I placed back in their home.

Motrin. I need a damn Motrin. Sharae pulled open her desk and went for the case where she kept her pills. She took a swig of water from the bottle sitting on her desk. Sharae swallowed, closed her eyes, and took a deep breath. She clenched her fist twice before opening her eyes again.

When she returned to the conference room, her manager Carol and the unnamed human resource representative were seated at the conference table.

"Rae, this is Mr. Varson from Human Resources," Carol began speaking once Sharae and Mr. Jenkins joined them at the table.

"Hello, Mr. Varson."

"Pleasure to meet you, Dr. Jones," he spoke, reaching his arm across the table for a handshake. "I wish it were under better circumstances," he added taking his seat.

Sharae frowned and turned her face to Carol who shifted her view to avoid Sharae's glare.

"Do you know why we're having this conference?" he questioned.

"No."

Mr. Varson shifted back to open the folder in front of him. He put on a pair of thin- rimmed glasses. "DHS takes customer complaints against its employees very seriously."

Unfazed, Sharae waited for him to continue. She rarely had direct contact with clients or their families, and when she did, her behavior was always above reproach.

Or, had been.

"I'm not following."

"A customer accuses that you used DHS files at your discretion to obtain her address so that you could use it for your own purposes..."

Sharae put up her hand to signal for Mr. Varson to stop. "Wait? What? No, I have..."

Clearly unmoved by the Sharae's reaction, he slid a sheet of paper over to her. "This is a petition for a restraining order from the client, waiting to be approved by a judge. The customer alleges that you have been harassing her on social media and that you showed up at her house and had to be removed by police."

Sharae stood up and pushed away from the table as Mr. Varson words began to make sense.

She shot an accusing glance at Carol, who again turned away to avoid Sharae's stare.

No fucking way.

Rage made its appearance with quick flickers of heat. Sharae fought to listen to Mr. Varson.

"Ms. Roberts' case was recently reviewed by one of your workers and her actions on the case were approved by you."

"This is a personal matter that has absolutely nothing to do with my job."

Mr. Varson cleared his throat. "The Department of Human Services: Office of Children, Youth, and Families vehemently disagrees."

Breathe...Stay calm. 1... 2... 3... 1... 2... 3...

Sharae closed her eyes as she prayed for the strength not to scream.

"It shows that you not only had access to Ms. Roberts' information as a DHS worker but as an employee of DPW as well."

"Wait one darn minute. I don't know Ms. Roberts personally and can assure you that any action taken on her case was unbiased."

"Again, given your relationship to the customer, all action taken against this woman and her family by you and anyone in your unit is now question."

Deep breath... "I *don't* have a relationship with the client. And until five days ago, there was nothing personal—"

"Dr. Jones, I don't think you understand the severity of these complaints and accusations against you and the department because of your five-day personal relationship with Ms. Roberts. Among the accusations is that you used your power as a supervisor to deny the reunification of her family—"

"Carol, you're just going to sit there and let him attack me and my credibility?" she asked of her supervisor whom she once considered a friend. "The client is lying because she is fucking my ex-fiancé."

Carol's face was void of emotion, same as she'd witnessed at any other disciplinary hearings.

"Under the circumstances and upon further review, we regret to place you on unpaid administrative suspension, or leave, if you'd rather call it that. Your reinstatement is pending the outcome of the investigation, of course."

"What?!" She turned to look at Mr. Jenkins for the first time since Mr. Varson had taken over the conversation. "No, wait; can they do this?"

"We can appeal it to have it removed from your file, pending the investigation," Jenkins advised her.

Sharae shook her head. The emptiness expanded more. The nothingness she was running from had followed her to work. The heat from the rage steeped and then became cold. She could swear she felt the warmth of her heart turn cold as it turned to stone.

"It was brought to my attention by Ms. Roberts, who is stalking me on social media, that she and my fiancé were having a sexual relationship. I did show up at her house, which used to be his house before we bought a house together to confirm, and I was not removed by the police. I left before they arrived. You can investigate until your face is blue."

"Dr. Jones, please be advised—"

Sharae laughed. "Be advised of what? That anyone can say anything against me, and the infallible career that I have earned is disgraced by someone who doesn't have the drive or desire to take care of the babies she brought into this world?"

It was too much... She felt the tears forming but fought them. She'd be damned if a nobody and an asshole was going to drain her well dry.

"Don't worry about the investigation. I'm gonna do you one better. I quit." She stood up. "I fuckin' quit."

"Rae!" Carol snapped. "Don't be hasty. This is procedure and nothing personal. Honey, we—"

"Mrs. Jeffries," Mr. Varson interrupted.

Sharae smiled, despite the range of emotions she felt. "It's okay, Carol. I quit. I'll drop you the resignation letter before I leave." She took one last look at Carol, rolled her eyes at Mr. Varson, thanked Mr. Jenkins, and left the room.

Don't cry. You can't cry. Don't give any of them the satisfaction of seeing you broken. Sharae coached herself with every careful step towards her office. This situation had given her the heart she required to take the next step in her life.

The fact that she broke down in tears in the bathroom and had to have one of her unit workers assist her out of the stall before security went in to get her did embarrass Sharae, but not as much as being escorted from the building with a box of your neatly-packed personal belongings. So, she was grateful that she had an anxiety attack instead of a fit of rage.

Tamika had been called and had gone up to pack those belongings for her. "I'm going to need a drink and a sleeping pill," she told Tamika when she returned with the huge box.

~ ~

Curtains drawn, no light, only darkness accompanied the silence of her bedroom. As a child, she'd picked out imaginary monsters hiding in every crack and crevice of all her darkened bedrooms. In her teenage years, darkness became more of a metaphor for the human behavior displayed that had the power to test her will for all the years that were to follow.

Sharae pressed her palm to her heart and counted the beats. *It's broken but not beyond repair.* It may have been beat down, but it still maintained its purpose: life.

Heavy eyes roamed and searched for light but found none until the sheen on the barcode of the pill bottle made her realize that she had not needed to take them. The unopened pill bottle and filled-to-the-brim wine glass sat untouched where she'd set them before climbing into her bed of clouds. Sharae lay listening to the battling voices in her head vie for her undivided attention, and she smiled.

The life that she had carefully planned had somehow now become meticulously unplanned. She laughed and promised herself that she would proceed with caution but would live a life with no regrets.

The Aftermath

Maybe I'm done running...

Chapter Sixteen

*T*he *freedom to wake up with absolutely* nothing to do frightened her. But so did continuing with a life that she'd built with the intention of living to the fullest, only to come to the startling realization that it wasn't for her. Being able to accept and adapt to change was how the winners played it. The soft and weak were left in a tangle of tears trailing behind the people who refused to lose.

Sharae got up from her bed, looked back at the covers, and shook off the loneliness of the night. If she allowed her emotions free range, she'd still be tucked away safely in the bundle of sheets underneath the down comforter.

She flicked on her radio and Adele's sultry voice flowed from the speakers and demanding her lover to let her be his, *"One and Only"* Sharae sang along to it, *"I don't know why I'm scared..."* She turned and looked at herself in the mirror. *"I've been here before..."* Poured her soul out in the words that she'd previously directed at James but had now required them of herself. *"... let me be your one and only... I'm worthy..."* Her eyes stayed on her reflection and the energy from words seemed to flow into the woman in the mirror and shot back into her.

She finished her song as if she were Adele herself in a concert hall full of screaming fans. In her mind, Sharae took a bow at the waist and waited for an eruption of applause.

Fuck James.

Fuck Matthew.

No more tears... She breathed, wiping the ones she'd shed during her solo performance.

"No more sadness," Sharae encouraged, shaking off the air of it as it crept up her spine. "I'm going to give you everything I have." That said, she blew a kiss at the reflection.

"Rae!" The knock at her bedroom door and King's voice startled her.

Sharae unlocked and opened the door. "How you get in?" she asked when he stepped inside the door.

King suspiciously glanced around the bedroom. He zoomed in on the untouched wine and pill bottle. Big brother mode instantly took over. "Are you okay? Mika called and told me everything. Why the fuck didn't you call me?"

Sharae smiled. "King, I'm fine. How did you get in?"

"Since your phone has been off all night, I grabbed Mika's key before she went to work."

His face was frowned up, and he was prepared for a fight, Sharae figured. "You want some breakfast?"

King stood in the middle of her bedroom and scratched his head. "What the hell is going on?"

"We can have this conversation over some food," she told him, backing out of the doorway. "I'll meet you downstairs. I gotta wash my face, brush my teeth, and..."

On his way down to the kitchen, King noticed that James's things were missing. The piano and drum set, previously a focal point for their musical entertainments, was now an empty space. The Italian street scene painting had been taken down and leaned against a back wall. Beside it was a box, filled with pictures of them as a couple, along with other items he assumed to belong to James.

He smirked. Looks like James had finally received his long overdue walking papers. Women had fickle hearts though, so the outcome remained to be seen, he decided.

She didn't appear to be as wounded as he'd expected she'd be. King didn't know if he needed to be wary or be worried. After speaking with her, he'd have a better understanding of the depth of the situation. Until then, he decided to make himself useful by cooking her a meal. She'd enjoy that.

King made his way to the kitchen. He put his jacket on the back of a chair, washed his hands, took out the fixings for eggs, turkey bacon, and home fries, and then went to work making her breakfast.

"Just how I like my man," Sharae joked when she joined him.

"I thought it was the least I could do," he returned.

King gave her the once over. Her face was bright. Though her eyes weren't glazed over with happiness, he didn't find sadness in them either. His heart tumbled as he smiled with pride.

"So, you quit your job and got rid of your dude in the span of a damn week?" he mocked softly when she came near him sniffing at the food cooking on the stovetop.

Sharae shrugged and swiped a small strawberry from a bowl and popped it in her mouth as she sat folding her legs Indian-style on the cushioned bench beneath the window. "Umm. This was sweet," she complimented the berry and ran her tongue over her teeth. "I could no longer see having a future with either."

Though her answer was tough and cut and dry, the woman he knew and loved was not. "Rae? Are you okay?"

"I thought I wasn't going to be. But now I know I will be," she replied back. "I had that resignation letter in the top drawer of my desk for as long as I can recall. I was just too afraid to actually use it. And James... Well..." she shrugged again.

"What happened?" he asked.

She rolled her eyes. "Basically, the girl that James is cheating with reported to my job that I was stalking her and that she got a restraining order on me because I'm mentally unstable and capable of anything. To top it off, she claimed I used my DHS power to keep her from getting her kids back."

King turned abruptly from the stove where the home fries sizzled to look at her. "What?!"

"Yeah. You heard me correctly."

"Fuck nawl," he growled.

"Crazy, right?" she replied.

"From the beginning." King made their plates and sat down and waited for her to begin.

"Awww. You really felt bad for me. Potatoes," she joked.

In his eyes, carbohydrates made everyone feel better. He'd allow her to have one that wasn't a part of her meal plan, King nodded in agreement. "It's one red potato made with my secret recipe. First off, do you need me to fuck James up?"

Sharae rolled her eyes, 'What?" laughed and flagged off the idea. "No, of course not. Listen..."

She shared her account of the last five days. She'd spoken to him three times, making excuses about missing training sessions. "Dudes be out of pocket for no reason. I'm so sorry, Rae."

"Don't be because I'm not. I'm pretty sure I was going to forgive him until the job ish." She scrunched her face up at her honesty. "I know, pathetic, right? Just being honest."

He nodded his head. He understood. "I know how it go. I'm a man and have wanted to be forgiven for shit I know better than."

"The only thing that bothers me is that she nothing like me. No job. Ratchet as hell. Three kids, with three different fathers, who were all taken by DHS, mind you. On welfare. I'm a freaking Doctor—" Sharae shrugged her shoulders. "and he wanted to be with her. So, fuck it. I actually want to say thank you to her ass. I hated my job but would have stayed there out of fear, job security, and playing it safe. And James, I would have probably ended up being cheated on a million more times before he married me. So, she thinks she won and she really— she saved me on all accounts." Sharae stood up and began to clear the table.

King listened to the words as they left her mouth, and as her voice penetrated his ears, he wasn't overly confident in his friend's newfound clarity.

"I hear you saying you're happy and all, and I want that for you. I mean, you fucking deserve it from a decent-ass dude. But it's okay to be sad, angry, or even hurt. You have a right to be all those things—"

Sharae shook her head and turned the handles for the water, letting it run. "I was sad. For days. I'm not happy to have this happen to me, but today I choose to be happy. I choose happiness because if I spend a moment too long dwelling on everything that's happened to me, I'm lost in a dark hole that feels larger than anything I could ever climb out of. With no damn hope." She turned the water off and turned to face him.

"Aww, Rae." King stood up.

"I know you know me, but you don't know how it feels to think that you're nothing. How thinking that you're nothing somehow translates into being nothing. You don't know how that feels. Inside." She motioned with her hands to gesture her heart. "I no longer give people the power to control how I handle my emotions. And if I can handle that successfully, I win and they lose." *James and Matthew.*
 King hugged her close. "You know you're a damn winner." He kissed the top of her head. Sharae hugged him back and because she was close to shedding tears that she said she wouldn't, Sharae pushed him away.

"Do you have any idea of what you're gonna do?" he asked.

"Nothing at first. Just a break from life. But in a good way," she added when he stared at her. "Hopefully, I'm able to get GLOSSY started."

King smiled. "There's my girl."

"Whatever. Follow my dreams. Wherever they lead me. I'm gonna get the butterflies tattoos on my back today, and this cute lil' pulse line inside a heart on my inner left wrist, maybe cut my hair short." She shrugged; the list could go on and on. "Think I'm going to be man-hating for a while."

"I can definitely understand that."

"And y'all nuccas be fraudn'. 'Cause them side bitches don't even compare to what dudes have at home but that don't stop y'all." Sharae shook her head. "Stupid. I swear."

King laughed. "Why you keep saying y'all? I'm not with that shit."

"First off, your freaking name is King."

"My momma named me King."

She rolled her eyes. "And you be demanding that that's how these hoes gotta treat you. You moody, surly, arrogant, ignorant—"

"Nawl. I'm honest. I'm all that shit you said too, but I keep it straight."

Sharae sucked her teeth. He was honest to a fault. She assumed something was wrong as Kyrie had been trying to reach her. "Poor Kyrie is all over you, and you keep pushing her off. Giving off conflicting signals, just like a man."

"Told you me and Kyrie are over. And how we get on me?" he asked, his promise to Ava replaying in his mind. And while he intended on honoring that promise, now was not the time to divulge that he was now in a committed relationship with her twenty-three-year-old sister.

Sharae shrugged. "Well, you're a man."

Chapter Seventeen

Sharae waited another week to tell her parents, attempting to summon the emotional strength required for the conversation she was now having with her mother. Thirty minutes after placing the dreaded phone call to her parents, Sharae rolled her eyes. "Momma, I most certainly will not call to ask for my job back." Sharae scoffed at the very idea of it even as she realized that her mother was hyperventilating. "Rae, you need your work. You have so many financial responsibilities," Lorraine Jones advised her daughter.

"I'll have GLOSSY to work on. My car is paid for. And I have a healthy savings so, I'm really fine until I figure out what's next."

"Do you need to come home for a while?" Lorraine offered.

It thawed her heart a few degrees to know that regardless of her choices, she could always go home. The Jones's door was always open.

"And you're sure that it's over for you and James? That you can't forgive him?"

Sharae shook her head, realizing that she was speaking to her mother, a woman who believed that a man's indiscretions could be overlooked, given what was at stake if they weren't.

"Bye, Momma," Sharae said, pressing the call end button on her phone.

That's her, not you...

Sharae was not surprised by her mother's response as it was a known fact within their family that her father had cheated on her mother, had produced a child with the other woman, which had been stillborn, causing minor ripples in their wave pool. It was said that Lorraine had accepted her husband's apologies and forgiven him as well.

Wives with men who traveled regularly for their jobs were known to put up with a lot in her day, Lorraine had explained. It was difficult living so far from where your husband was stationed. Lorraine had traveled from base to base, year after year, trailing a young Sharae in tow. The need for stability grew once Ava had been born. Still, more traveling and tours of duty continued for her father. And then one day a woman— fucking Jalyn Isles; her father's mistress from the last city he'd been stationed in had showed up at their front doorstep in Fairfax, VA seven months pregnant with her father's baby. Her parents had separated for about three months if Sharae remembered correctly. She briefly frowned over thoughts of her stillborn baby brother, Jalen. Her father had been almost inconsolable at the news and regardless of the infidelity that caused the rift in his marriage and everything that had transpired between her father, mother and his mistress, her father had wanted a son. Had openly mourned the death of the child to her mother's heartbreak and despair. Then there was another six-month trial separation to see if her mother had really wanted a divorce. They'd both agreed to marriage counseling and their lives seemed to have been getting back on track. The week before Gregory had been scheduled to return home the son of a close family friend and neighbor had changed

Sharae's life forever by abducting her and holding her captive for three days before being found. That one occurrence had finally grasped her father's attention, and he realized that his family needed him more than the United States Army and any of the woman he'd slept with across the country. Her father, Lt. Gregory Jones, had settled their family in Bucks County, PA., and the rest had been history. Once Ava entered college, her father had accepted an engineering consultant position in Arizona. By all accounts, her parents were enjoying each other as if they had just met.

The thought made Sharae smile. Everything that happened in their thirty-two years of their marriage had strengthened it. Time, distance, infidelity, and obstacles aside, their love for one another remained. When she turned fifty, Sharae hoped that she had what her mother did. And regardless of what she thought of her mother, Sharae admired the way she loved her family. Lorraine loved without conditions and gave without reserve. As a mother and as a wife. Neither she, Ava, nor her father could have done better.

Sharae took a deep breath. Gym bag perched on her hip, she stuck her earbuds in her ears and climbed out of her car. When the world is crazy around you, you could always count on some machine and full-body cardio to help you navigate through it, Sharae thought as she started her workout playlist and made her way across the parking lot. She checked in at the front desk, put her clothes away in a locker, selected a treadmill, and got to work.

Almost four miles into her run, she was rapping along with Lil' Wayne to one of favorite rap verses.

I'm Dapper Don and after mine, there will be none. Damn, I mean I there will be none.

I will be one… of the greatest things you've ever felt… you ever seen… or heard…

Carter… Harvard, ya'll scared. Not me, not I, call me young Popeye…… … … I be wildin' like capital one, what is in your wallet?

She decreased her speed as it clocked the completion of her fourth mile. Proud of her completion time, she registered it as just under an eleven-minute a mile. She checked her watch for calories burned, satisfied with the displayed number. *"And you ain't gotta nothin' on me,"* Sharae murmured the last line of the rap, encouraging herself as she simultaneously begged for air to be reintroduced to her lungs. She snatched the earbuds from her ears in the unfounded belief that she'd start to breathe better if she didn't have the music pounding in her ears. She decreased the speed again and wiped at the never-ending sweat streams with her shirt. She closed her eyes for a second but kept the slow walking pace.

"You murdered those miles, huh?" Aaron questioned.

Sharae's eyes popped open immediately. She gave a hesitant laugh and a shrug. "It's weird; I love trap music."

Aaron nodded. "Nothing wrong with that. How have you been? Haven't seen you here in a while." It was an observation, but he'd meant for it to come off as a question. He couldn't explain how'd he'd ended up on the treadmill beside her, willing her to turn to look at him for what seemed like that last five minutes of her run.

Hadn't he decided against her?

Hadn't he instructed himself to ignore the feelings she stirred within him?

One year of observing and another six months of working up enough nerve to speak to her only to find out that she was off limits and the wife of an acquaintance whom he knew was not worthy of having her felt like it was all for nothing.

He didn't question the timing of things, though. He firmly believed that the Creator's timing was perfection. Aaron also knew that she and James were currently separated due to the man's indiscretions. He'd been in the studio recently during a studio session in which James was instructing all its inhabitants to not allow admittance to the girl he'd always assumed was James' girlfriend. From what he understood, all the codes had been changed, and she was forever barred from the building. From what he could piece together, James was attempting a reconciliation between him and Sharae.

There were some advantages to the state of their current separation. With Sharae being separated from James, Aaron figured he wouldn't be imposing on Sharae's sense of morality by enticing her to cheat. He could openly pursue her if that was what he decided he wanted. Whether he was ready to take them on was another situation altogether. Aaron needed to think clearly but couldn't when Sharae was standing in front of him in all her radiant beauty.

Fresh from her run, he wanted her.

"Actually, I was avoiding you," she answered.

Both were thrown off by her response. It was far from the actual thoughts in her mind.

His smile was slow; there was hope. "And why would you be avoiding me?"

"Shit," she murmured, sucking her teeth. "Because you are dangerous." With that said, she stepped off the treadmill.

I so don't have time for no bullshit right now.

Fine men always mean bullshit, honey.

The walk to the back to get paper towels gave her the opportunity to calm her nerves for a moment. Aaron was still on his machine when she walked up to wipe down the one she'd used. "So, are you going to explain that statement?" Aaron asked.

"You know what it means," she replied as a matter of fact. "And I'm—"

"Married?" he answered, following her.

Sharae stopped in her tracks, turned to him, and said, "James just said that. Definitely not married. We are no longer together. I have too—"

"You're not ready for another relationship?"

Sharae smiled despite the fact that her stomach was in knots. "I'm so off men right now," she informed him with only an inkling of regret.

Aaron nodded at the rejection and shook it off. The feeling of it felt so foreign that he immediately mistook it for a challenge. Women literally threw themselves at him at every chance they got.

Sharae had not. She was different. With her, there was no room for ego.

"We could be friends," he offered.

"You're friends with my ex, and I'm sure you not even tryna be my friend," she quickly replied.

"No, ma'am. I want you to be my wife, but I can understand why you're not ready for that."

Smirking with raised brows, Sharae aimed her hazel eyes directly at his. "Y'all men."

Aaron would not be deterred. "Don't confuse the few with the many," he told her.

Sharae had to hold back her tongue before the age old arguments of men not being shit began to spew out of her mouth. "You know what? You're right," her unemotional, clear head stated.

"I'm right? A woman after my own heart."

Sharae smiled. "Don't get used to it. Do you like Mexican? We can grab something from Qdoba and talk?"

"I'll buy."

"Let me freshen up."

Less than thirty minutes later, they were tucked away in a corner booth, learning more about each other over guacamole, quesadillas, and tortilla-less burritos. She'd changed into a comfy-looking, gold off-the-shoulder sweatshirt that exposed a number of freshly- inked butterflies, making their flight over her bare shoulder. She added some chocolate tights and brown knee-length boots.

This was different than he'd imagined their first date.

Damn, I'm already considering this a date?   She was so inviting. Sharae tilted and cupped her head in her palm as she sipped her water through a straw. Her cheeks were rosy and her eyes, filled with amusement, aimed directly at his which reflected flecks of *"I'm so serious, you have no idea"* in them. She had no idea how serious he was. The curls surrounding her face were unruly, with tendrils of hair escaping the remaining mass of curls she pinned up into a ponytail. His thoughts twisted at the sight of her beauty. He had to consider that James would not be willing to let go and would put up a fight.

"Is this breakup permanent or are you considering getting back with James?" Aaron questioned.

Sharae laughed. "Oh, it's permanent." She spooned pico de gallo atop her quesadilla triangle. "The forever type of permanent. I have no immediate plans to be with anyone, but there is no way in hell that I'm getting back with him." She watched for his response intently as the tip of the triangle disappeared into her mouth.

Aaron didn't blink an eye. "How long were you together?"

Sharae sipped her water and cleared her throat. "Is this an interview?" she returned.

The smile was slow as it took over his firmly set lips. "Please pardon the repetitiveness of my assertion, but I want you. I don't want no bullshit or mess in between. It's complicated because James is a business associate. But I've been eyeing you for over a year now, and I've only known him for three months.

Sharae took a deep breath. She wasn't looking to get tangled. Men were off limits. She had her entire life to plan and the leg work for GLOSSY to do and didn't need the distraction, especially with someone so intense and commanding. Wasn't he already telling her that he didn't have time for BS and how she was his? No, she didn't have time for another possessive, arrogant man.

There was something, though...

Aaron straightened his back against the seat. "He wants you back. That's simple. People's emotions; now, they are not. You have a life invested with him."

Sharae sucked her teeth. He was offering her a relationship with him at the same time, testing to see if she still had feelings for James. "Since y'all are cool, I know you know that he is a liar and a cheater.

155

And that violates and invalidates everything between us. This might be too weird—"

"Have you ever experienced something you couldn't explain? Have a reaction to a situation that is so far off from your normal?"

This was that situation for him. It would be difficult to explain it to her when he wasn't all too sure how to explain it for him.

Her heart strings tugged at the sincerity of his tone.

You don't have time for no lying-ass men. Fear spoke out against the complicated feelings he evoked.

We can't handle another heartbreak. The battered heart chimed in.

She was about to concede to those voices when Hope whispered, *Not every man is James.*

Sharae bit the inside of her cheek. "This is completely unexpected. Is there a woman? Someone who thinks that she is your lady?"

"No." The answer was quick and decisive.

"No? As in, there is no one claiming your fine, successful ass as theirs? Or no, you're just not claiming them?"

Aaron smiled. "Nothing like that. Of course, there are women. There are always women around in my business. None who holds my heart, none of whom I would have to make any concessions to. I have a ten-year-old daughter; Chloe. Her mother and I have joint custody. No drama. I'm really low key."

"I'm not quite sure how to handle you," she conceded, exhaling the breath she held as she awaited his reply.

"Alright. That makes two of us. Can we start over?"

Apprehensively, Sharae looked at his outstretched hand.

Live... She mentally threw caution to the wind and grasped his hand in hers.

"Hi, I'm Dr. Sharae Jones but everyone calls me Rae. I'm twenty-nine years old, single, no kids, recently unemployed but am starting a project to enhance the lives of young girls. My life feels like an absolute mess right now. But I love long walks on the drive, have a love/hate relationship with food, and I enjoy reading and working out. So how about you? I would love to know more about my…" Laughing eyes stared at him. "future…"

"What kind of doctor are you? I think my heart stopped." Still holding Sharae's hand, Aaron turned her palm up to face him and was intrigued to notice that she had a red tattoo of a heart and a thin black pulse line there indicating an increased pulse rate. He smiled when he wanted to place a small kiss there. Instead, he gently rubbed his thumb over it, feeling the rough lines of the healing tattoo and watched her eyes cloud with the type of curiosity that couldn't be feigned. Aaron made it so they were palm to palm before he intertwined their fingers.

Chuckling, Sharae shook her head. "Ph.D. I am an economist—a statistician. I have mostly dealt with behavioral analysis within the workforce."

"Damn, that's like saying aka, "I'm intelligent as all get out and I know it. I don't know any women with doctorate degrees."

She laughed some more, it was almost a snort. Sharae could only imagine the type of women that flocked to him. *Every woman with a pulse*, she concluded. "That's surprising. I see hordes of all type of women knowing you."

Aaron smirked and shook his head from side to side. "Well, Dr. Jones that goes to show that you have a lot to learn. My name is Aaron Myers. Most people call me A. I'm thirty-five, single— never been married with one daughter. I am an Information Security Specialist by day. I dabble in real estate. I love music and have a good ear so I make beats and produce tracks when time allows. I see something that I want and I go after it."

Sharae smiled as she took it all in. "Information security?" She sipped from her straw then tilted her cup toward him. "Is that like internet policing? That's decent."

"More like cyber bouncers for companies. The most basic way to put it is that we safeguard all of a company's important data. We

157

make sure nothing gets in and nothing gets out. It allows me to travel all over the world and I love it. I also enjoy working out, long walks on the beach, a good book. Looking forward to one day having you to come home to."

The rose color of red rushed into her cheeks as Sharae blushed at the thought. It was as if the butterflies on her shoulders had somehow found their way into her stomach as she felt the flutters of their wings. "Still to be determined," she laughed. "Let's try this friendship out."

Aaron kissed her side of their joined hands. "Agreed. As long as you promise to let me know when you ready for more," Aaron murmured.

Chapter Eighteen

"Y ou have reached Dr. Sharae Jones, and I am currently unavailable. Please leave a detailed message, including a contact number, and I will get back to you." Sharae's voice repeated the same message for the last twenty calls he'd made. James cursed when the automated system informed him that the voicemail box was full. He ended the call.

The silent treatment was getting ridiculous. He'd allowed her more than two weeks.

Fifteen days to be exact.

James paced the front lawn. Given the circumstances, he understood her position but at the same time, he concluded that she completely misunderstood his. All of his calls were being declined and sent to voicemail. None of his texts had been read. It irked him to know, thanks to iPhone, that she hadn't even opened any of the hundred text messages he'd sent, begging for her forgiveness.

Just today, he'd received a note with a single key, informing him that all his personal items had been moved to a self-storage unit. He'd checked their joint account to find that she'd taken half the funds and had removed her name as an account holder. A new auto insurance card had also been delivered, showing that she'd removed her car from his policy and had changed his resident address to that of the studio.

In a fury, he'd shown up at her job to have been informed that she no longer worked there. They wouldn't even allow him entry to the building. He'd contacted Tamika through her husband Stephen who confirmed that Sharae was well and basically just ignoring him.

Nerves completely fried, James looked down at his watch. It was after eight p.m. and the cold air whipped across his face, reminding him that it was November. James stalked back to his car where he decided he would wait for her. The fallout was lasting fourteen days longer than expected. To quit her job and make foolish life-altering decisions without discussing it with him was not characteristic of the person he knew. The Sharae he knew overanalyzed every situation to death. She had to have been acting under the ill advisement of her therapist and single friends.

There was no way she would sever ties completely with him.

They shared an unbreakable bond.

James had come to the conclusion that Sharae was holding out for the ring. He nodded; he didn't blame her. Couldn't find fault in her. She deserved it. James pulled the ring box from his pocket. He opened the box, gazed at it as the diamond sparkled like a promise of her acceptance.

It would make her happy. Who would've thought it? Coming so close to losing her to make him realize how much she meant to him? He was finally ready to make her happy.

There were no sparkles in her eyes when Sharae pulled into her driveway beside James' Audi. She sucked her teeth and nervously bit on her bottom lip as she rolled her eyes and reached over to grab her tote. She'd already been prepared for him showing up, given that she'd been ignoring his texts and phone calls. Tamika had called her and told her that he'd called Stephen.

The nerve of men these days. Barricade up. Back straight, head to the sky, Sharae went to meet him. She was ready if he decided to put on a show.

James was out his car when she reached him.

"You quit your job?" James questioned her before she even had an opportunity to speak.

"Well, hello, to you too," Sharae responded as she breezed by him.

The instrumental to Ginuwine's, *Last Chance* began to play inside his head. James took a brief moment to take in her appearance. She was dressed in black sneakers, a black hoodie, and navy vest with workout tights.

Inappropriate thoughts of how appealing she looked had him biting back the urge to tell her how he felt.

He followed her to the front door but stopped abruptly when Sharae turned around to face him before she opened it. "What do you want?" she asked him. "Why are you even here?"

James cleared his throat and looked down at her. She had one hand on her hip while the other made gestures. "I was worried about you. You haven't answered any of my text messages or phone calls, and I received a storage key for my stuff."

Sharae frowned up at him, trying to figure out if the ball in her stomach were nerves or if she was just hungry. "And?" She wished she could read his mind but knew that she would not have to. James was cocky enough to lay all his thoughts and plans on the line.

"Sharae?" He searched her eyes for traces of naiveté but found none. "Are you okay?" His voice was sincere, and the touch of his hand to her cheek was meant to soften her towards him, but she backed away at the intimate contact.

A quick retreat and eye roll accompanied the words, "I'm fine. I sent the key through the mail because that saved us both any added

161

drama. I don't answer your text or calls because there is nothing else to say."

"Babe, you quit your job."

Sharae shrugged. "I hated my job. So, no big loss there. And considering that your girlfriend called my job and made false accusations, resulting in a suspension, I figure that she did me a favor. You can tell her I said thanks."

"Hold up. She called your job?"

Sharae spared him a glance. "Yes. I guess she was trying to get me fired."

James was lost for words. Completely speechless. There were no apologies to smooth the bumps in the road. "No, that bitch didn't."

"Yes, that bitch did."

"Rae, I had no idea."

"There's nothing to say, James. After this, there is no way that we are ever getting back together—"

James frowned and put his hand on the door over her head, closing her in. "I didn't know."

"What does it matter now?" she asked, pushing him away from her. "When y'all stupid nuccas out here doing a bunch of shit behind y'all girl's back, y'all really think y'all can control it. Can control the other person, and you can't. Don't try to control this side of it. I'm good."

"Can we go inside? Talk?" James asked when a stream of cold found its way between the two of them.

As cold as the crisp air, Sharae answered, "Out here is fine."

"We can work it out."

Thousands of thoughts and emotions were brimming to the surface. Sharae yearned to humble his arrogance by making him understand her side, but it no longer mattered. None of it mattered. No words could take back everything that happened over the past weeks. No words could erase what had transpired between the two of them.

She shook her head. "This is beyond us working it out. I'm going to speak to my lawyer to see what the best options are for the house."

"Fuck!" James growled, removing his hat and rubbing his hands over his head. "I know it's not right to ask you to marry me right this second, so I'm going to hold on to this ring until I fix this."

"You didn't even hear one word I said."

James nodded. "I did hear you. I know my apologies don't mean shit, but I'm sorry for all of this. I'm going to show you."

Sharae shook her head and waved him off. "I can't with you. Goodbye, James."

James stepped back. "I'ma call you," he told her as he backed away, still facing her.

"I'm not going to answer," she responded.

"Rae, answer the phone when I call," he told her and then turned to walk away.

Still making demands. Their relationship status was beyond his demands, and he was too arrogant to accept it.

Sharae rolled her eyes as she let herself into the house. Locking the door, she leaned against it and took a deep breath, wishing that it would hold her up. *Is it possible to be amused by his actions?* The thought that he was serious about his intentions to be reunited, let alone married, was quite laughable.

Too entertained to be annoyed, Sharae pushed off the door as she came out of her vest and hoodie. She stepped out of her sneakers at the base of the stairs and took them two at a time on the way up. She went into the bathroom, turned on the faucets to the tub, and poured some of her bottled *Relax* bubble bath by *Lollia* into the water stream. She watched as the bubbles began to form before going into her bedroom.

Sitting at the edge of the bed, Sharae dropped her purse on the floor, but quickly picked it back up when her mother's voice reminded her that was the sure fire way to become and stay broke. She stood up and placed it on the footstool beside her bed instead.

163

Sharae threw her hands up and fell back onto her bed. It had been a long day. A bubble bath and a movie would surely put her to sleep. That was better than needing the aid of pills.

We don't need that... We're good... You're good... I'm good...

She had already picked out *Something Borrowed* and had loaded it in the DVD player before leaving her house that morning. She turned her radio on and twirled around, dancing out of her clothes. Sharae walked naked out of her bedroom as the sounds of Norah Jones and Ray Charles drifted into the hall, following her into the bathroom as she decided that candlelight would complement the bubbles. She opened the bathroom closet and quickly set up tealight candles all around the tub, the sink, and toilet seat.

Sharae stepped into the tub and sat down, causing water to slouch around the edges of the tub onto the floor. She closed her eyes as the heated water rushed up to her shoulders, much like the water rushing the coastline at the beach. She sank deeper until she was submerged neck- deep. Her only regret was that she'd left her book in her bedroom.

Time spun out, becoming irrelevant as she imagined the lapping water carrying her worries away. By the time the forty-five-minute bath ended, she'd reheated the water twice, dipped her head beneath the surface, and washed the suds from her body with her massaging shower head.

Thoroughly lotioned, powdered, and now bundled in her white robe with her hair wrapped under a towel, Sharae crawled beneath her covers. Music and lights now off, she pressed play to start the movie. She glanced at the clock and figured she'd be asleep in less than ten minutes.

Damn, Lollia is definitely worth the price. Sleep was calling her name. At this rate, she'd have to watch *Something Borrowed* at least ten more times before she saw it to the end.

Forty minutes later as she felt herself drifting into sleep, the vibration of her cell phone beneath her pillow brought her attention back to the movie. Sharae smiled when Aaron's name flashed. "Hey," she answered, voice husky with sleep.

"I thought of you, multiple times today. So I felt it my duty to call and make sure you were tucked away in bed all safe. Were you asleep?"

The sound of his voice coaxed her to snuggle against the fresh pillows she'd bought after James left.

"No, not sleep," Sharae lied. "But I am all tucked away." She yawned. "Excuse me." She rolled onto her back. "Had a long day." She yawned again. "I'm sorry. It's that time."

"That's okay. Get some sleep. We can talk tomorrow," Aaron, himself now yawned.

Sharae laughed. "Aww see, yawns are so contagious. How was your day?"

"Great now. How about you?"

Sharae rolled her eyes despite that she was smiling from ear-to-ear. "It was good. Very productive."

"Can you cook?"

It wasn't a question of could she, it really was more of if she like to. So, brows knit together, Sharae answered, "Yes. Can you?"

"I've been known to put it down in the kitchen. Maybe one day you'll allow me to cook for you."

"I'll have to take you up on that." Another yawn. "Oh gosh. Once you get started."

The velvet warmth of his laugh all but came through the phone and made her cheeks flushed.

"Go ahead to sleep. I'll call you in the morning."

"No, just talk to me," Sharae responded. She held back another yawn.

Aaron chuckled. "Tell me something weird about you."

Sharae thought it an odd question but was game for answering it. "Random weirdness. Okay. Don't judge me, but I can't smell under pressure."

Aaron was quiet for a moment, which was quickly followed by a burst of laughter. "Really? Can't smell under pressure. That is funny as hell."

"See? People be like, *'you smell that?'* I'll sniff, but I never smell whatever it is."

More laughter on the other end.

"I'm so serious. It's the weirdest thing ever." She had to laugh at that herself. "Now you." More intrigued with him than sleep, Sharae sat up against the headboard.

"I'm all kinds of weird. Even though I'm all tatted and I workout, I guess I always assume people perceive me as this macho type dude, I secretly enjoy romantic comedies."

James hated romantic comedies and swore up and down that real men didn't watch them. She almost rolled her eyes as she thought of him. She would have to stop comparing at some point. "No? I love romantic comedies! Supposed to be watching *Something Borrowed* right now."

"It was alright. Left me questioning the girl code, though."

"You really watched it? Wait, you saw it on a date?" Aaron could imagine the expression on her face and had the overwhelming urge to see her. "Can I facetime you? Maybe we can watch it together?"

"I just got out the tub. You trying see me looking a mess?" she asked.

"I'm just trying to see you. Any way I can." The intimacy of his words caressed her.

"You're not naked or anything, are you?" Sharae asked, her desire to see his handsome face battling with her thoughts that he was indeed some pervert trying to show her illicit images of himself.

"No. I'm just getting home. Still in my suit, got a drink, and put my feet up. If it makes you feel uncomfortable, it's cool. I can wait to see you in person."

Sharae nibbled nervously on the inside of her lip. She pulled the towel from her hair. Damp curls fell down, framing her face. "You don't have to wait," she told him, pressing the facetime option on her screen.

Aaron answered quickly, his handsome face filling the box when it appeared.

If smiles could match, they would be identical.

Would it be an accurate description to say that he is hands down the most attractive man I've ever come in contact with? Sharae wondered as she drank in the sight of him. His gray tie was loosened at the collar of his black dress shirt. From a certain angle, she could see he'd also unbuttoned the top three buttons of his shirt and that he was wearing a tailored vest.

Damn. Her mouth was dry.

"Why are you so damn beautiful?" he questioned her, wishing he had the magical powers to reach through the screen and touch her intimately. Is it *possible for her to be more beautiful without makeup? Naturally curly hair framing her face, skin fresh and wrapped all up in a fluffy white robe.* He wondered if her skin was as soft as it looked.

Sharae blushed. She'd had men tell her they thought she was beautiful and was learning how it deal with it. It wasn't always easy taking compliments when your experiences taught you to wonder about the intentions and actions behind the words. "Thank you. So, you gonna watch this movie with me over the phone?"

"You watch the movie, and I'll watch you until you fall asleep."

Do men receive special training on how to make a woman feel tingles all over?

Strategically put-together words and sweet pickup lines should not work on her, but this one had hit its target.

She smiled. "Really?" She drawled sarcastically.

"This will have to do until I get the privilege first hand," he told her.

"You are so very sure of yourself, Mister."

167

"Of course I am," he responded.

Distracted by the word **Bitch,** displayed as a purple text banner across the top of her screen, Sharae minimized the call to read the text. With a fading smile, she read the text from an unknown telephone number. ***"HE DON'T WANT YOU BITCH! KEEP FUCKIN' AROUND AND YOU GON' LOSE MORE DEN YOUR JOB!!!!"***

"Rae, what's wrong?" Aaron questioned, his voice ripe with concern as he witnessed the twinkle in her eyes dim like fading headlights.

The sound of Aaron's voice brought his face back into focus. Sharae sucked her teeth. "A, do you mind if I call you back?" Sharae asked.

"That's fine. Is everything okay?"

Mind already racing towards her next move, she murmured, "Yeah, I'll call you back in a lil' bit."

Sharae disconnect the call right as he said, "Night, then."

No, this hoe didn't.

Get a drink and call this bitch.

Just show up at her house and fuck her up.

The voices offered suggestions galore, but Sharae just shook her head.

The high road took a back seat to the pettiness. Sharae pulled up James' text messages and opened them for the first time in two weeks. She screenshot several messages where he was begging, pleading, loving, and frustrated by her nonresponse. She then text messaged the woman over ten screenshots and included a message of her own:

"You should focus on your dude wanting to be with me, stupid. I dismissed his ass and am allowing you to have him. Now, say thank you and please keep him home. Tired of him showing up begging to get back with me. I have no intention of ever, and I mean ever, being with him again. As I've stated before, please don't come for me, or I will have to fuck you up. Bye hoe; be happy. I am."

x

Instant response: *"What, Bitch? Don't make me show up at your house."*

"LMFAO, you nothing-ass trick. Know that I don't want James but be prepared to get fucked up if you plan on showing up here."

That is it… and that is all. She mentally dusted her hands, and Sharae powered her cell phone off. Maybe, just maybe, she would contact AT&T to get a new telephone number. She loathed the thought of having to go weeks of back and forth with Daneen over James. She was not interested in entertaining either one of them.

Sharae let out a frustrated sigh as she sank down into the middle of her bed. She'd had the same phone number for the past ten years. She wasn't sure if she could give it up but contemplated doing just that if it meant getting rid of Dumb and Dumber.

She would have to sleep on it.

Chapter Nineteen

ays passed into a week and then a week into two and so on. She'd changed her cell phone number but had also received harassing messages on Facepage, so Sharae resolved that by disabling her account. She hadn't wanted to, but after blocking the girl, making her page private, and weeding through tons of wall postings from random people, she had just chalked it up as a loss and deactivated the account. It was necessary to maintain her sanity. She figured that Daneen was gearing for a fight; she wasn't likely to get one, but the girl was definitely trying all of her patience and all of her nerves, not to mention the remainder of her resolve not to stoop to the heifer's tactics.

James was popping up unexpectedly every other night, stating that he just wanted to see her. She was on the verge of asking King if she could stay at his place for a while until she figured out what her other alternatives would be. Sharae shrugged it off as she had other more pressing situations to concern herself with, situations that held the promise of great things to come.

Girls Living Outcomes of Successful Starts at Youth was no longer just an idea she'd penned in her mid-twenties. In the last month, she had used all of energy to turn her dream into a reality. She designed a logo and trademarked the name. Now, she not only needed willing and available mentors, but she also required sizeable donations to actually help fund the project.

Raising money had never been a problem for Sharae. She'd use a small portion of her own savings as a start-up until the donations began to pour in. She'd worry about securing funding once she secured the professionals who were willing to help make a difference.

The thought of taking a chance on herself to give others a chance gave her a thrill unlike no other. Her rationale was if young ladies in the inner city were given the chance to see things beyond their communities, then it would expand their scopes of reality and show them that dreams could be limitless. During her test trials with the self-sufficiency initiatives, she'd come across women who had never been outside the city of Philadelphia. It had blown her mind to discover that there were actual adult women who had only traveled as far as different counties to visit shopping malls. Sharae had high hopes of changing that for all the women who entered her program. There had been considerable effort put forth to have a formal informational session for GLOSSY prospective mentors and contributors. E-vites, formal invites, and information brochures were all officially mailed out to every professional woman she knew. The list of twenty-five distinguished women included friends and associates that Sharae considered would make excellent mentors if they elected to participate in the program's initial cycle. So far, she had confirmations from a lawyer, a writer, a real estate broker, a hair salon owner, a clothing boutique seamstress, a high school principal, a bakery owner, and a health and fitness specialist.

Yes, some lucky ladies and girls are about to be all GLOSSY and will *have a better life because of it*, she thought as she checked her cell phone for text messages.

Hey, beautiful. Things were a lil' hectic today but I should be settled by ten. Facetime?

If I'm not asleep by then... she responded quickly.

Aaron's response was lightning-quick: **You know you want to talk to me.**

Sharae narrowed her eyes and typed back, **You swear you know me but you're right this time, I do. So ttyl.**

Then there was Aaron and the beginnings of something that could potentially be very nice once she was ready to commit to another relationship. He was so serious yet possessed a sense of humor that had the ability to make her laugh. He proved to be a match for her wittiness and was quick to check her on her sarcasm. She'd discovered that he was the owner of the securities firm he'd spoken of on their first date. He was an entrepreneur; something like a self-prescribed hustler who had his dollars invested in several different prosperous businesses. And from what she could see, his pockets and prosperity ran deep.

Aaron was used to being in total control and came off as very cocksure and demanding, but in the few dates they had, she saw a softer and kinder side that was also giving. They bumped heads because she was also a control freak who planned every detail meticulously while he worked off a schedule but was far more flexible about things. They'd worked out together a couple times, and he joked that no other guy from the gym would ever approach her now because they knew she was his. They'd gone to the movies, attended a Legends of Hip Hop concert as VIP guests, and taken a day trip to Washington D.C to visit the National Museums.

But no sex. Not even a dry hump. By the third date, even though they'd held hands in public, she assumed there would at least be a kiss but still nothing except a brotherly peck on the cheek. When she'd initially informed him she wasn't ready to be in a relationship, Aaron had taken it to heart and let her know that he wouldn't take the next step until she let him know she was ready. Aaron had been the perfect gentleman when it came to respecting her wishes that they just be friends.

More than a month later, Sharae wished he'd stop being so damn respectable. It was driving her absolutely crazy! The thought of him made her smile as much as being in his presence did. He was out of town on business, but she'd check his plans for the weekend. With special plans for Aaron in mind, the dopey smile plastered on her face turned into something much more wicked.

"That stank face cannot be because of GLOSSY luncheon invites," Tamika teased as she walked around the other side of Sharae's desk. She rocked her fussy six-month-old daughter, Camille, in her arms. "It's okay, Pooh," Tamika cooed as she expertly unfastened her blouse and almost had her left breast out before King said, "Whoa! Whoa! You just gonna pull them out like that?"

Tamika rolled her eyes at King. "Pass me that receiving blanket right there. She is about to have a heart attack." Camille hated having the blanket over her as she ate.

King laughed and cleared his throat. "I'm just saying they belong to your husband and your baby. I don't want to see them."

Tamika's eyebrows creased as she looked accusingly at King. "All the titties you see, nucca? Please."

Sharae laughed at them. It never failed; they had to go back and forth about something. "You're right, Mika. GLOSSY is going to be a huge success. The swag bags are going to be the best. Makeup, gift cars, test her tickets and more. And I'm kind of seeing a new guy."

"I see you tryna slide that in there. James is gonna kick ya ass," Tamika joked as she sat beside King.

King frowned. He'd seen her workout with the guy Aaron from the gym. The smiles that had passed between them. "It's kind of early for you to be dating. I thought you were going to focus on getting

173

GLOSSY started and…" he used air quotation marks when he said, *"be off men"*.

"I said kind of dating, and I am focused. I'm so hype right now about my project," Sharae said as she pushed away from her computer. She handed them both the informational brochure. "I have a logo and a mission statement. And I'm going to, with the assistance of my friends, change and possibly save the lives of young girls. How freakin' great is that?!" She clapped excitedly.

"Awww, honey, I'm so proud of you," Tamika winced as Camille used her nipple as a teething ring. "Shit!"

"Yeah, Rae. I'm really proud of you. Who are you using for marketing, promotions, networking, and your website?" King asked.

Sharae shrugged. "I don't know; I was going to try and do it myself."

Tamika chuckled. "Warning: Do-it-yourself project on deck," she said to King. "Tell your friend that she needs to hire a professional."

Sharae rolled her eyes. Her friends made fun of her DIY projects, but they had saved her hundreds of dollars. "Why? I can do it. It's really not that hard." Sharae dismissed the notion of spending money on something she could do herself.

King cleared his throat, straightened up, and sat closer to the edge of the couch. He rubbed his hands over his head. "I was thinking that Ava could help you out with that. She recently took over social meeting marketing, promotions and networking for me and has already increased my client list within the last two months."

Sharae frowned. "My Ava?"

My Ava, he thought territorially. This was going to be harder than he expected. What he felt for Ava had been unexpected but was important enough for him to share it with Sharae. "Yes. Rae, she's a damn genius at what she does." His pride for Ava shone in his eyes.

"I guess I never thought of her. I mean, I know she does it to make a 'lil side money. I know she's good, and I love her blog."

"It is good. I love her diary of a fanciful fashionista indulging in food and love. I think she's dating someone too," Tamika added. "The tone of her writing when she speaks of going out has changed. It went from straight partying to more dining and romantic-type things. She has a new column about dates."

This was his opportunity to jump up and say, *'Yup, she's dating me.'*
But King said nothing.

Sharae considered Tamika's comments. Ava had been glowing the last time they had lunch, but Sharae assumed it was the excitement over her upcoming graduation that had her floating on cloud nine.

Sharae shrugged. "I guess with all that's going on with me, I haven't been all up in her business." Her focus on Aaron, GLOSSY, and preserving her mental sanity had taken precedence and had left little room for her to be overly active in Ava's life. "I'll definitely ask her if she'll look it over for me," Sharae decided.

She reached over to stroke Camille's cap of curly hair. The baby contently suckled at her mother's breast, blissfully unaware of the struggles of being an adult.
Sharae smiled; life for babies was so simple. She turned her attention back to King. "Don't forget to text me Kyrie's number so I can call her about the details for the luncheon."

Surprised at the mention of his now ex-lover, King frowned. "Rae, we've been over for months. I know she called you. And I told you twice."

Sharae shook her head as she pointed accusingly at him. "Hmm. I knew you was gonna fuck that up."

While Sharae had been hopeful that their friend would settle down with the real estate agent, Tamika had seen the writing on the wall. King was still restless while he was with Kyrie. Though, she noticed the edginess dissipate in the last few months.

"What did you do to her?" Sharae wouldn't admit that she'd ignored more than a dozen of the woman's call before having her number changed.

"I didn't do shit," he flagged. "She wasn't for me. My mom didn't like her, and y'all two only tolerated her because she was with me."

They both mentally agreed and nodded their heads.

"She was so cute, though," Tamika said.

"Well, another one bites the dust," Sharae added.

"I'm going to have to find you a nice, feisty thang," Tamika offered.

King made the X sign with his arms as he shook his head, recalling the last three disasters Tamika had sent his way. "No more hookups from you," he laughed. "I'm definitely cool. And besides, I have someone."

Sharae swiveled in her chair, giving him her full attention. "Someone like what?"

There was a flicker of light in his eyes, and his lips displayed a hopeless grin as he thought of his someone. "Let me find out," Sharae murmured, clapping her hands.

"Well, who is she? How long? And when are we gonna meet her?" Tamika bombarded him with a barrage of questions.

Sharae took a moment to inspect her friend. "Oh, my gosh; your black ass is happy. Who is she?" she pumped for an answer.

There was breath he was holding that he expelled with his response. "Ava."

There was the truth of it. He was in love with her, King realized. The rush of emotions he felt smoothed out his apprehensions.

Dead silence. Even Tamika was taken aback. Sharae's eyes clouded with confusion. Tamika adjusted Camille onto her shoulder to burp her. After a moment Sharae indulged in a conversation with herself. *My lil' sister Ava. I'm sure that's not what I heard.*

Yes, honey you did...

But King is... Is a damn womanizer.

"My little sister, Ava? King, she's a damn kid," Sharae said to him, standing up. She immediately began to pace the room to soothe her nerves.

"Oh shit," Tamika let out. She decided to remain silent until her friends required a referee.

King stood up and blocked Sharae's path. "Yes. She's not a kid—"

Eyes wide, Sharae pushed at his chest. "Why would you think it's okay to date my— my baby?"

King held his hands up. "I know it's a touchy subject but, I love her."

Wrong answer. Sharae shook her head. "I'm not hearing this. You're a damn dog, and she is a kid with no experience at doing anything. My parents still support her, for God's sake."

Irritated but rational enough to understand her concern, King said, "I'm gonna say this 'cause I love you. You know absolutely nothing about her. Not the life that she has or what she's built for herself because all you worry about is you," he told her. "And if I'm not mistaken, mommy and daddy paid for your shit til' you were twenty-four," he added angrily.

Tamika stood up carefully. "Okay, calm down."

"After I'm done. You guys are a lot alike. She admires you more than you know. Your success makes her feel so inadequate that she downplays her own success so that she comes off as the needy lil' sister. She knows nothing of your failures. You never let her see you that way. She takes your elderly aunt out once a month for brunch. She feeds the poor and volunteers at CHOP. She's hoping that you look at her and one day see a woman. You think she's a pampered princess cause you're the damn Queen. But you see none of that, so please tell me who is fucking trippin'?" King demanded of Sharae.

Speechless and motionless, she considered Kings words, the weight of their impact pounding in their meaning.

177

Detach; take a step back from your emotions.

Reason; how would you handle the situation if you were not involved?

Shit...

"I'm sorry, King, but I'ma need a minute to adjust. You're my best friend, and she is my baby. I know you, and despite what you're saying, I know her. I just don't know y'all the way y'all know each other."

Overwhelmed, Sharae flopped down onto the couch. She stretched out dramatically then sat up straight. "Are you serious about being in love with her?"

"Yea. I am."

Emotions swirled. "Don't break her heart, King, 'cause I would have to fuck you up," Sharae said sincerely to him. Then it hit her. "I can't. You were her first." Sharae pretended to gag. "I think I'm going to be sick."

Seems like her baby wasn't a baby anymore after all.

Chapter Twenty

*I*s there a right time to tell to someone you love them? Is there some unwritten rule on how it should be done? Maybe there is a manual? Is it supposed to slip out at the pinnacle of orgasmic release or be a well-put together string of lines designated for a certain occasion? King wondered. He imagined being lost in the sea of Ava's gaze as he buried himself inside her and how they warmed the moment she reached her peak as he whispered the magical words. Would her heart melt? He smiled to himself as he thought about Sharae's threat.

"Rae said she would fuck me up if I hurt you," he said to Ava.

Ava laughed, her voice warm and rich like the hot chocolate she'd just given to him. "I know that's right."

King took Ava's hand into his, intertwining their fingers. "I wouldn't, you know." He was sure of that now. King kissed their joined hands.

Ava shrugged; she understood how relationships and good intentions worked. "No one ever intends or sets out to hurt anyone they care about, but sometimes it happens despite our best intentions." *Wasn't Sharae in her big old house crying her eyes out over James? Well, she couldn't really use James as an example, could she?* "I'm so proud that you had the courage to tell her about us. *And* that you kept your promise. I don't know how much longer I would have been able to keep it a secret," Ava added.

King shrugged. "We weren't a secret. I just had to work out how to tell her. It's not your typical situation." Secrets were usually something people kept out of shame. "In any case, it kind of just came out 'cause her and Mika was talking about hooking me up, and as a defense, I was like, 'Nawl. I have someone.'"

Ava smiled. The admission made her want to kiss him. With a nod, she playfully agreed, "Yup."

"You sure you don't want to go out tonight?" King inquired.

"Yes," she quickly replied. "Everything I need is right here."

A quiet evening in sounded just about right. It was cold and rainy out. She didn't feel like getting dressed up for an outing. No reports or assignments were due for school; there were no emails or blog postings to respond to, and season one of Game of Thrones was finally listed on *On Demand*. "Game of Thrones and a fine man cooking me a three-course meal sounds so much better."

King smirked. "You ain't slick. You only like Game of Thrones 'cause of the boah."

Her and every other woman with a pulse, Ava mentally agreed. And while Jason Momoa's Khal Drogo was definitely fine, she actually enjoyed the premise of the show. "Awww, you jealous?" she joked with a kiss to cheek.

"Nawl. I'm straight," he replied with a compensatory pat on her thigh.

"You shouldn't be 'cause you my Khal Drogo every day."

King rolled his eyes. "We on episode six," he laughed. He had to get off the couch because he would soon succumb to all her flirtations and dinner would not be had. She'd end up bent over like Khaleesi from a couple of episodes before. "I prepped a citrus spinach salad, garlic herb salmon with grilled zucchini and squash, and chocolate strawberry trifle for dessert," he told her, getting up.

Ava stretched out and rubbed her stomach. "Daaaamn, can I get some rice, though? And do you need a sous chef?"

"You're not that good at taking orders, babe."

Offended, Ava stood up and sucked her teeth. "I can cook," she said defensively.

King shook his head. "I didn't say you couldn't. I said you don't listen, and this will end up being Ava's dinner."

"Whatever, King," Ava said as she followed him to the kitchen. "You don't want me to help you?" she pouted a couple of minutes later.

"Everything is already prepped," he said to appease her. "What you can do is grab a bottle of wine and turn on some music and just watch a master at work," he told her as he put his customized black apron on.

~ ~

"In all these years, I swear I didn't know you could cook so well. All those hoes would have been getting the business," Ava admitted later, looking down at him as he lay across the sofa, head in her lap.

"It's always a plus when it come to the ladies. A thorough nigga who is handsome, athletic, can cook, *and* got bread. I was a definite commodity."

Ava laughed. "You a'ight. And now you off the market."

Damn. All the way off the market and could care less. "You saved me from the misery of single life, babe," he laughed. "It ain't nothing out there, though. Plus, stupid niggas be messing up good shit with good women for nothing-ass hoes," he said, thinking of James and Sharae. There was no love lost over their breakup because he was never particularly fond of James because of his dating habits. Not that he'd been a saint when it came to dating, but he was always honest. And that made all the difference in his mind.

"I know, and since I had time to think about it, Rae wouldn't have to intervene on my behalf 'cause I would kill you," Ava stated as a matter-of-fact.

King tilted his body back to get a good look at her face.

Ava blinked at his blank stare. "What? Yes! I said it. I'm crazy, and I'm not for no whole bunch of mess," she laughed but was very serious.

"I don't want no trouble, Ma," he laughed back.

King's stomach was full, and there was no other place he would rather be. The fact that she matched him in his moodiness intrigued him more. She was demanding of his time and space but wasn't easily sated just by being in his presence. She thrived off their interactions with one another. He loved to cuddle, lounge around on the couch, talk about everything, and sometimes, nothing at all. He'd learned that some women just wanted to be in the same place as you so you weren't in another place with someone else. It didn't work that way with them. She forced him to watch more of the world news and less of Sports Center and ESPN, challenged his sometimes limited views on society, and debated endlessly, even if her view was flawed. She could handle his temper and talk him down when it got the best of him. She had patience for all the small things he did not.

Plans for a meal prep option were being implemented as an additional service for his clients.

Ava had bullied her way into his life, and after all the positive additions she'd brought, he couldn't fathom it without her. Certain it was love, still not exactly sure how to share it, he just lay back on her lap and enjoyed the comfort of her touch.

Chapter Twenty-One

*T**he doorbell chimed as soon** as she reached the base of the stairs. She remembered her FedEx delivery and was happy that she was still there to receive them. She was already running late to meet Ava for their scheduled lunch.

The joy of receiving packages was replaced by confusion as she was handed a certified letter by the mail carrier. Sharae signed her name when prompted and waved the goodbye after giving the carrier the receipt.

After recognizing the Commonwealth of Virginia stamp, Sharae stared down at the letter and tested its material weight. Not quite sure if she was ready to address the situation that lay inside, Sharae quickly weighed the emotional impact and set the letter in the mailbox on the table and decided that she didn't care what it said. She would not allow the contents of the letter to dictate her emotions for the day or for the rest of her life for that matter. Hadn't she just told her own mother that a little more than a month ago when she decided not to attend Matthew's parole hearing?

"I'm not going, and I don't want you to go either. I just want for it all to be over."

Sharae cringed when she heard Lorraine's gasp for air. "Sharae Jones! You need to be there. He needs to remember what he did to you."

"I can't. I see Matthew's face in my dreams. I hear his voice when I'm sleeping, and I don't want to. I wasn't right for weeks after the last time. I used to freak out when James put his arms around my waist in the middle of the night."

"Rae, we cannot allow Matthew to get away with what he did to us," Lorraine pressed.

"No, not us, Momma. Me! What he did to me!"

"Exactly! Fifteen years is not enough. His sentence was twenty years, and he deserves every single second of it. You should make sure you do whatever you can to see to it."

Sharae could feel the darkness cover her heart but also felt the flicker of an unwavering love that would not give up on her. "GLOSSY is how I make things right with me. I don't want to dwell in the past for the next ten years of my life."

"Gregory!" Lorraine said as her husband took the phone from her. "Baby, I want you to think about it."

"I have thought about it and I'm not going..."

Her thoughts lingered back to the letter she'd left at home as she poured over web page layout designs and drank iced coffee with Ava. They'd managed to tie together the loose strands that made their six-year age difference feel significant. The majority of the blame, if it had to be assigned went to Sharae because of the boundaries put in place that kept them separate. And more because of Sharae's insistence to treat Ava like a child. It was the bond she had shared with Ava that had literally saved her life after Matthew's abduction. The precious eight-year-old who had no idea of the very adult things going on around her was relentless when it came to hounding Sharae for attention. Ava didn't seem to care that all she wanted to do was fall into a black hole and die in an abyss of darkness. There she was carting that rugged stuffed rabbit and the special edition copy of The Velveteen Rabbit because it was her favorite book and she wanted Sharae to know she could now read. She had pressed and pressed, and no matter how much her mother had insisted that she leave Sharae alone, Ava would not. In the end, Ava had become the light in her very dark world, had made her feel real again, and had drawn Sharae out of her depression. She had been her source of joy for years that followed and still held the softest spot in her heart. It pained Sharae to think that she had somehow discounted Ava while holding her close so that no one could hurt her.

Witnessing the adult Ava work in her element gave Sharae a little more insight as to who she was. She could remember Ava spinning around to her computer during conversations many times but assumed it had been for fun, the blog and the many social media sites.

How ridiculously blind of her to have not seen that gleam of happiness radiating in Ava's eyes as it was now. She wasn't sure how much of that gleam had to do with King but was diving in to find out. "I guess I didn't realize how serious you were about King," Sharae admitted to Ava. She spread her arms wide. "How serious you were about everything."

"I love my work and I love him," Ava returned.

It was something she hadn't disclosed to King yet, but now that she'd said the words aloud to Sharae, Ava was going to be sure to fill him in at her first opportunity.

"Why didn't you tell me that you wanted King that way?" Sharae asked her.

Ava shrugged on a hearty laugh. "Of course, I did. Several times, but you just didn't take me seriously. Neither did he at first, but I was able to persuade him otherwise."

Sharae smiled as she read the pure love for King in Ava's eyes. She felt it as it smoothed over and coated her own heart as she touched it. "I'm sorry that I treat you like you're a baby. But you are my baby. And if I ever gave you the impression for even one second that I don't value you, then I am sorry beyond words. You made me feel real."

Genuinely touched, Ava shrugged off the weight lifted by Sharae's admission. "I guess it's not really— I mean I can't explain it. I know you love me to death, and I may have wedeled myself into the pigeon hole you have placed me in by acting so needy. I know we're not 'tell every single secret, all up in each other's business close', but I'd like for us to be," Ava admitted.

Sharae nodded in agreement. "I would like that. I told King I would kick his ass if he hurt you."

Ava laughed. "He told me. I'll keep that in mind, but he has been nothing but wonderful to me." Her smile was so bright; it could light up the darkness night. "Are you good, though?" Ava's voice hinted at concern.

"I'm as good as I'm gonna be. I had a lil' rough patch, but now I'm as right as rain." She decided not to speak about Matthew's parole hearing.

"Rae, I'm so sorry about everything. Your job. James. What are y'all gonna do? Your house?"

Sharae shrugged. It was, after all, just a piece of property. Another illusion built to keep her invested in their relationship to nowhere. "Daddy warned me that it was a big decision to buy the house with him without being married."

She'd already contacted the mortgage company, her financial advisor, and lawyer to gauge her options. Recently unemployed, there was no way she could arrange to take over the mortgage payments on her own. She'd tried every angle, and the finances were not adding up for the unforeseen future. Sharae rolled her eyes at the thought. James was still stalling on his agreement to sell. In the past two months, he'd paid his half of the payment, but she couldn't expect him to continue doing so when the reality set in that they were never going to be a couple again.

"I want to sell. James won't agree to anything unless I speak to him directly. He doesn't have my new number, and I'm figuring I'll just move out sometime after the new year."

"Hhmm. Damn, that shit sucks. How does your heart feel?"

Sharae rubbed her chest, where it had previously hurt, to feel every single beat and smiled. "Healed. Free."

Ava took in the sight of her older sister and knew that she spoke the truth. Her eyes were bright, her skin was glowing, and her smile was unfazed by their discussion.

You selling this shit hard, girl...

You can cry at any time. I got you., The voice of misery reared its ugly head, flexing her untapped and vulnerable emotions.

No, I have you... Love jumped in.

"It'll get resolved, one way or another. I'm not pressed. And I'm excited about GLOSSY, and there's a new guy."

"I heard. He handsome too. You aren't wasting no time," Ava joked, throwing her hand up for a high-five.

"Not one second on that ass."

"Sharae... Ava..." They both turned to see their newly-married cousin Celena waving and walking up to their table.

Sharae smiled and stood up to embrace Celena. "Look at you. Married life treating you right. You're damn near glowing." She hadn't seen her since the wedding and hadn't spoken to her since before she'd changed her number.

Celena kissed Sharae's cheek and then hugged Ava next.

"You want to join us?" Ava offered.

Celena flagged off the invite, "Oh no, Ant is over there at a table. I had to come over and say hey. I been trying to call you since the other day. And you... you deactivated your Facepage. My mom had to call your dad to get your new number."

"Why? What's wrong?" Sharae asked.

"Nothing. Are you okay?"

"Yea. I'm fine. I was having an issue and had to get a new number. No big deal."

Celena bit her lip as she considered her options. "Okay, I'll just call you." She huffed, but Sharae read the confusion in her cousin's eyes.

"Lena, I'm fine."

"I don't know how to say this, but I saw James at my doctor's office with some girl."

With her smile still in place, Sharae shook her head. "Oh, don't worry about it. We broke up."

"I saw him at the OB, so I spoke. He spoke back, and that lil' ratchet thing he was with was like, "Who the fuck is she?""

"OB? As in you're having a baby? Celena!" Sharae shrieked happily, ignoring the fact that she'd said James was at her OB with another female.

"Yes, we're having a baby. What the hell is going on?" Celena questioned, clearly confused.

"We're done, so I don't give a damn about him having no baby."

"Since when? The girl damn-near showing."

Pregnant and showing... Sharae's heart skipped a beat.

I can't care... I— I don't care...

"Lena, cool out," Ava jumped in to shield Sharae from the onslaught of questions from what felt like an interview from the Daily Inquisitor. "They've been broken up for a while," Ava added.

"I'm sorry. I didn't know. I was just trying to let you know."

Chapter Twenty-Two

*S**harae observed the fire* as the flickering orange flames with traces of red danced across the darkening logs. Its ferocious appetite as it ate at the burning embers matched her current mood. She couldn't honestly say that running into Celena hadn't partially precipitated her overwhelming need to basically fuck the shit of out Aaron. That the court's decision regarding Matthew's parole, although unknown to her, meant that people's lives went on. She couldn't always be stuck in the same place, basing her life off how others lived theirs.

Neither James nor Matthew would get one ounce of credit for her decision to share herself with a man who was so worth it. Without another thought to either, Sharae decided she had much more promising things to concern herself with.

There was a ball of fire burning beneath her cool and contained edges. Lust-filled gazes over intimate conversation of music greats inspired her to be tuned into him. So while they spoke of great hip hop beefs, rock and roll royalty, and the softer side of pop, Sharae planned her seduction.

"Don't judge me," Sharae laughed. "My favorite female rapper is Ms. Jade. The street- I'm-hungry-version."
Surprised, Aaron rolled her choice around in his head, processing his approval. "Ok. I guess I can see that."

Switching iPods, they had the opportunity to go through one another's music library. Aaron was initially surprised with what he'd found. He'd suspected that she would enjoy R&B legends and throaty ballads from both Mariah and Whitney but had also found multiple DMX, Nas, and Jay-Z albums. Of course, there were multiple Beyoncé and Mary J. Blige's albums, in his mind, that was a given. She also had an extensive soft rock and pop selection, songs, and artists from every genre except techno made up her music library of sixteen hundred songs.

"It was her verse on "*Nizzo*" that had me like, 'Yo, she is really hot," Sharae announced. "I mean— I really enjoyed, *"Girl Interrupted"* but that was for mainstream. That verse was raw…" She murmured the words to the rap she knew by heart… "skills so cold, they crush your instrumentals…"

Aaron clapped, impressed by her flow. Admiring how she lost herself in the idea of the lyrics, his smile spread across his face. It was gratifying to be with someone who loved it as well. "Look at you. I'm even more convinced that you're the one."
Sharae laughed as her stomach did flips. *Damn his sexy ass to hell*, she thought, but her tone was mocking when she spoke. "You're convinced?" She drew her eyebrows together and spared him an unconvincing glance. "Aww. You soft on me now 'cause I can rap?"

Aaron moved closer, closing in on her personal space. "I'm soft on you for a number of reasons." The hunger of his desire reflected in his eyes as he inched even closer to her. Their eyes locked, and he continued, "How you speak of hip hop culture as easily as you can discuss the economy and societal pitfalls."

The heat from the fire must have crept into her. With flushed cheeks, Sharae sat up from her leaning pose as Aaron closed in on her circle by joining her on the rug, his eyes still locked on hers as if the lion had found its prey. "Because you want to mentor young girls, because you like museums, long walks on the drive, and working out; because you are unlike any other woman I have ever met."

Sharae feigned putting out the imaginary flames with waves of her hands. "Whew. You are laying it down pretty thick." She wanted more, and in her head, she was igniting the flames with some imaginary lighter fluid rather than dancing them out.

Aaron inched closer yet again. "I'm not *laying* anything..." the word *'yet'* lingering in his thoughts but went unsaid.

It had to be the image she made, curled up on the rug with a mound of pillows surrounding her as the fire crackled behind her that had him reneging on the bargain he'd made not to touch her first. She was always wearing an oversized sweatshirt that hung off her shoulder to display those hopeful butterflies for his viewing pleasure. Ooh, how he imagined himself kissing each one of them. Aaron couldn't be sure if it was the light playing tricks on him or if he saw actual flecks of red as the flames swam in her hazel eyes.

Hadn't he dreamed of her here? Lounging in front of the fire after dinner with a glass of wine, a tray of fruit, light music, and conversation with laughter, lingering looks, and desire pumping from them both in waves?

Aaron settled for the spot on the other side of the pillows to sit facing the fire. He leaned back on his hands. Quickly, he talked himself into backing off and giving her space. She needed time to see him, to want him, and to choose him beyond simply keeping her company as he had these past weeks.

"Why haven't you," Sharae followed up the moment she saw him bank his desire, "laid anything down yet?" she added, crawling beside him.

There was no telling who moved first as swift movements of arms and legs brought them together. Torso to torso, a tangle of arms, lips touching, plundering tongues, linked fingers, heat transferring as they both fought frantically to just be a part of one another. Heightened senses and edgy need seeped from her to him... him to her. It was raw and primal lust that had him pulling her onto his lap.

Sharae opened her eyes to stare up at Aaron, becoming lost in his as his lips descended upon hers. Her lips parted on a sigh captured by him as she drew him closer.

Yes. Honey... Yes... the voices in her head, in unison, melded the words together.

Sharae shivered as his lips left a trail of kisses over her bare shoulder. Their lips soon reunited as his hand roamed beneath her cropped shirt and his fingers trailed heat across the planes of her skin, delicately tying up the loose ends of her heart, making it whole. Cradling her with one arm, Aaron used the other to massage his way up to her breast. Carefully palming one, he squeezed lightly, enjoying the weight of it beneath his touch.

Sharae hummed in appreciation and let her hands roam free as his lips switched places with his hand. She arched her back like a bow, inviting him to take his fill. Lust filled haze clouded her eyes as Aaron's hand slipped into the waistband of her pants. Her thighs spread at his silent commands. Searching fingers delved into the welcoming warmth of her femininity and played there, stroking her intimately as she murmured fervent pleas for more.

As tingles of climatic sensations grew within her, Sharae bucked beneath the onslaught of his lips and hands. "Aaahh!" she breathed.

"That's right," Aaron coached, lifting his mouth from her nipple. He sucked at it again as his fingers played her body like a fine-tuned violin. "Give me you," he murmured, kissing her lips.

Sharae moaned as her hands slid over his chest while she made quick work of unbuttoning Aaron's shirt. She licked at his nipple and felt his lips form a smile against her breast. The manipulating strokes of his fingers quickened their pace as she lapped at his nipple with her tongue and stroked the other with her fingers.

"You gushing. I want that," his voice thick as he spoke against her ear. "I want all that," he added. His hand, slick with her juices, captured hers and guided it to join in on his play. He covered her hand, sliding his fingers between hers and continued to stroke her until he felt the tell-tale tremble as she began to quake as her buttocks clenched and thighs shook as she fought the urge to tumble recklessly over the edge of orgasm's cliff. They both stroked her into taking that last leap.

"Hhmmm. Shiiiiiit!" Sharae squealed as the last of her climax trickled out of her. Her body convulsed uncontrollably as Aaron laughed, pressing his forehead to hers.

"We not done," Aaron warned as he maneuvered their bodies so that he could pull her legs free of the pants that were already halfway off.

Spikes of excitement flowed through her as the husky threat translated as a promise of more to come. Her heart swelled with anticipation as he kneeled behind her, and the kiss at the base of her neck had her hairs standing at attention awaiting their next command.

Sharae lifted her shirt from the hem and pulled it over her head. Aaron quickly found the front-fastening clasp of her bra and freed her plump breasts into his waiting hands. Sharae rolled her neck over his shoulder as he kissed the side of her neck. He used his teeth to nip at her ear and whisper everything he wanted to do to her as she raised her arms above and behind her to hold his head.

Aaron kissed down the underside of her arm as his tongue licked a path to the first butterfly. He led a trail of wet kisses diagonally from her shoulder across her back to the base where the dancing woman seemed to have set them free. The discovery that those butterflies weren't alone but that were a part of a massive work of art covering her

193

back made his manhood throb. "I'ma make these butterflies fly tonight baby," he murmured as he kissed his way back up to his original starting place.

Sharae turned in his arms to face him. She nibbled her bottom lip then went in for a kiss, her hands unfastening his belt. She quickly pulled at his jeans to get them below his waist and off of his hips. She pushed him playfully onto the floor and pulled his jeans and boxers from his body. She crawled to him and made no secret of her appreciation of his sizable contribution to their party. Sharae tilted her head to the side and licked her lips as she envisioned pleasuring him with her oral skills.

"Ahhh," Aaron moaned as he watched his lengthy shaft all but vanish into Sharae's warm, wet mouth. His hands crept into the mass of curls as she stroked his dick with her lips and tongue. Sharae flexed her throat muscles so that they contracted to massage the head. "Fuck, Rae. I want to be inside you," he breathed out but continued to guide each up and down stroke with the handful of hair that he held steady.

Sharae rolled her head from his grasp and made a smacking sound as she popped his dick from her mouth. Aaron's eyes darted to hers as she placed her hands on his shoulders settling over him. Teasing, Sharae began to lower herself onto him but strained against his upward thrust.

Exercising tenderness and patience, Aaron captured her waist with his hands, and with his eyes directly on hers, he carefully lowered her onto him.

Breath skittish, Sharae rocked as she settled onto him and took all that was inside of her. She bit her bottom lip in pleasure as he filled her. "Yesss," she moaned as she closed her eyes and began to ride.

Lost in her warmth, Aaron allowed her to set the pace and enjoyed the slick heat that embraced him. She lifted up slowly and circled her hips, coming down and rocking her hips when she reached the base of his shaft. Sharae repeated it until he mimicked the same alternating motion.

Aaron bit her neck where she tilted her head. She quaked but continued to ride him as his hands, still in her hair, brought her face level to his and willed her to open her eyes to look at him. Sharae sensed that Aaron was willing her to open her eye but she didn't know if she dared, so she quickened the pace instead.

"Look at me," Aaron ordered. "Open your eyes and look me."

She was overwhelmed with emotion and didn't trust herself to make eye contact when she emptied all of the feelings he'd evoked from her in waves of her release. She felt him shift, allowing him to change their position. Her back was now against the rug as he hovered unmoving over her. She circled her hips in invitation but Aaron did not budge. "I wanna see your eyes when you explode."

Lids and lashes fluttered open to meet his gaze. "I'll never hurt you," he assured her as he slid an inch into her.

His words produced its intended effect. Her newly-bandaged heart was slowly being pried open, and she wasn't entirely sure if she could trust them.

"Let me love you," he murmured against her ear but gasped as he sank deeply into her welcoming center. She was so deliciously warm that knew he'd never allow anyone else to have her.

"Yes," Sharae breathed as Aaron staked his claim with a searing kiss to her lips.

Her heart was fully opened, and he was diving in. She couldn't fight any longer against what she needed. There was no pain and fear quickly dissipated as her heart accepted its newly-appointed partner.

"Hmmmm," she moaned, matching him stroke for stroke. Aaron linked their fingers over her head with one hand and captured her right thigh in the other. He pushed it high and delved deeper inside. Sharae was sure she saw stars, that everything went black except for the direct view of his face as she closed her eyes and her orgasm rippled through her.

Aaron kissed her forehead then trailed a path of kisses down her face as he continued to stroke inside of her. Sharae engulfed him, hugging him close with her arms and legs. The kisses to her lips were tender, complementing each down stroke. As Aaron stared intently into her eyes Sharae turned her head attempting to break whatever invisible links that held them captive to one another's stare. Feeling overly emotional, exposed, and open Sharae wasn't entirely sure if she was offering what she thought Aaron sought to pull out of her. It felt that he was without words or making any request demanding that she give herself— not just herself but that she give her heart to him. And for that one moment in time when nothing else mattered except them, Sharae decided that she was willing to give that and everything else. So they continued to give one another all themselves completely until Aaron finally grunted out his release.

Moments passed as he gathered his senses. His breath was ragged as he attempted to withdraw from her. Sharae, still warm beneath him, tightened her arms around his neck. "Wait. Not yet," she whispered, not ready to break their physical connection. After her heartbeat slowed and she let her arms and legs fall from his body, Aaron gathered her close and rolled them over so that she lay atop of him. He kissed her forehead and Sharae murmured something inaudible but snuggled closer. "Hmmm."

"I told myself that I wouldn't touch you until you verbally said the words," he murmured, fingering her tousled curls. In his mind, his pride had her owing him that much. Pride aside, Aaron had done just that, without the actual words and was already interested in doing it again. "Now, I don't know how I will stop."

His words hit home. "I missed you while you were away," she yawned.

"I can tell. I got the 'Daddy's home' treatment."

Sharae chuckled. "Can't tell a nucca nothing these days without it going to his head."

"It definitely goes to my head alright."

Sharae smiled as she felt him stiffen. "I need a nap first."

Sleep came later after they'd moved from the living room to the stairs, and finally the bedroom.

It was in her sleep that she cuddled with Aaron but awakened to dreams of Matthew murmuring, "Mine..." in her ear.

"No... No. Please." Arms tightened around her waist and brought her closer to him. "Please don't," she murmured. "Matthew, don't." She pried the arms from around her waist that held her captive. She quietly rolled to the edge of the king-sized bed and sat up.

"Rae?" Aaron's voice, not Matthew's, spoke, still partially asleep. "You alright?"

Sharae shook her head to clear it. "I'm fine," she told him even as her stomach clenched and her heart beat erratically.

Unsure, Aaron held his hand out to her. Though his own mind was foggy from sleep, he could swear he heard her murmur "No" in her sleep. "Come back to bed."

"I have to go to the bathroom is all," she told him as she stood up and put on the t-shirt that hung over the back of a chair. "I'll be right back."

Inside the bathroom, Sharae sat on the top of the toilet seat and nervously combed a hand through her unruly hair, wondering if Aaron had witnessed the nightmare. She hoped he wouldn't pry; she didn't want to have to lie to him about it, but she also wasn't ready to share it with him either.

"You okay?" Aaron inquired as Sharae returned from the bathroom and settled beside him. Embarrassed to find the overhead lighting on when she returned, Sharae laid her head on his chest.

"Just a bad dream."

Sensing something was wrong, Aaron tilted her face up to his. "Wanna talk about it?"

"No. How about we make some dreams of our own instead?" She reached up to bring him down to her with a kiss.

"How about we try this instead?" Aaron kissed her forehead, wrapped his arms around her, and whispered soothing words to coax her into sleep.

Chapter Twenty-Three

*A**va Jones," the keynote speaker announced.* Amidst the cheering of the roaring crowd, he watched with very proud eyes as she walked across the stage to accept her diploma. In true Ava fashion, she turned to where she knew her family was seated and held up her degree and flashed them the most magnificent smile ever.

"That's my baby girl!" Gregory Jones cheered with thunderous claps. Despite the call for quiet; whistles, and well wishes could still be heard throughout the auditorium.

My girl, King thought. Possession was nine-tenths of the law, after all, King reasoned as an overwhelming sense of ownership radiated through him as he watched Ava take her seat amongst the other graduates.

Over the course of their four-month relationship, Ava had singlehandedly done what no other woman could claim to have done:

she'd taken ownership of his heart. He'd balked at the thought as he'd never loved a woman enough to have shared those words. Just that morning as the pre-winter sunlight crept through an opening in the curtain, streaming its rays while illuminating her honey-toned cheeks, he laid watching in amazement that he somehow hadn't fucked up what he'd started to build with her. Ava looked positively serene as she cuddled closer to him in her sleep. Without overthinking it, he tested the words with a whisper against her ear. "I love you."

There, he'd said it, and no greedy succubus had swallowed him whole.

Sleepily, Ava had rolled over so that they were face-to-face. Her lashes fluttered open until her hazel eyes focused on his. She touched her hand to his cheek and held it there as the love spilled from her heart. "I love you too."

It was that love that had him anticipating the customary drink and talk of his intentions with her father. Instinctively, King glanced over his shoulder at the man he'd previously only known through his interactions with Sharae and now saw him through the eyes of a man hopelessly in love with his youngest daughter. Gregory was giving him the once over and nodded his head in what felt like a disapproving father saying, *"I know you fucking my lil' girl, and now you gonna have to answer to me."*

"Ummm, hmmm. Greg is giving your ass the death, I'm-a-solider eye," Sharae laughed as she nudged him with her shoulder.

"I know. I'm not looking forward to this discussion. I remember when I first met him, and he told me that he would kill me if I ever broke your heart."

"That's Daddy for you," Sharae shrugged. "Momma is silently ecstatic. She absolutely loves you. And I don't know why 'cause you are such an asshole!"

"I'm the closest thing to a son she has, and she loves me, and your dad will remember his fondness for me as well."

Sharae laughed. "You're a big boy. You'll be okay. Plus Aaron will be here to share in the scrutiny soon enough."

His eyes searched out Ava in the crowd below. King shrugged. "She is worth it."

"She is definitely worth every ounce of love you have in there," she agreed as she pointed at his heart. "Hmmm. King in love. Who would have thought it?" Sharae murmured.

"Not me."

But he found himself explaining his intentions to Gregory an hour later.

"Mr. Jones, I would never intentionally hurt her."

"Now, it's not that I think you will, son, but those are my babies," Gregory motioned to the dining area where his two daughters sat with their mother, his wife.

They were his world. He turned his attention back to the men who wanted to make them theirs. "I don't make a habit of getting in my girls' business, and I'm not gonna start now," Gregory stated to both King and Aaron. "But I would like to know what your intentions toward my daughters are."

King cleared his throat. Aaron twirled his scotch around in his glass.

"I've waited forever to feel this way about a woman, Mr. Jones, and I just want it to last," King explained truthfully. He took Gregory's partially upturned lips as a half-smile instead of a sneer.

"And you?" Gregory gestured toward Aaron.

"She is going to be my wife one day, Sir. Sharae doesn't believe me yet, but I still have some convincing to do." Aaron swallowed the last swig of scotch in his glass.

"That-a-boy." Gregory held his hand out for Aaron to shake it.

"My youngest, she's tough as nails with a mouth like a motorboat, but she is as genuine as she is materialistic," Gregory warned King with a slap on the back. "Gonna put a hurting on those pockets, Boy!"

King nodded in acknowledgment.

"Now, my oldest, she's a sassy something, but she soft as cotton, sweet as candy with a heart deep as the ocean. It's been bruised, battered, and broken to pieces. A lot. So, it is fragile, and I expect that you'll handle it with care. Not like that last piece of shit she was with. Would like to break that pussy's neck!"

Aaron coughed in his hand to cover his smirk and then shook his head. "Nothing like him, Sir."

"Glad to hear it. Never liked him."

They finished their drinks and rejoined the ladies at their table. Ava's smile widened as she received her father's seal of approval with a nod. King leaned down to kiss her on the lips.

"Guess I was barking up the wrong tree," Kyrie's voice came from behind him.

What are the chances of this dumb shit happening while out to dinner with everybody present? King wondered.

"Kyrie," King straightened and turned toward her. "How are you?"

Kyrie didn't pretend to smile or make pleasantries as she aimed hateful eyes at King and then followed up with a same intense stare at Ava as she stepped closer to the table. The man she was with was so busy talking on his cell phone that he hadn't realized that she'd stopped at their table.

"I've been better," she responded bitterly. "Y'all looking fine, though. Sharae." Sharae spoke back.

Kyrie didn't miss the fact that King had clasped Ava's hand and squeezed it when he turned. "And Ava, right?"

"Yea. It's Ava; nice to see you again, Kyrie," she responded quickly but didn't state that they'd previously met several times before, that she'd done an interview with her about real estate for her blog, and that she shouldn't have had a problem remembering who she was.

That was okay with her, Ava figured. Kyrie could pretend not to remember her, but she was damn sure that she'd remember that she was with King.

"Well, it looks like I finally see why we're still not seeing one another," Kyrie answered and walked away.

"Well," Lorraine said, "someone isn't happy," she finished as she watched the angry woman join her companion and angrily lift her arms in the air after the man said something to her.

"King stopped seeing her to be with me," Ava filled her parents in. "I'm glad she decided not to make scene."

Chapter Twenty-Four

*I*t *was a cute movie, Sharae* thought sometime later that evening as Gwyneth Paltrow's character, Kelly Canter, finally sang her heart out with a movie-stealing performance on the movie screen-sized television. Sharae handed Aaron his Corona and curled up beside him.

It was a cold winter night, but Jack Frost wouldn't get an opportunity to nip at her nose. She was warm, inside and out.

All was right with her world. She'd seen her parents and that made her immeasurably happy. Sharae hadn't realized how much she'd missed them. Interacting with them. Seeing them interact with one another. Her mother had made a big deal about her weight loss, and it would have embarrassed her if she hadn't already known Aaron from the gym. *"The pictures really just don't do you any justice. You look so beautiful,"* Lorraine had complimented. King had earned some tears from her as she expressed her sincere gratitude for taking care of both her girls. Aaron had also been a hit with Lorraine and had received her father's stamp of approval with a nod and a quick squeeze of her shoulders when they had returned to their table after drinks.

"Would you have made a scene?" Aaron inquired.

Share laughed when she caught the gist. "Fresh out? Hell yeah. Not four months later, though."

"I've had women show out," Aaron said with a reminiscent smile.

Sharae playfully frowned at his lingering smile, grabbed a pillow from beside her, and hit him with it. "I bet!"

Aaron shook his head. "Nawl, when I was younger, Janelle, Chloe's mom used to show up at shows. I mean— she would literally pop up at an out-of-town show and just start wrecking shit."

Sharae could picture it as he spoke about it, and she just shook her head. "I'm not doing none of that."

Aaron clasped her hands and tugged. "Wait? What you mean?"

Sharae frowned, pulled her hands away, and playfully slapped at his but aimed serious, somber eyes his way. "If a nucca don't know who he belongs to, ain't no point in my trying to convince him. That's not what I'm here for."

His eyes suddenly became serious. "So, you know who you belong to?" Aaron returned. She was exactly whom he wanted. He meant to have her, for her to acknowledge it.

Sharae felt the intense heat of his stare. "I still need convincing," she slowly played.

Aaron smiled. Lucky for her, he was in a convincing type of mood. He leaned in. "I can handle that," he drawled as he nuzzled her neck.

Sharae closed her eyes as she took in the realization that this good man wanted her. "Ummm," she murmured.

He don't know your ass is crazy... the slick one whispered.

Not crazy... Love shielded her quickly. *Hurt... maybe a little broken...*

Sharae opened her eyes, catching sight of what was playing out on the movie:

Beau was yelling, "How many did you take?" at an unresponsive Kelly who was lying flat on her back, arms stretched out.

Sharae held up her hand to stop him as she focused on the movie. "Oh, my gosh," she murmured. "She tried to kill herself?'" she asked him with confused eyes. She watched as the doctor came out to James, shaking his head. When she saw how James shrank down onto the floor and Beau walked away from the hospital, she knew that Kelly was dead.

"What type of crap?" Her eyes filled with tears for the fictional character who thought she had no other choice but death.

Clearly concerned, Aaron brought his face back to hers and used his thumb to wipe away a tear as it made its way down her cheek. "Are you okay?"

Sharae shook her head and touched a hand to her racing heart. "I'm sorry. I'm a softy, and that was completely unexpected."

Aaron attempted to lighten the mood by kissing her lips in a soothing way and pulled her back close to him. Sharae wrapped her arms around him and hugged him close.

"I picked a lousy movie. She was crazy, though."

No. Someone like him wouldn't understand the loneliness you felt and the overwhelming need to escape it by any means. "You don't have to be crazy, just irrevocably lonely and broken."

"It's okay, babe," Aaron kissed the top of her head.

"I have something to tell you," Sharae said, freeing herself from his comforting embrace.

She needed to walk. To pace. She bit the inside of her lip and thought, *Here we go...*

"Then you can decide if you still want to be with me."

Aaron sat up to the edge of the sofa, hands clasped together visibly curious. His expression hinted at concern. "Okay, go ahead." Mr. Jones's words came back to him, *"...heart as deep as the ocean. But it's been bruised, battered and broken to pieces. A lot..."*

Sharae bit her lip just to the point of pain. "I've been there. Felt that consuming darkness that strangles the will to live. I suffer from anxiety, have bouts of depression, and am prescribed a couple different medications that help me to cope. Currently, I'm not taking anything. I used to see a doctor twice a month, sometimes weekly. When I quit my job, I lost my insurance coverage, so I haven't seen her in that capacity in over a month. She's a friend, though."

Sharae stopped pacing and looked at Aaron to gauge the expression on his face. She sighed heavily when she couldn't read him. His body wasn't as relaxed as it had been just moments before when she was curled beside him.

There was a possibility that he wouldn't want her after she was done, but he deserved all of the truth.

All of what made her... her.

Aaron held out his hand for her to come to him, and her heart sank for sure. *All the way in love*, Sharae thought as a fresh surge of tears welled in her eyes. She sent him a weary smile but stayed where she was. She hadn't shared this in years.

"Babe, whatever it is, I will still want you," Aaron reassured her as he stood up and walked over to her. He made a motion to hug her, but Sharae backed away, putting distance between them.

"When I was fourteen, my nineteen-year-old neighbor kidnapped and held me captive in his soundproof basement for three days. He chained me to a bed and took my soul away. I was happy before that." The tears slipped easily down her face as she remembered. "Normal, naïve, and innocent. And his desire to possess me destroyed that. I didn't even know that he looked at me that way. My momma and daddy were separated for a moment so he wasn't home. I mean he was away at boot camp anyway. And Momma— she had taken Ava to dance rehearsal..."

Aaron rubbed his heart as it beat painfully for the fourteen-year-old girl she spoke of and even more so for the woman who stood in front of him. The woman he loved. The sometimes-restless nights of indecipherable murmurs now made sense.

"Matthew," he murmured as he'd been able to make that out one night. He knew there was something there but didn't press and figured she would open up to him when she trusted him enough to share.

Sharae was surprised that Aaron knew his name. That surprise was clear as her eyes met his. "Yes, Matthew. I had the biggest crush on him. But I wasn't fresh, so all I ever did was crush from a distance. And he was five years older than me. He wanted to be just like his dad, an army lieutenant. He was in ROTC for as long as I can remember and had joined the army after graduation from high school.

When he came back, after a year, he was different. More mature, more handsome, but hardened somehow. We had a picnic about two months before, and I can remember him staring at me every time I turned around. I didn't know if I was flattered or uncomfortable." She began pacing again. Aaron stayed where he was and helplessly shoved his hands in his pockets for fear dragging her to him and never letting her go.

"Momma and his mother, Ms. Melanie, were really good friends, so we were always over for dinner or parties or whatever. He told me that his momma had made something for my momma and that I had to come see it." There had been a thrill that he'd sought her out. They'd made small talk about her starting her sophomore year of high school. She was kind of surprised that he'd even taken any interest in her. "Once inside the house, he offered me some lemonade and joked about how much older I was looking and if I had a boyfriend. I had butterflies in my stomach. He was like a big brother but at the same time not, you know? We laughed and talked, and the next thing I remembered was waking up in a bed with my hands bound, a leather collar around my neck, and dressed in a lace, babydoll nightie." She wiped the tears from her eyes and winced at the memory of his voice when she began crying and struggling. "He'd said, *'It's okay to cry.'*"

"There were thoughts running through my head. I just didn't understand it all. His eyes were completely blank. He was void of all emotion. That handsome smile was replaced with this bone-chilling sneer. I yelled and I— I screamed. Had no idea where I was. He raped me, held me to him in my sleep. Whispered the word *Mine* in my ear. And for three days, I was. My eyes were bloodshot red from crying, my throat completely raw from screaming. I thought I was gonna die, and my momma wouldn't have known where I was. I thought that he was— going... to kill me…"

Restraint be damned. She had to know what love felt like. Aaron pulled her into his arms and rocked with her as she unleashed a flood of tears. "Babe, I got you. No one will ever be able to hurt you again."

Aaron's arms felt like home as she breathed him in. "The room was like some kind of sex room for his parents. Apparently, Ms. Melanie liked chains. So, his dad had come home from boot camp, and they'd come down for some much-needed whatever and found Matthew passed out on the couch and me balled up on the bed in chains. *It had been the piercing scream of Melanie that jolted her from her half sleeping state. Sharae had been drifting in and out of sleep — a kind of unconscious sensitivity that made her aware of her surroundings even when everything else inside her felt as cold as the handcuffs that bound her hands together.*

"What the fuck, Boy?" Matthew Sr. yelled taking in the sight of his neighbor and very close friend's missing teenage daughter laying in the fetal position atop his bed.

"What did you do?" Melanie screamed in horror.

Someone's here… Get up. Get up someone's here. The voice spoke. Sharae moaned in pain. She couldn't recall what Matthew had put into her wine to "help" her sleep, he'd said. Coming to, Sharae shivered as the cold from the air conditioner crept from her ankles to just beneath the hem of the fuschia babydoll nightie he'd made her wear, causing goose bumps to appear. Dazed, Sharae struggled to open her

209

Hurricane

eyes against the weight that seemed to force the eyelids to remain closed.

"Help," she thought she screamed but there was no sound. Her throat was on fire and was completely dry. She couldn't remember the last time Matthew had allowed her to have a drink of water. Instantly her hands went to her neck, the collar was gone. Sharae squeezed her eyes tighter when the memory of Matthew removing the collar from around her neck replayed in her mind. He'd promised to take it off if she promised not to attempt to escape. She would have agreed to anything he'd offered.

She could hear Ms. Melanie and Matthew Sr. frantically yelling at their son to awaken him. Finally, Sharae heard his disgruntled and boisterous voice exclaim, "Get— Get the hell off me." To his father as Matthew Sr. attempted to shake the man awake. Sharae willed her eyes to open enough to focus on Matthew and his parents. Matthew Sr. was pulling on his son to get him to stand up. Matthew wasn't budging except for to push at his father to ward him off. Sharae remembered him popping a handful of pills out of his cupped hand and then chasing it down with alcohol before falling soundly asleep. She had made a hundred desperate wishes that he died from whatever he'd taken. Her insides clenched in fear as he glared directly at her from across the distance of the room. "Don't be afraid, he can't hurt you." A voice of hope squeaked out. Her heart sped up so quickly that it felt as if it was going to bounce right from its place in her chest.

"Boy, what in the san hell have you done?" Matthew Sr. dragged him bodily from the couch. His feet dangled in the air as Matthew Sr. held him up. "God, Mel, get Rae."
Slick streams of tears made their way down Melanie's face when Sharae looked at her. Hand pressed up against her mouth as if to hold in her screams, Melanie shook her head.

"Rae, baby, it's going to be alright," Melanie said cautiously taking steps toward the bed. Sharae nodded as she accepted the fact that she was recused. That someone had found her. There was so much joy

that she couldn't contain it. Sharae sat up linking her fingers together and began rocking her body front to back murmuring, "Thank you, thank you, thank you, thank you, thank you..." She rocked and cried. God had been listening to her prayers. She'd solemnly relinquished all her faith in anything after that first day. There were no windows or outside light in the room and the deep red and black trim of the walls gave no indication of the sun rising or setting. Sharae had no idea how long she'd been where ever it was that they were. She'd lost track of all time. He'd taken her favorite watch; a gift from her father and smashed it to pieces before her very eyes telling her that the only time she needed to concern herself was the time she had to spend with him. And as Matthew had said, she didn't need no damn clock for that. Moments passed, time became an endless cycle of nothing and no one except for Matthew.

The sight of Melanie coming toward gave her back that faith. It quailed her mounting anxiety of being bound and ultimately killed at the hands of the woman's own son. She'd struggled against the handcuffs which were attached to a long thick chain that went around her waist. Sharae held them out toward an approaching Melanie.

Recognizing that Sharae was not only bound with handcuffs and a chain at her hands but that there was a large chain wrapped around her waist that was somehow attached to the headboard of the bed, Melanie briskly walked back to her son and slapped him on his face to bring him out of the haziness he was experiencing. "Matt, what the fuck did you do to her?" she cried.

Matthew struggled against his father's hold. "Where's the damn key?" Matthew Sr. shouted at him.

"Rae is mine," he spat out, feeling invincible. The sick thrill of being caught fueled his rage. A pair of deranged eyes met Sharae's. Afraid to meet his eyes in a full on stare down, Sharae glance back toward Melanie. Matthew didn't stop talking. "Tell'em you ain't going nowhere, Baby" he chuckled, the sound rich and sadistic.

Out of breath, Matthew Sr. huffed. *"Where are the keys, Boy?"* Towering over his son by almost a foot, Matthew Sr. maneuvered his son into a headlock, controlling the now belligerent man's jerking motions by using his body as a barricade. In muscle and body mass Matthew senior outweighed his son by at least twenty pounds and used it to his advantage. The situation was literally unfathomable. Twenty years in the military hadn't prepared him for this.

"Mel, check his pockets, baby," Matthew Sr. barked out the order to a clearly shaken Melanie.

With unsteady eyes and blurred vision, Sharae watched as Melanie nervously dug into the pockets of Matthew's basketball shorts while her husband held Matthew against his body. Her head throbbed at her temple as thoughts of freedom and a future— a future until this moment she was not entirely sure she was going to have overwhelmed her.

Bucking for release, Matthew hurled obscenities at his mother as she continued digging, undeterred by her son's words until she retrieved the circle key ring with two keys and a dancing woman clad in a red bikini keychain.

Winded, Melanie scurried over to Sharae almost tripping on Matthew's sneakers. With long delicate and shaking fingers, shades whiter than Sharae's own, Melanie unlocked the handcuffs, rubbed her thumbs over the chaffed skin the friction from the handcuffs had caused. Melanie rubbed a caressing hand over Sharae's cheek. *"It's gonna be ok, babygirl,"* Melanie murmured into her ear. Melanie was nodding excessively as if also reassure herself. Strands of her blonde hair stuck to her face as they became dampened with her tears.

Matthew shouted, *"Don't, motherfuckas. I love her. She loves me"* as he tried to wrangle himself from his father's vice grip. Though he was anchored firmly by an unmoving Matthew Sr. he continued to yell, aiming his angry black eyes at Sharae. *"You are mine. You hear me, Rae? Mine!"* as Melanie freed Sharae from the chain of large metal links.

Arrested by fear, Sharae did not make one single motion to move when the heavy links fell from around her waist onto the bed. She lowered her gaze from his as Melanie hugged her. "We gonna get you to your momma," Melanie assured her. Sharae was cold to the touch, Melanie observed as her skin covered the young girl's. She rubbed her hands up and down Sharae's arms to generate heat as the goosebumps pricked to attention beneath her palms. This could have been her child. Some sick and twisted person could as easily hurt her twelve-year-old daughter Gabriel. The image of Sharae displayed this way burned forever in her mind. Melanie shook but managed to remain in control of her emotions enough to say, "We have to move, babygirl. Can you walk?"

Shivering, Sharae nodded her head. She had to move "I have to get up," she muttered painfully to Melanie who was attempting to pull Sharae toward the edge of the bed. Just get up…

Sharae inhaled the stale air, remnants of cigarette smoke ripe in the air infiltrated her lungs. She expelled with a shaky breath. And for one moment Share tuned them out and concentrated on how she was going to will herself to get on her feet. She wasn't given the option or the luxury of time, at the urgency of Melanie tugging hands, Sharae's confidence arrived giving her the courage she required to move. That was all she needed, Sharae leaped off the bed. She stumbled slightly and put her hand on the bed to steady herself. Melanie came to her side to hold her up. "Let's go," she murmured.

"Don't you leave me. Rae, I love you," Matthew roared as he fought to pull free from his father. "Where ever you go I will find you."

Frighten beyond words, Sharae halted in her tracks. The distance between the bed and door suddenly felt miles away. Warm streams of liquid trickled down her leg as she stood too afraid to move. Trapped like a deer caught in headlights, urine pooled at her foot as she stared at him.

She had peed on herself.

"Get her out of here and call the police, damn it. Fuck," Matthew Sr. grumbled when Sharae came to a surprising halt at the *sound of his son's voice. He'd known the devil was inside of the boy, for years now. Hadn't Matthew been accused of inappropriately touching the sitter one night and at the time he'd sworn it was a "misunderstanding of intentions" on the frightened sitter's behalf? He'd been fifteen then and though he'd believed the sitter, Matthew had taken his son's side. Possibly wrote it off as something that young boys did.*

The reason for Matthew's discharge from the army was for deviant sexual assault on a local woman who generally handed out her favors freely to the officers, but hadn't been interested in Matthew. He'd been accused of beating the young woman and had held her against her will overnight into the early morning. With all things considered, Matthew had been attending the mandatory therapy sessions ordered by the court, so he and Melanie had allowed him to stay in their home. Not once since they'd received the word that Sharae had been missing did he fathom that his own child was responsible for it. Not one second. Not an inkling, a notion that he was capable of taking someone who was like a sister to him.

Shit, Matthew Sr. thought. It had taken his twisted son three days to unravel ten years of friendship.

As Melanie pulled Sharae out of the secret room, through the darkened basement Sharae recognized Gabriel's bike. It still had the flat the twelve-year-old girl had gotten the morning Sharae was taken. She noticed more items familiar to her as she climbed the steps from the basement into the kitchen, Sharae sobbed as the realization that she was three houses away from her families' home sank in.

The lights were so bright, Sharae winced against the pain she felt and closed her eyes.

Breathlessly, Melanie grabbed the cordless phone from the counter and punched in the 9-1-1. "This is 9-1-1, State your emergency," the police dispatcher answered.

"Please come, we've found the missing girl, Sharae Jones..." Melanie rattled off their address as she rushed out of the room and came back with a white faux fur blanket and put it around Sharae shoulders.

Melanie opened the back door of her kitchen, let the cool September air in. She replaced the phone back on the receiver and dreaded what she had to do next.

"Sharae, I'm going to take you home now, hun. Your momma and pop been looking for you tirelessly. I'm so sorry, babygirl," Melanie said to Sharae as she rushed toward the battered girl. "Let's get you clean up."

Sharae didn't hear Melanie. Blocking out all her thoughts and Melanie's voice. In the quiet, she could hear Brownstone's, "If you love me," softly drifting from the living room speakers.

She screamed, her voice erupting above a whisper for the first time since being discovered. The song made her entire body ache, the sound of the chorus drummed in her ears as her body pulsated uncontrollably beneath her skin. Matthew had played that song on repeat for hours on end she vaguely recalled. She knew that she would hate it for the rest of her life.

Sharae screamed a gut-wrenching growl again as she spun around and ran toward the front door. She was out of the house with Melanie running behind her. "Momma," she cried as she hurried across the two neighbor's lawns between their houses. It had rained the day before and the fresh cut blades of grass mixed with small patches of mud coated her bare feet.

"Lorraine! Gregory!" Melanie called as Sharae's voice rose to shouts.

Lorraine burst out the front door of her house. The screen door pushed open so wide that it cracked against the wall before closing on Gregory as he followed close behind her. Lorraine's eyes immediately falling on her daughter as she raced across their lawn to meet her.

Taking in Sharae's appearance, Lorraine shook her head to dismiss the how, the why as she pulled Sharae into a hug and held on for dear life. The blanket Melanie had given her had fallen off during her run. Gregory stepped up, encircling his daughter into his arms as he kissed the top of her head. His heart stopped at the sight of her; weak and battered. He pulled her back to look her directly in the eyes and to study her. She was hurt, beyond hurt, Gregory surmised. She was shivering from the night air and stood on bare feet, he noted. "Daddy," Sharae murmured as she melted into the warmth of her parents.

"Mel, what the hell is going on?" Hands shaking, Lorraine frantically demanded of her friend who stood just off from where they were huddled on the lawn.

Melanie held her hands to her mouth and shook her head from side to side. She couldn't explain in words the events that had just transpired. She threw her hand up in the air, "I can't— I don't know how— ooh fuck!" Melanie said shaking as she laced both hands on top of her head and rocked from side to side.

"Rainey, I didn't know.—" Melanie began.

Lorraine frowned, stepped toward Melanie and gripped both her arms when she was close enough. "Didn't know what? Where was she?" she demanded shaking her friend. "Where did you find her? Mel?" Confused, Lorraine turned back to Sharae and her husband. "Rae, where were you?" she cried.

"Let's get her in the house, Babe," Gregory said when Sharae didn't respond verbally but she had tightened her hold on him.

Lorraine whirled back to Melanie. "Tell me where you found her," she shouted to her friend.

She was going to be sick, Melanie thought. Right here, right now. Melanie doubled over and threw up. Oozing green bile soaking the white canvas surface of her converse sneakers. "I— ugh— I called the police as soon as I found her," Melanie struggled as she swallowed some of the acidic bile.

Minds muddled, Lorraine and Gregory turned their gazes to their friend. "What is going on?" Lorraine questioned her friend.

Throwing her hands in the air in frustration, Lorraine screamed, "You better start talking now."

Melanie shook her head again. "I didn't know," she repeated. "Matthew. he had—"

Surprised at the mention of Matthew's name, both of them turned so they were facing Melanie. Sharae tightened her hold and buried her face into Gregory's shirt.

"Matthew what?" Sharae squirmed, shook her head against his chest. Her tears soaking the front of his gray T-shirt.

Melanie's squeezed her eyes tight as if telling them with closed eye made it better because she wouldn't have to look in the faces. "It was Matt. He took Rae," she stuttered. Melanie sank knee down into the grass after delivery the heart-wrenching blow.

Reeling from the shock of the news Melanie had just delivered to them, both Gregory and Lorraine stared speechless at Melanie as if she'd just told them that she herself had abducted their fourteen-year-old daughter.

Gregory took a deep breath and took a step forward instinctively shielding Sharae from Melanie's view. "Whoa, what did you say? Your fucking husband—"

Melanie shook her head. With pleading eyes, she held up a hand. "Noo. Little Matthew."

Instantly, Lorraine cried out placing one hand over her heart.

"Get Rae inside the house now," Gregory ordered his wife. He stared blankly across the distance of their front yards. "Get her in the house now," He repeated balling his hands into a fist.

Lorraine quickly retrieved Sharae from his side and began ushering her toward their house when they noticed the flashing red and blue lights of two police cars speeding up their street. Coming to her feet, Melanie said, "I called the police and an ambulance for Rae" as she began to walk toward the house.

Adrenaline pumping, Gregory started to run to meet the officers as they came to a stop in front of Melanie's house. As he approached the patrol car, Gregory recognized the car pulling into an empty space closer to his house and stopped. The familiar faces of Detectives Turnbull and McDonough climb out of their beat-up Chevy Caprice did little to assure Gregory that he wouldn't end the evening being placed police custody.

"Lt. Jones, Sir," McDonough addressed Gregory. "Shift was almost over when we received the call. Came right over," he added. Detective Turnbull came up alongside Gregory. "She say anything, Sir?" he asked attempting to divert Gregory's attention from what was taking place between Melanie and the officer back onto Sharae.

"Let's go take care of Rae and your wife, Sir," Turnbull suggested as he gave a nod to the other set of officers that he'd secured Gregory's attention and then they could proceed with what they'd came to do to place Matthew under arrest.

"Dispatch called for an ambulance, not sure if you need one. You and Mrs. Jones can drive over to the hospital and we can take Rae's statement there," Det. McDonough said as he started to walk back towards the Jones' residence. Partially distracted as he tried to focus on the detective's words, Gregory shook his head and glanced over his shoulder to where Melanie was sobbing while speaking with two officers.

"Y'all need to get out there find Matthew. If I get my hands on him. I'ma— I'ma kill that son of a bitch," Gregory forcefully said to the two detectives making their way over to Lorraine where she Sharae stood huddled on the front lawn.

"Suspect's mother said he is unarmed and is being detained in the basement," said a crackling voice from the device on attached to the lapel of Turnbull's faded navy blazer.
Gregory's eyes widen as the message sank in. He whirled back to the direction of Melanie's house.
Close on his heels, Det. McDonough reached to grab his arm. Gregory evaded him and approached the front steps to the Hall's house. "You mean this degenerative fuck is in there?" He made another attempt to

go up the stairs and enter but was blocked at the front door by one for the policemen. "Bring him out here." Gregory demanded.

Det. McDonough approached Gregory with his hands up. "Lt. Jones, you have got to let the officers do their job, Sir. Now we can't bring him out of the house if you stay here and we can't allow you to go in. Look at your daughter, Sir"

Gregory angrily punched one fist into the other hand, took a quick glance to where his wife stood with their first born, his princess. She was shivering. He was grateful that his wife had covered Sharae with the shirt she'd been wearing over the piece of adult woman's lingerie. Gregory shook his head, torn with indecision. It was hell having to see his baby this way. Gregory kicked their wooden porch swing with so much force it cracked up again the side of the house. "He has to pay. He's gonna have to pay now!" Gregory roared and he charged towards the front door.

The officer blocking the front door pulled his service weapon. "I can't let you do this, Sir," the nervous rookie officer spoke, aim dead on.

"Stand down." Det. Turnbull ordered with a warning and cautious hand. The rookie maintained his stance., gun at attention. "Lt. Jones, I promise you, he is going to pay for what he did to Rae. But she is safe, she is alive."

Alive? She would be scarred and torn and irreparably damaged, Gregory thought. "Can you imagine what that sick fuck did to her? That's my baby," he broke. He doubled over as the dam of emotion inside him broke. He groaned as Det. McDonough lead him off the porch.

Gregory raced across the lawn, upon reaching them, he gathered Sharae into his arms and was carrying her into the house. Just as they opened the screen door to enter into their home, Matthew, who was surrounded by three officers was being brought out; hands handcuffed behind his back. Sharae couldn't see him but heard him when he shouted, *"You are mine. Mine—"* *And for the second time that even she peed herself.*

It seemed like a lifetime ago, except when she was in dreams. In dreams, she was a fourteen-year-old scared out of her mind. The smell, the sound of his favorite love song still had the power to make her insides curl.

Sharae shook her head to bring her back to this time, this place, with this man. "I was a minor so I testified on a recording, didn't attend the trial." Sharae shrugged a shoulder, cleared her throat and took a deep breath. "Intent to sexually enslave is a class three felony in Virginia and carries a maximum sentence of fifteen to twenty years in prison. He did go to prison, Daddy moved us back to PA. He's originally from here. And life dragged on for me. I hated myself, life, everything. He's now up for parole, and I decided not to go to the hearing because I want that part of my life to be over. They sent a letter over a month ago, and I haven't even opened it up. I don't want to know if he is walking the streets." She tried to release herself from his tight embrace, but Aaron held onto her. "I don't have a job. I have a mortgage with my ex that I can't afford. I'm broken and my life is a mess and I..."

"I love you," Aaron said as he kissed her forehead. "I love you. From the moment I heard you singing Layla off key in my shower."

Sharae let out a muffled cry of laughter.

He would have to make some serious inquiries into finding out more about Matthew and his current whereabouts. King would know.

That night, she slept dreamless, and the arms that banded around her did so in protection and love, not obsession and domination.

Chapter Twenty-Five

*T*he remainder of the holiday season came and went quickly after Ava's graduation, and as December melted into January, all Sharae longed for was a nap to go along with her hot tea and the new year.

The thought of being able to snuggle into a mountain of pillows was a long shot with the day she had ahead of her. She'd spent most of the night before, much like the past month, burning up the sheets with Aaron and had awakened to him playing, *Bomb (A.P.)* by Trey Songz, which had prompted multiple morning love making sessions.

She giggled at the thought of him nuzzling her out of sleep with Trey's lyrics.

Things had finally fallen into place, she figured. Aaron hadn't turned away from her. Instead, he'd delved deeper, seamlessly becoming a part of her everyday world. He had surprised her by taking her to his family's house in Maryland for Christmas and introducing her to his mother, stepfather, and siblings.

Sharae laughed when his brother had teased him. "She's the one? Mom, you know this boah stalked this woman for like a year before he even spoke to her, right?" When Sharae had looked over in his direction, he'd shrugged easily as if to say, "I told you so."

As a sincere gesture of his affection and appreciation of her love of jewelry, he'd added to her collection of mismatched bangles with his own platinum one with the agreement that she'd never take it off.

They'd brought the new year in with champagne, his daughter; Chloe, well wishes, and amazing sex.

Yes, the new year looked promising. So promising that she'd set up a new Facepage profile and had been confident enough to post a picture of Aaron and herself as a couple. It was their coming out picture in which she'd tagged him with blown kisses. She had a multitude of new things to look forward to, but a nap was not one of them.

The first GLOSSY match-up reception was happening in less than eight hours. All the work of pouring over profiles and selecting mentoring candidates had been tedious and trying but was worth it when she reviewed what she'd like to call her roster. All the GLOSSY girls had been selected and paired with their prospective mentors based on their interests and needs. She was disheartened that she couldn't take on all the girls who had applied but had plans, based on this season's success, to expand the number of mentors and mentees for the next cycle. Sharae glanced down at her watch. *Make that seven hours.*

Sharae bit her bottom lip and rolled her eyes. *No damn nap and something else is gonna end up getting pushed aside.* One thing for certain, it wasn't going to be her scheduled quickie with Aaron.

She also had a training session with King, a hair appointment, a last minute check of the event venue, though she was fairly confident that she could arrive late and that her friend and go-to event specialist Catrina would have gotten the ball rolling in her absence.

Sharae cautiously picked up the oversized mug filled to the brim with hot tea, hoping not to spill any of the boiling contents as she walked towards the stairs. The doorbells chimed, followed by impatient pounding. Sharae frowned as some of the hot water sloshed over to burn her hand.

"Shit!" she yelped, putting the cup down on the mail table. "One second!" she yelled, shaking her hand to ward off the pain. She was still swearing at the pain when she opened the door to find James standing on the other side.

"You fucking somebody I know from the studio, though?" James started in on her as soon as she opened the door. He was livid when Daneen had told him that Sharae was dating Aaron and showed him the pictures as evidence. He had to look on Facepage for himself to believe it. She'd all but dropped off the face of the earth only to resurface unavailable to him. Despite never being home when he'd shown up, James was sure that Sharae would come around. Now he was sick... emotionally and physically ill knowing that she'd shut him out and had allowed another man in.

Amused, Sharae leaned into the door frame. "Did you come to talk about agreeing to sell the house?"

James eyed Sharae. She looked beautifully unfazed by his unannounced appearance, her hazel eyes teasing him with an annoyed sparkle. She'd lost more weight, her neck appeared longer, and somehow she looked more regal… more royal. Even the black T-shirt with the glittery written word Glossy across the front of her chest sparkled. He smiled at the thought of a tiara perched atop her head of lush curls. He hadn't seen her face except for when he desperately needed to and gave in to peeking at the wallet-sized photo, which he kept hidden behind his social security card, of her clad in a sexy corset and boy shorts. James hadn't heard her voice in nearly two months, and his heart wept at the fact that he couldn't take her in his arms and show her how much he'd missed her.

Sharae folded her arms and debated letting him in. There were more pressing things that needed to be discussed other than her choice of bedmates.

"Come on in. We may as well get this over with," she said.

Surprised, James followed her inside. The entry way was the same, but everything he remembered about the home he'd built with her had changed. She'd painted the rooms a warmer shade of ivory and outlined the woodwork with a brown hue instead of the charcoal one that had once been there.

The oak hardwood flooring was practically gleaming under a fresh coat of varnish. James took note that she'd replaced the furniture with the faux leather and microfiber sectional that used to be in her apartment before they moved together. She'd always loved the couches for she said they offered deep couch sitting and cuddling opportunities. Cuddling opportunities with her new man, James mentally surmised. And in *his fucking house!*

"You letting that nigga sleep in my bed?" he angrily asked once he settled at the dining room table. James envisioned Aaron insisting that they rid the place of every trace of him. Knowing that he would have done the same didn't make this change any easier for him to accept. Truth be told, if he'd asked her, Sharae would have told him that she'd done everything herself because she couldn't live in *"His"* house with all of *"His"* things but hiring a professional to remodel and redecorate her home was not financial feasible at the moment. And, she was, after all, the Queen of Do-it-Yourself projects.

Sharae arched a brow and frowned at him. "James, you should be more concerned with your own situation rather than worrying about what's going on with me in my house. I'll be right back."

She went to her office to retrieve the agreement to sell the house. When she came back, James was standing up, hands on his hips and looking into his grandmother's wall-length mirror.

"You always loved this mirror," he murmured.

"Here." She handed him the agreement to sell documents that her lawyer had drawn up. "You can have it back if you want," she told him.

James flagged it off and took a seat. "Nawl, you so beautiful, I wouldn't do it any justice" he replied to her.

Sharae rolled her eyes. "This is really a win-win for both of us. You get to be happy with your new life, and I get to be happy with mine," she happily suggested with a shrug. "No ties. No nothing."

James shook his head, looked down at the paperwork, and then looked back at her. "You changed your number, deleted all your social media, stop answering emails, and now you actin' like I just saw you yesterday."

"Your side bitch was harassing me. We're no longer together, so what I'm acting like is that I want you to agree to sell this house that ties me to you for the next thirty years."

"I miss you. I want you back. I can even forgive that you fucking someone I know.

Sharae burst out laughing. "What?! You're going to forgive me?" she shouted incredulously, pushing away from the table. "You're fucking delusional. Let's just cut our losses and keep it moving. We can probably get some bread out of this," she added to make the idea more appealing to him.

James stood up and grabbed her by the wrist. "Fuck bread! I want to wake up with you forever. I want babies. I want to turn the key in my front door again. I want to sleep in my bed, in my damn house!"

"That's right! Congratulations are due, I hear," Sharae laughed as she pulled her wrist free.

"What is that supposed to mean?"

She wouldn't go there. "Don't worry about it. I'm all out of any feelings for you. I promised myself that I wouldn't waste another moment of energy on you and I won't. I will not. I'm happy, James."

"With that nigga? He worse than I am!" he shouted.

"This is not about him. If you have any love for me, please agree to sell the house. My sincerest hope for you is to experience a love so great that it will change your selfish ass."

James looked down at her. "Not having you changed me. I love you. Now stop playing, take me back, and marry me."

"No," Sharae answered. "You've cheated on me with like three different bitches." In her heart, Sharae suspected that there had been more but at this point, didn't have one iota for care if there were a hundred. Sharae touched her chest. "I gave entirely too much of myself to someone who wasn't worthy. I don't care if the grass ain't as green as you thought it was gon' be. Fuck outta here with all that. I loved you— I mean, I was damn near out of my mind with love for you and none of that meant shit to you. So nawl— we ain't ever getting married. We not even gonna be speaking after this."

His nostrils flared. "I don't want that nigga in my house. Be respectful to me and the fact I'm still paying the fucking mortgage."

The nerve of men to speak of respect as if it applied solely to them. "Thank you for continuing to pay the mortgage. If it were not for your complete male stupidity, you would still have keys that worked in the front door, and I would still be trying it make it work with your undeserving ass. And for what it's worth, Aaron won't be with me here because you still pay the mortgage."

James looked around the room. It too had been redecorated, and except for the mirror, nothing else of his had made the cut. James realized that the *him* in his own house had been replaced with everything *her*. There was no room for him here. Her life had gone on without him. She was already moving on without him. Justifiably so.

And yes! He would take responsibility for it all. The irreparable damage he'd done to the foundation of their relationship demolished any hopes for even a casual friendship. He had no options, no leeway, or leverage to keep her tied to him. The beautiful twenty-five hundred sq ft house would simply be a shell without her, so stalling to keep it was pointless. He'd come to rant and rave and curse and intimidate, but when he looked at her, all he had was heartache and regret.

Sharae deserved to be happy. She wanted the things that he'd only dreamed and planned to give her without any real intentions or course of action to make them a reality. His life had been a mess, and he still had too much shit on his plate.

"Still got a smart ass mouth, I see. Can I get your new number?" James inquired. The boyish grin returned.

"Another thing you shouldn't be worried about. Now, are you going to sign or not?"

"Can we fuck one last time?"

Sharae frowned, trying to figure out if she heard him correctly. When he stood up and stepped closer to her, she put her hand up. "You so damn disrespectful. Get out now."

James caught hold of her as she made a motion to mug him in the face. "Rae, it was a damn joke." *Partially*, he reasoned with himself as he held his hands up.

"Watch what you say! I'm not no whore. And we are way past our fucking days. I'm dead fuckin' serious about when I say I have absolutely no intention of ever talking to you again."

Bullet straight to the heart. James rubbed it as he echoed the word, "Damn." He took a deep breath and let her go. "For what it's worth," he began as he turned back to the table and scrawled his name on the document and turned back to her, "I really loved you. I still love you. If it don't work out with boah, look me up." And for what he knew to be the last time, James took Sharae into his arms and kissed her forehead along with all his dreams of a future for them goodbye.

And as James climbed inside of his Audi, Sharae stood in her doorway happily waving him out of her life. Down the block within the confines of a black Ford Five Hundred, plans were being made for someone else's happiness.

Chapter Twenty-Six

Well, she's safe and that's all that matters. Too bad for boah, though. Karma is no damn joke," King said into his cell phone as Ava peeked her head into the bathroom. "I'ma hit you back," he added when she stepped in.

Ava scanned the room cautiously. She'd seen his phone light up, and instead of answering the call while in the room, he'd left and took the call in another room. "Who was that?" she asked as nonchalantly as she could.

"Aaron," he responded quickly. Aaron had called to fill him in on what happened in their search to discover the outcome of Matthew's parole hearing. The investigator that they'd hired to get the information on Matthew had given his final report. Matthew had been released and fatally struck by a car three days later. Because the investigation had been done without Sharae's knowledge, King wasn't prepared to be so forthcoming with Ava. He certainly did not want to argue because of it.

Ava sat on the toilet and closed her eyes. He didn't exhibit behavior of a cheater, but she had rationalized early in their relationship that she'd have to act crazy every once in a while, just to keep him on his toes. "So why you take it in here?"

King sat on the edge of the tub. "Say what you mean."

"You've had your phone on silent for like the last two weeks. I saw it ring, and then you came in here to answer it. Why?"

"Ava," King sighed.

Her heart raced at his tone, but she continued. "Don't 'Ava' me. Why you in here talking to Aaron? What's going on?"

King was silent as Ava fixed herself up and washed her hands. "Well?" She prompted for him to continue.

"My phone has always been on silent, so don't do that." He grabbed her arm as she shook off the excess water. "Don't insinuate shit; be clear. I'm talking to Aaron in here because what I'm talking about is none of your business."

The frown was immediate; she was feeling moody and out of sorts for other reasons, and although she would normally enjoy a round of back and forth, she figured it wasn't worth it. Not when she had other news to share. "Okay," she agreed.

Now, King frowned. "Just okay? Nothing else?"

Ava shrugged, "What else is there?" Surprisingly, and thoroughly confusing him, Ava leaned in to kiss him.

He'd been bracing himself for a barrage of accusations and an onslaught of smart-mouthed quips that came out as hard as a champion fighter's jab. "My woman agreeable? Something must be wrong."

Ava shrugged again. "I guess that depends on how you look at it," she said quietly.

There was something in her eyes that he'd missed before. A sadness. A mild confusion, he figured. She'd seemed quiet for the past couple of days, but he'd assumed it was because she hadn't heard anything back from the top Philadelphia marketing firm she'd done two interviews with prior to graduation. Or... maybe she had heard something from one of the many prestigious firms she'd applied to, and they wanted to hire her for out-of-state employment, so she was going to end it because she had more of the world to conquer without him.

"Well, what's wrong?" he asked as he became overwhelmed by the ideas of what could be wrong.

Ava leaned against the sink. "I'm pregnant." A visit to her doctor's office had confirmed it after she missed her period in December and the two weeks since January had begun.

"Pregnant?" King repeated aloud more to himself than to her. "Like, a baby?" he asked, the idea being foreign to him.

Defensively, Ava folded her arms across her chest and rolled her eyes. They'd spoken of wanting children in passing as new couples do but had made no mention of actually having one anytime soon. "Yes, like a baby," she sighed. "I know that it's not what we planned or that we haven't really discussed, but—"

King pulled her to him, swallowing the rest of her sentence as he crushed his lips to hers.

Ava was close to tears when he caressed her face with his hands and just stared into her eyes. "So wait. You're not upset?" she smiled.

His heart swelled. This was that moment his father spoke of when he said, *'And in one instant, everything will be right. And you will know it.'*

King picked her up, carried her out of the bathroom and into the living room in long quick strides. He sat down and cradled her in his lap. "Far from it," he laughed, grabbing his house phone. He pressed some numbers and held on as he waited for the other party to connect.

"Ma, you gonna be a grandma!" he happily spoke into the phone. "Yes, Ava is pregnant," he continued. "I don't know, Ma. Here, ask Ava," he said, pressing the phone into Ava's hand.

"Hey, Ms. Rashida," Ava said nervously into the phone. She blushed at whatever his mother said. She relaxed in his arms. "I went to the doctors today, and I'm about seven weeks."

Ava stared back at King as she listened to his mother's words of excitement over the news of her first grandchild. "Alright, Ma," King said from the sidelines. "We'll call you back once I convince her to marry me," he added, taking the phone out of Ava's hands.

At the mention of marriage, she turned in his embrace and straddled both legs over him so that they were face to face. "I've been agonizing over this since Christmas, and from the looks of it, for no reason," she murmured.

King shook his head and kissed her nose. "For no reason," he agreed. "You're having my baby. You're everything I've ever wanted," King told her, leaning back so that he could look at her stomach. Amazed with the thought that inside there was his son or daughter, King continued to smile, pouring every ounce of his heart into it. He reached under her shirt, placing his hands over her abdomen.

Relieved, Ava's accepted the joy of her pregnancy. King was okay with it— more than okay with it. He was ecstatic, and she'd been afraid that he wouldn't be.

"So, about this marrying you," she said, placing her hands over his, her gaze never leaving his.

"Will you?" he asked, playfully kissing at her lips.

Ava tilted her head to the side, squinting her eyes at him. "Will I what? she asked.

King loved that she sought clarity in all things. "Be my one and only baby mama, take care of me when I'm old and sick? Share all of the days in between now and then?"

Ava continued to smile but arched a brow. King continued, "Marry me so no other man can ever have you."

"Ava Mathison?" Ava tested the names together aloud as if she'd never done it before silently. "Has a nice ring to it, right?"

He kissed her roughly. "Fuck yes! Now, for the record, is that a yes?"

Ava threw her head back, laughing and answered, "Fuck yes!" just as roughly. King hugged her close to his body.

A wife... A baby... Yes, it was time. He breathed deeply, inhaling her in, knowing he could never do without the subtle scent of Lancome's Miracle ever again.

"Umm," he heard Ava's muffled utter. He loosened his hug and looked her in the eyes. "Does this proposal come with any diamonds?"

Chapter Twenty -Seven

M*ade it, with twenty minutes to spare*, Sharae thought as she pulled into a parking space at *A Manor of Dreams*. Sharae stepped out of her car and smiled with pride. The Manor was a dream alright, more of a fantasy. While it was more of a pre-war plantation home than a manor, Catrina had done well for her event planning business with an expansion to include it and had transformed the manor into a luxury event and ballroom venue. She'd acquired the sprawling estate after her wedding there the year before. It was a breathtaking sight, Sharae thought as she walked up the paved walkway. The pearly mist and fog added a sense of intrigue to its opulence.

The historic dwelling stood grandly with its overstated, two-story columns of ivory and muted cream. The double staircase spiraled upward to the second floor, wrapping around the building to enclose it and served as a focal point and entryway for the ground floor. It housed three, lower-level ballrooms and one grand ballroom on the top level. Tucked in the corner of the property near a small pond was an elegant farmhouse restaurant.

Catrina waved her off at the door as she approached. "I swore you were going to be late," she said to Sharae as she stretched her arms out for a hug.

Sharae rushed up the walkway for a laughing embrace. "Nag. Nag. Nag... late for eight years' worth of events, and you get labeled as the late person," Sharae said. "You cute."

Catrina rolled her eyes, put one hand on her bulging belly, and the other one to her back. "I feel like a damn whale. And when you're late for every event for a decade, you are the late person," Catrina informed her. They walked inside and made small talk about the expected arrival of Catrina's first baby. "Girl, your cousin is acting like a damn fool 'bout this baby. Don't be surprised if he just happens to show up." Sharae laughed at the thought of her older cousin David popping up and knew that he would.

"You have to send someone back out for the boxes in my car," Sharae warned Catrina. "I really appreciate you hosting this here for me."

"I'll send a couple of the guys out, and it's the least I could do since I couldn't participate. Next time I got you," Catrina told her. They walked into the ballroom and Sharae's mouth dropped opened.

Score! Catrina smiled with pride.

"It looks wonderful," Sharae breathed. String lights, potted plants, and floating clouds of silver, black, and pastel pink balloons all dressed the room. Round tables were scattered throughout the room and topped with black linen and silver sheer fabric tablecloths. Catrina had broken out the good serving china and flatware for her very momentous occasion. Sharae dabbed a finger to her eyes.

"You the shit," Sharae said, giving Catrina a high five.

~~~~~~~~~~~~~~~~~~~~~~~~~~~~~~

Sharae closed her eyes and repeated the very same words that she'd spoken to Catrina no more than an hour before as she walked across the room to stand behind the speaker podium. She was close to puking when Catrina pulled her into and embrace and whispered, "*You got this*," as encouragement. It was silly to be nervous, she off-handedly reasoned as she realized her palms were sweating. After all, she had completed a magnitude of presentations and speeches in her lifetime. This was different, though. All of those were not personal and while she had been very effective statistician and a somewhat passionate DHS supervisor none of that was hers. There was no vested interest beyond wanting to be the best at whatever task she took on. Now that her palms were sweating she almost— very nearly forgot where she was and would have wiped them on the front of her dress. Sharae couldn't possibly do that now that she had the undivided attention of the fifty females in the room. Sharae cleared her throat and scanned the room. Zeroing in on the potted orchid; focal point she'd picked out shortly after her arrival, Sharae placed her hands on the either side of the podium, dug in. A few pieces of copy paper stared up at her, she'd placed her speech there before so her hands would be empty when she walked up.

Sharae smiled a cheerful smile, it was so wide that the corners of her upturned lips almost touched her eyes. "First, I would like to say, Welcome to the first official Glossy match up reception. Without you ladies, this night would not have been possible. So give yourselves a round of applause." She clapped and waited for the audience's cheers to subside. "I am ecstatic and honored to be standing in a room full of such esteemed women along with bright and promising young women."

She aimed her eyes and a warming smile at her matched teen; Tatiana. "I was a small child when my mother and father started to instill a sense of responsibility in me. In most cases, they would allow me to choose what I wanted to do but made sure I knew what was on the other side of my decisions. Like many girls; I was lost, wishing that I had someone who would take the burdens of my heart and just make them all just disappear. It took the love and care of my baby sister to show me that sometimes the world is not just about me. But about the "me" I was to other people. From then on I volunteered as a big sister during the summers and then all through college. I thought, maybe I could help shape the lives of others so I drummed up twenty-five ladies who were interested in doing the same and made this happen. I still can't believe that you are all here. I need everyone who has a name card in front of them to stand up." Sharae waited a moment as all the teens in the room stood up.

There was laughter as the girls realized that none of the adult women had stood. "Okay. Each one of you is going to call the name you have and that woman will stand and then she'll come over to you and the two of you can go somewhere in the room to get to know one another. On the back of the card is five questions. This is kind of like a mini interview. You ask them the questions and then come back to introduce them to everyone else."

Once the last person was teamed up with their match Sharae herself began to walk over to a waiting Tatiana. She observed the room with pride as she walked over to her teen. *You're definitely the shit...*

Those were Tamika's exact sentiments three hours later when she and Sharae took in the sight of one generation of women imprinting on another. The last time she was in a room of twenty-five teenaged girls, she was one herself, Tamika thought with a laugh.

"Yes, she is," Ava agreed, coming to hug her from behind. "I love my girl. A little shy, but I can get her out of that," Ava said, taking a seat on Sharae's lap.

Sharae shook her head. "Not everyone is meant to be the prom queen."

Ava stood up and swiped at the front of her dress to smooth the invisible wrinkles. "I can't tell," Ava joyfully said, spinning around to show off her long legs in her four-inch, glittery gold Jimmy Choo's and BCBG black sheath dress.

"Don't you just have southern Belle written all over you?" Sharae laughed.

"Your girl seems kind of shy too, Rae," Tamika said as she spotted Sharae's matched teen sitting at her table alone while the other girls were buzzing around her.

"Well, Rae definitely matched you up right," Ava joked with Tamika, turning their attention to Tamika's match who had become the center of most of the girls' attention.

"Yup, she rowdy. Smart too," Tamika assessed. "She probably uses her assertions at the wrong time, but we gon' be good."

"I'm jealous that I don't have no girl," Catrina joined in.

Sharae held up her hands. "You're about to pop like tomorrow. One girl at a time," Sharae told her, holding up one finger.

Ava was already imagining her own baby bump and had been waiting for an opportunity to get her hands all over Catrina's stomach. "You look good, Trina," Ava complimented.

"Doesn't she?" Sharae agreed. "I'ma need your stylist when I'm pregnant and large as all hell," Sharae added.

Catrina's hand stopped midway to her mouth, and she frowned. "Is that your nice way of saying that I'm fat?" All three of the other women laughed.

Sharae stood up and held her hand in the air. "I damn sure didn't say that." She danced around Catrina, rubbed her belly, and placed a playful smack of her lips on Catrina's cheek before she slipped away.

"Can you take a picture with me?" Sharae asked with a tap to the table to get her mentee Tatiana's attention. The girl had put headphones in and couldn't hear when Sharae had initially called her. Alarmed, Tatiana looked up from her cell phone.

Sharae held her cell phone. "For our Facepage and Instagram pages?"

A brief smiled appeared before being replaced by a smirk that came along with an uncaring shrug. "Sure. Why not?" Tatiana answered.

Happily, Sharae tugged the girl from her seat and into a hug and quickly snapped a picture with her iPhone.

Don't force the relationship, Dr. Trainor's voice echoed in her mind as if she were standing in front of her instead of across the room.

"Do you mind?" Sharae asked once she weighed it out in her mind.

Tatiana stared and then shook her head. "Can we take one with my phone? For my page?" she asked.

"Of course," Sharae answered. They ended up taking enough on both of their phones to qualify as a photo shoot.

"That was fun. I love taking pictures," Sharae added.

"Dr. Jones?" Tatiana said nervously. "Can I ask you a question?" she added.

"Please, call me Rae. And ask away," she replied.

"What made you come up with this group?"

Sharae narrowed her eyes in genuine thought and smiled. "I want to make a difference, and I want to help someone else make a difference," Sharae answered. It was as simple as that.

"Well, thank you," Tatiana responded and unexpectedly hugged Sharae.

She hugged the girl back and promised herself that she'd make good doing just that.

~ ~

A fresh batch of overwhelming happy tears flowed as Sharae pulled her car into the driveway of her house. Her dream had materialized before her very eyes in the form of twenty-five matched teams of promising teens and professional women who would represent GLOSSY.

It's foolish to still be crying, Sharae thought, wiping the tears away. But the afterglow of what she felt could not be matched by anything at this very moment. She pulled down the driver's side mirror, took a quick glance in it, and giggled as she remembered the smiles on the faces of the girls, every one of their names whom she'd remembered. Sharae had never experienced or thought it possible to be drunk on success. She'd heard people speak of it, had watched the joy of it spread across a person's face, but had never actually felt it herself.
She breathed deeply and allowed it to course through her veins like a life source.

Five of the young ladies selected to participate had given her a hug... A real -touch- your-soul hug of gratitude. She had kind of bawled then too.
And Ava. Ooh, Ava. Sharae's heart melted. When the evening was over, Ava had shared her pregnancy and engagement news. *A baby.* A niece or nephew to spoil. A wedding to plan. Her heart tightened with envy, a natural human response as she wanted those things as well. At some point, she had been desperate to have it. At this point, though, GLOSSY would have to be enough. She would have to be enough, Sharae decided, taking a quick glance at her watch.

It was late, and Aaron was waiting on her. Because it was later than she'd anticipated and because he had an early morning, Sharae contemplated just calling him to say she would meet him tomorrow after he returned from his first meeting. As if he sensed, her thoughts her cell rang.

"Where are you?" Aaron questioned, his voice light and fun.
Sharae laughed. "In the car bawling over how great everything went," she told him. "I was just about to call you, though. I forgot my overnight bag, so I had to come home," she explained.

"That's why I told you to leave some clothes here," he reminded her.

It was supposed to rain and would probably start by the time she was back on the road. Sharae wished she had listened. "I was thinking about just coming over tomorrow. I didn't want you waiting up for me."

"Nawl, I need you now," he told her. "And I have a surprise for you."

Sharae smiled. "You know I love surprises." She got out of the car and shrieked at the frigid cold air. "It's cold as shit! I'ma change my clothes, grab my bag, and be there in like thirty to forty-five minutes."

Aaron nodded as if Sharae could see him. "Leave the dress and the heels on," he told her. He'd been fantasizing about peeling her out of her black corset-inspired cocktail dress since she'd sent him a picture of her earlier that evening.

Already imaging a slow seduction, Sharae started across the walkway in hurried strides. "Sure will. I'll call when I leave back out." She disconnected the call with an air-smacking kiss and walked as quickly as her high- heeled feet would carry her. She danced from side to side to generate heat as she stuck her key in the door to unlock it. She opened the door but turned back briefly when she heard what she thought was the wind.

The fuckin' hawk is out... she thought, and as she stepped inside the entryway, her peripheral caught sight of the figure coming towards her. Sharae felt a quick prick as the figure jammed what she assumed was a needle into her shoulder. She winced as she went down, the figure towering over her as Sharae sank to the floor in a cloud of confusion.

Chapter Twenty-Eight

lick... click... click... click... the chain locked in place.
Nooooo, she screamed or at least thought she had. Was that her voice or her imagination? Hesitantly, her bound hands went to her neck, searching for the leather collar but found none. Lost in a state of semi-conscious, Sharae struggled to open her eyelids, the grogginess dissipating with each attempt. Nothing was clear but it had to be a nightmare. "Matthew?" she sounded out.

Bet you wished you opened that letter now... the slick thought seeped out, permeating hope with fear.

You have no place here, Love spoke against the traitorous thoughts.

Sharae could hear laughter somewhere in the distance as she struggled to gain control of her senses.

Just a trick of your mind. Open your eyes. She attempted to.

Open your damn eyes! Body paralyzed, fear spread through her like the creeping fog of predawn mornings. *Where am I?* The question seemed to have the resounding echo effect as it bounced around in her brain.

Her mind, recovering from the lull of the drug and sharper now, was already piecing together patches of memory. The last thing she recalled was being stuck with a needle and someone pushing her into the house and onto the floor. Not Matthew's basement but her house.

Focus, her mind ordered, but her mouth had other plans. "Matthew, please..." she pleaded as the past tumbled tumultuously into the present.

The room was dark except for a spill of light from the kitchen. Through hazy eyes, Sharae saw that she was on the floor in her living room and her hands were bound with plastic zip ties.

There was that wicked, crazed laughter again. It was enough to make her cringe, but Sharae searched the room for the source of the laughter instead. Her eyes widened in horror and surprise as they landed on none other than Daneen.

Sharae weakly croaked out, "Why?"

Through the darkness, she could make out the gleam of the whites of her crazy, bulging eyes and sneering mouth. Daneen laughed again and turned the lamp beside her on. "Why?" she angrily repeated, mockery ripe in her tone. She blew a huge bubble of gum and popped it with a swift chop of her teeth. "Because you're you." And in Daneen's mind, that was reason enough.

Sharae focused on Daneen's angry face, and for a moment, she saw Matthew's. In that fleeting moment, although she had absolutely no idea as to how she would get out of this dangerous situation, Sharae promised herself that the outcome would be different this time. She was not going to end up being a victim again because if she did, there would no escape this time.

And that did not sit well with her plans for her future.

"And they all want you," Daneen spat, getting up from the corner chair. "I told you to leave James alone, but you wouldn't listen," Daneen reminded.

Sharae closed her eyes and shook her head. *What time is it?* she wondered as she scanned the room, finally focusing on the huge wall clock. It was after four a.m. And outside, the rain poured and the wind howled as it beat ferociously against the windows. Daneen had drawn the shades on the wall of windows.

"You won," Sharae conceded to appease the crazy woman. "He wanted to be with you." She'd seen enough episodes of Criminal Minds and Snapped to make an attempt at some sort of comradery.

If she could just befriend her, change her mind, getting her talking until...

Until she figured out how she was going to gather enough strength to overtake her. Or until someone showed up to save her. Sharae quickly assessed Daneen as the woman approached her. Daneen was furious but appeared to be weapon-free, Sharae gathered when she didn't see anything in her hands. Daneen squatted down in front of her. "Nawl, he wants you. I saw y'all earlier and you waved him off like the good lil' wife," she drawled.

Sharae shook her head again. "You don't have to do this."

Daneen squinted her eyes in disgust and grabbed Sharae's chin. "Don't I?" She pushed Sharae's face to the side. Hadn't she done every fucking thing she'd thought James had wanted? Shit, she'd aborted their baby early in her second trimester after James had promised that there would be time to have one once she'd gotten on the right track with a job and regained custody of her other children. They'd had to go to New York City to have it done. He had been out of sorts for months since Sharae had cut off all contact with him. She carried the hope that if showing him that Sharae was over him then James would finally move on with her.

Hadn't she gotten a job at the nursing home and started nursing school part time? And all he was fuckin' worried about was Sharae's too good, uppity ass.

Daneen gripped Sharae's chin again and stared her in the eyes. She blew another bubble, this one large enough to touch Sharae's nose before she popped it. "You're perfect in his mind." Daneen mugged her face aside, the mere sight of Sharae turning her stomach. "But if you were so perfect, why was he with me? Telling me he loved me and that he would marry me?" Daneen sucked her teeth.

Nerves shattered, Sharae's knees bumped together; she bit her bottom lip and silently prayed for a miracle. Although she wasn't overly sure that Daneen's true intention was her death, Sharae couldn't afford to underestimate the woman; she had been, after all, drugged and bound. "There is really no need for this," Sharae tried to reason. She scanned the room to catch sight of anything she could use as a weapon or that could free her from the restraints

Daneen glanced down at her. She hardly saw what was so special about her. "You can believe that if you like. James will never look at me the same way as long as you're around."

Defeating Daneen required strength on her part, and even if her teeth chattered and her knees buckled beneath her, Sharae was determined to survive. Mind clearer, she coached herself into a calmness that she was a very long way from actually feeling. First, she had to get off the floor. There was an ink pen under the ottoman that she'd dropped a week before and had forgotten to pick up. If she could reach it somehow...

Daneen paced the room like a mad woman, rattling off pieces of her life in incoherent sentences.

"Daneen, I haven't done anything to you. Please let me go and this will be a part of the distant past."

Daneen shook her head and let out a frustrated grunt as tears flowed from her eyes. "He made me get rid of our baby!" she yelled, coming back to her. "It's too late for anything to be in the past," she said tilting her head to the side.

Somehow, there was a faint pang of hurt for this heartbroken woman, intertwined with her fear. Then she heard the lyrics *I'm calling you Daddy...* start to play as a call from Aaron came through, and she breathed his name as if she were coming up for air.

Daneen sighed heavily, rolled her eyes, and stretched back over the arm of the chair so she could retrieve Sharae's phone. "And this nigga. He been calling all night." She shoved the phone close to Sharae's face so she could see Aaron's picture display on her phone. "I see you got him wrapped around your finger too." She'd come on to him at the studio once, only to have been ignored.

Daneen used the phone to trace the outline of Sharae's face. The stale aroma of cigarettes and weed lingering on her breath danced into Sharae's nostrils as Daneen inched closer, demanding that she look at her.

Sharae attempted to turn her face away from Daneen's forceful hands, which Daneen mistook as Sharae thinking she was too damn good to look her directly in the eye. "Bitch!" Daneen yelled, one balled fist striking out against the flesh of Sharae's cheek. Her head jerked back at the unexpected blow. Sharae winced and brought her bounds hands up to protect herself against another one. She had to get up.

Just let her take you away... It would be so easy...

Sharae shook her head to ward off the pain. She had to bide her time.

"See!" Daneen raged as she stood up again. "There you go thinking you're better than me."

If she could use the couch for leverage, Sharae thought she'd be able to get up. Once she was on her feet, the odds would be in her favor.

Just start screaming the house down. Get the neighbors' attention...

"How do you do it? Make them want you forever?"

"Daneen, James stopped being with me because he wanted to be with you. I don't want him, and today he agreed to sell the house so I won't ever have to talk to him again."

"This was supposed to be *my* house. He promised me I would live here with him once you moved out." Daneen waved her arms toward a mountain of Sharae's things. "I decided that I would help you move out." Clothes, bags, and shoes were all dumped in a heap on the floor. "No babies but a bunch of shit. How can one person own so much shit? You have an entire room full of clothes, bags, and shoes." Although the words dripped with hatred, they were also laced with unmistakable jealousy.

"Daneen, listen to me. You can have everything you want," Sharae said to her.

Daneen's phone rang; she pulled it from her back pocket and put on a deranged smile. "Finally, you called back. Say hi to your bitch," she spat angrily, punching a button to place the phone on speaker. She held the phone in the air. "Hello?" James's voice demanded. "Daneen, what the fuck is going on?"

"James!" Sharae called out weakly.

"James!" Daneen repeated on a whine.

Voice stronger, Sharae called out to him again.

"Rae?" Confusion tinged his voice. "Sharae?"

"Yes, baby, it's your precious Rae. I know it's raining, but you better get your ass here before it's too late."

"Bitch, I'ma fuckin' kill you!" James grounded out.

"Whoa-but you love me."

"We're at my house!" Sharae yelled just as Daneen ended the call and threw her cell phone against the wall.

"You think he coming for you?" Daneen laughed wickedly and bent down, furiously grabbing a handful of Sharae's hair. She twisted her face up to look at her. "Imagine him driving on the fuckin' expressway in the pouring rain," she hissed out.

Daneen stepped back and grabbed the water bottle from the lamp side table. Sharae watched as Daneen turned the bottled up to her lips, and then as if it was a second thought used the bottle to squirt the liquid onto the pile of clothes, onto the curtains, the couch and then the oversized black and white canvas portrait of Sharae.

Crazed, Daneen next squirted what smelled like lighter fluid near her.

"It's everywhere," she laughed hysterically, throwing the empty bottle over her shoulder. The look in her eyes was darker, but when Daneen clapped her hands together, jumping up and down, Sharae thought she looked downright giddy.

This bitch is crazy. Focus, Rae. Focus... You gotta get up. Mentally, Sharae was already on her feet, but her body needed a moment more to catch up.

"Daneen, you don't want to do this. Not for James," Sharae advised, trying to get past the gatekeeper of her crazy.

Up... Up...

"But I do," she replied very calmly as she quickly struck the match and let it drop to the pile of clothes. Instantly, the fire flared, illuminating the trail of the lighter fluid.

Like a starting gun shot at a track meet and the runners poised to take their marks, Sharae leaped up with a scream and rammed herself, full body, into Daneen who lost her balance and fell onto the floor. Then like a sprinter in the hundred-meter dash, Sharae ran with all her might, her heart beating wildly and so fast that it pounded in her ears as she raced toward the finished line; the front door.

Panicked, and still weak, she pressed the trigger button on her alarm system. It began to blare very loudly. Somehow, she'd forgotten to arm it when she'd left earlier but relied on it now to save her life. Behind her, Daneen pulled at the back of her dress, and Sharae turned, using both bound hands to push Daneen with all the force she had in her. Sparing no time on Daneen, Sharae's focused her attention on unlocking the door.

247

Sharae could smell the smoke as it permeated the air of the foyer. She sent one hurried glance over her shoulder as she opened the door and started running out the front door and down the walkway yelling, "Help!" at the top of her lungs. The air rushed out of her as she was plowed to the ground, scraping her chin as she fell. The palm of her right hand slammed onto the concrete causing intense pain. Daneen was on top of her, pulling her hair and trying to force her to turn around.

The ground felt like a block of concrete ice as she struggled to break free of the smaller woman's death grip. The rain poured from the sky, drenching them, and the wind pinched like ice needles against her bare skin.

"HELLPPP!" Sharae yelled once again. "Get off of me!" she gritted out as she fought to get onto her back. She wouldn't remember how until afterward, but she was somehow able to turn over onto her back and used her legs to confine Daneen around her waist. She was screaming, exhausted but desperate as she used her bound hands to place them over Daneen's head.

It's either her or you... She could take her. Sharae had watched all those years of wrestling on Saturday mornings as a child and thought that she could pin or subdue her in some type of figure four, or a half-nelson, or choke hold.

Daneen struggled, her body flapping and nails digging into her prisoner's skin. Sharae used her larger size to her advantage. Her eyes were closed so tightly that ribbons of light strands rippled beneath her eyelids as she imagined snapping off the woman's neck. Sharae squeezed her knees together around Daneen body as the woman struggled against them. Her arms flailed in the air with no reprieve. Her screams shrieked the early a.m. quiet as Sharae squeezed her arms tightly around Daneen's neck as she continued to struggle to get loose.

"Shit! Dr. Jones?" her neighbor; Peter asked, reaching in to grab Daneen from Sharae's grasp. He saw Sharae's bound hands and began to pull Daneen who was close to losing consciousness as the fight in her began to disappear. "Janie, honey, call the police!" he yelled back to his wife who was standing on their lawn, watching in horror from a distance.

"Dr. Jones. You have to let her go," he told Sharae.

Sharae let go, lifted her head up off the ground, and squinted one eye. The rain continued to pelt the earth as she stared at her usually unfriendly neighbor. His presence produced a flood of tears to her eyes. Sharae let her head fall back to the concrete and she cried.

~ ~

In the distance, Sharae watched as her old life disappeared in flames. Dark, furious hues of deep orange and red consumed concrete, wood, and glass, billowing clouds of thick black smoke. Firemen fought in vain, risking their lives to save something that meant absolutely nothing to her. The person responsible, so desperate in her need to have what the house and all the extras stood for, destroyed it all, and also in the process, destroyed herself, Sharae thought tragically of Daneen who was now handcuffed in the backseat of one of the many police cars that crowded her block.

"So, you'll just come stay with me," Aaron murmured when he joined her. She laughed a little and wiped at her already tear-streaked face. "That bitch tried to kill me," she told him, shaking her head.

But she was alive, a little bruised with some minor aches and pains, but she was alive. The entire chain of events was too crazy for even the wildest imagination.

Aaron had feared that she was in danger when she never showed up to his home. "Thought I lost you," he said. The frantic thirty-minute drive from his house to hers in the pouring rain felt like an eternity as he'd raced to get there. The entire time he was telling himself that she'd fallen asleep and she was not answering because her phone was still on silent from earlier. Those thoughts had gotten him here, but he couldn't explain the twisting horror he felt as he approached Sharae's home and saw fire raging from the windows as the house burned out of control.

His relief was indescribable when he spotted her standing on her neighbor's lawn.

"I love you," Aaron told her and kissed the top of her head.

Aaron... her knight in shining armor. He'd come to save her. She needed a minute. How close to death could one be without taking a minute to revel in their survival? And survival for her meant to be real... to love... and to be loved in return...

Sharae closed her eyes, allowing the words to sink in, to adjust to them, to believe in them, to trust them. He had spoken them to her before, but in this moment, she allowed that love to flow through her body and settle inside her heart, to cover and protect her.

As the sun rose out of the clouds and light began to shine on them, the last drops of rain cleared, and Sharae flexed her hand in Aaron's. "I love you too," she replied as she clasped his hand tighter and intertwined their fingers.

Aaron used their linked hands to bring her to him with a tug. "Let's go home," Aaron suggested.

The EMTs that had examined her highly recommended that she go to the hospital for more intensive testing, but Sharae declined. She was alive and breathing, and the police had already cleared her to leave the scene and had made arrangements for her to come into the police station to make to a formal statement later that afternoon. She heard her name being called and spotted James running up toward the barricades, searching the crowd for her.

Aaron spotted James next, sighed heavily. *Nut Ass Nigga had the nerve to show up here*. Deciding to make his position unmistakably clear, Aaron sent James a heated stare bridging the gap across the distance between them. Aaron made sure he had James' full attention when he tipped Sharae's chin up to him and covered her lips with his.

"Yes, let's go home," she agreed when she saw that James stopped in midstride when he saw them, his mouth open and eyes full of regret. He didn't say a word when they turned to leave.

Not everyone survives storms, Sharae concluded, mentally exhausted. The vast devastation and wreckage for miles to be seen tearing up shores and destinations alike. It seemed that during the last few months she'd been all but dragged out in the rain and left to drown. Then she figured that it was a choice. A conscious decision that she had to make to live. Not just live. But to live happily and free of fear.

So no... Not everyone survived, but with the dawning light, timidly emerging through the cracks of dark clouds and beaming down on the flooding waters, it reminded her that not everyone gets washed away either.

THE END...

Epilogue

Eight months later

"After this baby, I want a big-ass wedding," Ava screamed at King as he watched the lines on the monitor climb to chart the continuous contractions. Ava bowed back, head digging into pillows as another one started painfully at the base of her back.

"Breathe baby. Breathe. Just like we practiced," King coached Ava as he tightened his grip on her hand.

"Wheeeeew! Eeeeeh eeeeh wheeew…" Ava panted, as her unfocused eyes tried to settle on the damn machine that beeped every minute for no apparent reason. "Oh. Fuck breathing!" she spewed as she jammed the red button that supposedly injected her with morphine to relieve the unbearable pain. She threw it down when it didn't take any of the edge off. "I hate you. I really, really hate you!" she cried as she turned her head to Sharae. "I need you to fucking help meeee. Pleeeeease!" she begged.

"You have to stay down," a nurse told her, stepping into the room. The stupid machine alongside her bed beeped in alarm this time, and the damn contraption of a belt that they attached to her stomach was sliding off along with the circle monitors. "It has to be right here at the peak," the nurse advised, adjusting the monitor and strap again.

"Nurse? Is there anything else you can do for her?" King questioned. "We've been here for six hours. The contractions are back-to-back," he added as he watched Ava squirm under the pressure of bringing their son into the world. Wincing, he watched her clutch the iron railing of her hospital bed in one hand while digging her nails into his arm with the other.

Horrified, Sharae observed the laboring process as her own back tightened and a wave of uncomfortable contractions rippled throughout her own body. They were coming in every four to six minutes she mentally calculated.

Sharae ground her teeth and blew out a shaky breath. "Shit," she gritted and closed her eyes as she rubbed the space under her rib where baby girl B had decided to stretch out. She clenched her thighs as baby girl A kneaded her head against her cervix.

My babies, Sharae thought. *Impatient as hell...* She'd been experiencing the contractions for the past eight hours and had been dry-heaving before receiving the call from King that Ava had gone into labor. All the books she'd read suggested that these symptoms were the onset of labor but she'd just been seen at Dr. Prielou's that very morning and had only been dilated one centimeter. Dr. Prielou waved her off and had reminded her that she'd see her at her next week's appointment if not before.

"Rae, are you cool?" King asked her.

"I'm the one having a damn baby!" Ava let out on a shriek. There was a groan and a grunt that sounded like it came from the base of her feet up through her body and out of her mouth. "This is such a punishment!" she cried.

Sharae winced off the next wave of pain and shook her head at Ava. "I'm fine. They must be stretching out. I swear all day long, though. Two more weeks of this..."

"Well, I don't want no more minutes of this. Get this baby outta meeeee!" Ava yelled at the nurse who sat between her legs checking her cervix.

The nurse pushed back from between Ava's legs. "Ten. Looks like we're about to have a baby tonight after all."

Heart racing, King's eyes widened at the announcement by the nurse. "It's time now?!"

"We've paged Dr. Prielou, and she is coming up right now," the nurse told them.

"Aww, shit! Thank you, God," Ava said, her mind now relieved, yet the pressure building against her birth canal didn't allow her to resurface. "Rae come hold my hand," Ava called to her sister.

Nervously, King dabbed Ava's sweaty forehead and kissed her there. "You hear that? We ready," King said, kissing her brow again.

"Rae needs to sit down," the nurse instructed, taking note of Sharae finally relenting under the pressure of her own contractions. She glanced at her watch. The last one was three minutes. "I can't sit. I have to walk," Sharae said as she began to pace.

Two women dressed in pea-green scrubs came in and settled near the baby bed. The doctor came in, instructing the nurse to break the bed down.

Sharae took her place beside Ava and held her hand. "Are you able to hold her thigh up?" the nurse asked as she did a quick assessment of Sharae. She shook her head. "I need to walk," Sharae answered as she doubled over. She heard Dr. Prielou order a wheelchair for her to sit in as the nurse slipped in beside her to take hold of Ava's thigh. King was on the other side, holding the other thigh while he leaned over to watch the process.

Sharae rocked off the pain with a two-step as Ava was instructed to give her first push. Fighting with tears and the sudden wetness trickling down the leg of her yoga pants, Sharae watched painfully as her baby sister screamed her son into the world with five pushes in the span of six minutes.

~ ~

It was the most amazingly horrific event she'd ever experienced, Sharae figured she would say when asked, Sharae thought. But for the life of her, she would not have been able to recall anything except for the seconds that Aaron joined her in her own hospital room. He kissed her forehead, intertwining their fingers and tracing her wedding band while he murmured sweet nothings of encouragement.

Sharae bit down on her lip until she tasted blood. "I can't, babe. I can't," she shook her head as the pressure forced her into tears.

Lorraine came over to her, cell phone in hand as she continued recording the scene as it unfolded, reassuring Sharae that everything would be okay. Both Aaron and Lorraine had been in the waiting room during Ava's labor and had immediately rushed to meet Sharae when news that she was being admitted reached them. "Momma, I can't. I need drugs. I know I said I could do it naturally, but I lied!" she cried.

"Come on now, Rae. That's nonsense. You can do it.," Dr. Prielou encouraged. She'd come straight from Ava's delivery to check Sharae's cervix and was happily surprised to discover that she was ten centimeters dilated. "Grandma, Dad, I need you both to hold her knees and help her push back if needed," she advised Aaron and Lorraine. "Ava and baby Jordan are waiting to see you and your girls. Chin down and let me get a big push,"

Sharae bore down and pushed, but stopped when Dr. Prielou instructed her to.

Thirty-five minutes later and out of sorts, Sharae let out a frustrated, tortured grunt. Her mother had switched her position and now stood behind her near her head. Lorraine whispered words of encouragement to her daughter. "I can't do it anymore," Sharae breathed and closed her eyes. "Please!" she cried as the nurse took her hand and placed it between her legs so she could feel the top of her baby's head emerging. "Rae," the nurse said, her hand back on Sharae's knee, "they're ready, and you are not going to cry your babies into this world. You can do it," she finished as the doctor instructed her to push again. "Aaaah!" she grunted out a yell. Over the years, she had cried for many reasons. Shed millions of tears over people who didn't even deserve one, but her babies deserved them. But not the weak and weepy, *'I can't do it'* tears. She'd give her babies the strong and silent, *'I can do anything tears'*.

"Oh, baby. Mariah's head is out." And within moments, her body was out, and Sharae witnessed the most perfect sound she'd ever heard. Her daughter's first cry of life outside the womb pierced the air and brought a fresh flow of silent tears to her eyes.

Aaron cut the cord, and Sharae's eyes weakly followed her baby as the nurse wiped off amniotic fluid and cleared her mouth and nostrils. It was a blur as another contraction reminded her that she wasn't yet done.

"Malia is ready," Dr. Prielou announced. "Now, let me get another push." Sharae bore down and pushed again and again. Malia joined her sister, mother, and father three minutes later.

"Baby, I'm so proud of you," Aaron told her with a kiss to her sweaty forehead, "I love you," he told her.

Later, when the twins were cleaned and swaddled in pink hospital blankets and topped with cute hospital hats with tiny bows and sleeping, one in the crook of each arm, Sharae's heart swelled in a way she would never be able to explain. She murmured, "Mine..."
Somehow the word didn't frighten her into a panic but described a proprietary love that only a mother could have for her children.

Mine, she tried the word again and sent an amused glance at Aaron who was sleeping in the chair beside her bed.

Well, she shrugged, taking in the realization that she'd have to share and thought, *Ours...*

Bookclub Questions

Complete our book club questions, return by email, and enter drawing to win $50. Gift Card.

Drawing date 5/31/17

1. What is your overall thoughts on this book?
   A. What was your favorite part? Lease favorite part?

2. What did you enjoy most about the characters?

3. Do you think there is a biased notion that educated women don't involve themselves in relationships where they subject themselves to behavior like James? Is it different for women who lack education?

4. At what point, if any did you become emotionally invested in Sharae? Ava?

5. What did you think about King? James? Aaron? Do you think that they exhibit typical African American male behavior?

6. If you were Sharae, how would you have handled the issues she went through in the book?

7. How did you feel about Daneen?

NOTES

Other books available by
Elaine L. Allen
No Ordinary Love
E-book and Paperback

Check out
Briannah and Tyree's story:
Love is Blind
Available Now on Wattpad
@MsSheWrites

Briannah

Night breezes were quickly transitioning from summer winds to much cooler fall gusts of air. The sun had finally melted into the midnight blue sky; the stars, silvery flecks shined brightly, dotting the sky. Darkness crept though, clinging to every corner, shielding one's eyes from the sight of broken pavements littered with empty multi-colored weed packets, crack vials, and cigarette butts. The night and its despair weren't allowed to claim all things. Beneath the towering street lights, high as the row homes on the blocks they illuminated, dreams still lived. Hope still breathed daring breaths.

Briannah and Aylonah were both sitting out in front of Briannah's house, discussing their futures. Making plans, changing plans, and just living quietly for a moment in time just as best friends do. Having been born into a family with an affinity for clothing and expressive talents in fashion, Briannah had her life mapped out since she'd been ten and enjoying weekends playing dress-up in her grandmother's boutique. Aylonah's future, however, seemed just as distant and much like her past, bordering someplace between confusion and contentment.

"So, we got an invite to go to Bobby Dances on Saturday. And I'm hype because I talked to Trina, and she said Howard homecoming is in like two weeks," Briannah mentioned, her bright face shining with excitement. "That shit gon' be hot. So you know I'm tryna go," she added. "Do you know how many educated black men are going to be there? You think your gram gon' let you go?"

Accustomed to being rather involved with herself, it took Briannah a while to notice that she was having a one-sided conversation.

Frowning, she looked over at her friend and nudged her shoulder. "What's wrong with you? Why you so quiet?"

Aylonah shook her head and shrugged in response. "No reason. Don't judge me, but I feel like I need a Woolworth counter milkshake." she murmured.

"I'm talking about going to Howard homecoming and Dances, and you talking about Woolworth milkshakes, though? Girl, don't let that nigga stress you out," Briannah advised as she searched her friend's face. "'Cause you sound like your ass gon' get fat."

Aylonah laughed; Briannah could always be counted on for a little comedic relief.

"Whatever; I'm not even worried about him. And ain't nothing wrong with Woolworth milkshakes except the fact that I can't get one 'cause they closed down. I was thinking about the internship opportunity at Brown Publishing. It would mean more time with people in the business. I could get advice on my work from editors who work there. They could tell me what I'm doing wrong, you know? I submitted a book of poems earlier this year, and my agent says that they're still looking it over. Anyway, there are a lot of advantages to working for this company."

"Stop moping; you know you the shit. If they know what is most profitable for them, they'd publish one of your off-the-wall stories."

"You be thinking everything is so easy, Bri. You already have connections for your future," Aylonah confessed.

Briannah frowned and rejected the suggested theory. "That don't mean I have to work any less than you do to make it happen. You're seventeen; you don't have to have your future planned to the T."

Aylonah took a moment to digest the advice. "I guess you're right. Jay works there. It's his mom's company."

Briannah chuckled and tapped Aylonah's knee. "Ummm, now ain't that nice? I seen y'all together, and he is on you."

Aylonah sucked her teeth. "I don't even think so. He's on you," Aylonah divulged with personal knowledge. She smiled. "He be like, 'Yo, when you gon' hook me up with Briannah?'" Aylonah copied in her best impression of Jay.

Briannah had her own suspicions regarding the source of Jason's affection. "Well, he too late. I already got one— two— three men too many," she said jokingly, counting on her fingertips. "And here come one of them right now," she said on a sigh when a tall chocolate brother turned her corner.

Briannah sucked her pearly white teeth.

Damn, why he always gotta come around when I'm outside?

"Won't you just tell him you'n wanna talk to him anymore," Aylonah suggested under her breath.

Briannah frowned at the thought. *I know she ain't talking.* "Shh, here he come," she said instead. Bouncing off the steps with feigned enthusiasm, she greeted the approaching guy, "Hey Kendal." Aylonah shook her head and decided to reflect on her own relationship issues as Briannah chatted with her friend.

"You know you wrong, right?" Aylonah questioned with a laugh when they were alone.

Briannah smiled with sweet innocence. "What?" she asked, watching Kendal disappear around corner.

"Nothing. Where B at?" Aylonah inquired nonchalantly.

Briannah concluded that she was still watching her back after having mouthed off to Brian at school the day before.

Thoroughly disgusted with the happenings and less-revealed details of their relationship, Briannah squinted her eyes into slits. "You ain't tell him did you?" she accused.

"You'n have to say it like that. I'ma tell him."

Briannah rolled her eyes and said, "Aylonah, what I tell you? You betta—" Briannah let out a squeal when a black Ford Explorer turned into their street. "Oh my God! I cannot believe that he would come around here! Look at me! I got on sweats.!" Aylonah giggled after following Briannah's gaze down the street toward the oncoming vehicle.

"So what's up with y'all two?" Aylonah inquired, watching the Explorer pull into an empty parking space a few houses down.

The cool breeze danced across the base of Briannah's neck and slithered down the span of her back and length of her arms, creating a trail of chill bumps over her entire body. Suddenly, the protection of the sweatshirt wasn't enough to fight off the chill in the night air.

Briannah wasn't sure if it was the air or the thought of him that caused her to shiver. Instinctively, she rubbed her hands up and down the length of her arms to warm them. "Nothin'. He tryna play with my head. I'm not his baby momma or none of these other lil' hoes he be messing around with."

"You like him, though, so you sound upset," Aylonah noted in an amused tone.

Briannah squared her shoulders, shook her hair back, rolled her eyes, and said, "Please; too many niggas want this for me to be getting all mad over his black ass."

Aylonah cleared her throat. "So why is Ty the only one getting it then?"

"Only a few times and then he didn't call me for a while after that, so it's his loss. Now he expects that every time his ass pop up, I'm going to drop everything to go with him."

"Why you so worried about how you look then?"

Briannah rolled her eyes and neck. "'Cause I'm conceited within reason. Plus, I learned that appearances give off impressions, sweetheart," she explained seriously as if she were giving notes to Man-Catching 101.

Nervously, Briannah bit the inside of her cheek as Tyree stepped out of his car.

"Yeah, right. I got homework to do. I'll talk to you later?" Aylonah asked, noting that her best friend's attention had already been redirected towards the fine male walking toward them. "I guess I'll see you tomorrow then."

Briannah absently waved her off saying, "Night."

She took a seat and waited for Tyree to join her on the steps. The anticipation of sharing his company quickened her pulse, heated her heart, and aroused her senses. She was powerless to fight against what his mere presence did to her but she was determined that she'd never allow him to see through the façade she created. With the assumption that there was some sort of lingering expectation on his part for a grand display of excitement, Briannah did the exact opposite and waited for him speak first.

"So, what's up with you tonight?" he questioned. She didn't respond but continued looking past him, through him, thinking of him.

Tyree Gardener, known in the neighborhood as Chase, was twenty-two years old and completely out of her league. He was unlike any other guy she'd ever dealt with on any level. Tyree was handsome beyond words. He stood about six feet one inches in height. His skin was a mass of dark chocolate, covering a magnificently built body of long, lean arms and legs. His features showed strength. His eyes were a shade of chocolate brown.

"I thought you were coming over last night," she finally said, hoping traces of her disappointment didn't slip out in her tone.

"I got caught up," he explained.

Briannah smirked and slapped her knee. "And what's her name?"

Tyree laughed, finding her amusing. He found it even more strange that he actually liked her. More than liked her. As long as it had taken for her to decide that she was finally going to allow him to take her out, he better had liked her.
By his account, he'd been putting his bid in for her since she was fifteen. It had taken more time than he'd assumed, but as expected, Briannah had proven to be worth the wait.

He enjoyed everything about her. He appreciated her straightforward beauty that left nothing to be desired. Her eyes were the color of cinnamon sticks. Her skin was shades lighter than his own, a shade he described as honey. Her lips were thin but still managed to look pouty after being glossed. Her hair was the color of dark soil and fell about two to three inches below her shoulders. He also noticed that she always ran her fingers through it as if to make sure that it was all still there. It had taken her two years to get it to grow that long, he knew, and she seemed to love it. She stood five feet eight inches in height; she was thin and had slender arms and legs that were very well toned.

While the physical package was to be admired, Tyree found himself truly attracted to Briannah's wit. Her constant no holds barred attitude didn't turn him off. She was smartly sarcastic, slick, and quick-minded. He appreciated her relationship with her close friends, in her dealings with them, and in that, he saw into who she truly was. Her qualities extended far beyond those of the person she'd shared with him. She was fiercely loyal and as genuine as they came. He respected that she did not compromise who she was to fit other people's perceptions. It shocked him that he was waiting for her to give him a piece of that.

And he was, he admitted, waiting like a puppy dog for a real piece of her.

"Not a girl, business. And I just seen your boah Kendal come from around here. So who steppin' out on who?"

Briannah sucked her teeth and held her hand up to him. "Chase, don't go there with me okay? Bad day. I was waiting for you to bring your narrow ass around here all last night, so don't say shit. It's called common courtesy. I could have went out with my friends." She thought about adding, "or another guy," but was intelligent enough to use discretion, foreseeing his negative response. "Could've had a freakin' ball," she complained.

He smiled, acknowledging that she used his nickname and then coughed. "All that on a school night, hunh?"

Briannah narrowed her eyes to slits and glared at him. "Whatever. Y'all always tryna run games. I'm not on that type of time and you don't have to run no games on me."

"Come on now, Bri. We've known each other for years, so you'n even gotta go there."

Briannah stood up and folded her arms over her chest. "In two months, you've called me, what? Like fifteen times?"

"No, you've been home like fifteen times. Where you be at? I come by, you ain't never here. So what the fuck is going on with you?!" he exclaimed.

Briannah smiled, thrilled at her ability to get a rise out of him. "I'm busy. I have a job and friends." She shrugged her shoulders and sent him weary look and added, "Shit to do."

Tyree's eyes were serious when he looked at her. "Like I'm not busy? I have a million things to do too, and if you can't be number one, it's not my fault."

Absently, Briannah rubbed her hand over her heart to temper its beat. She didn't know where either one of them was taking the conversation. The undertones in his voice caused a ripple in her heart that she wasn't equipped to deal with. A relationship was not something she expected to want from him.

Casual sex… friendship… maybe, but love? Love was too much, Briannah decided. It made her feel too much, left her too vulnerable, she reminded herself. It required nurturing, time, attention, and consideration for others. It would make her responsible for another person's expectations, their feelings, and what love meant to them. She could already imagine herself falling in love with him the way Nora Roberts spoke of it in the novel Aylonah reads. She was almost certain that'd he'd only be playing at it.

She took a step back from her emotions and held up her hands in surrender. "Look, I'm overreacting. I'm not trying to be your number one, and you'n gotta be mine. But what's the deal? One minute, you on me, and the next, you ignoring me. I don't know what to think or how to deal with that."

Briannah swallowed the deep breath that she'd been holding as Tyree gently gripped her forearms, pulling her closer to him. "I'm trying to see you. At night, in the morning, whenever," he confessed.

Briannah sighed. She could feel the reigns of her control beginning to slip from her grasp. He was wearing her down with his endearing words. She was becoming undone with what she considered dumb-ass lines. She couldn't decide if the handsome face and good shot was what kept her interested or a combination of everything else. Her heart tripped a beat; he had the "everything" else, she thought dreamily. The same everything she'd already turned her heart against. The same everything that she's determined she just plain old was not ready for.

"That's a cute line. Don't say all this shit to me tonight and tomorrow I can't get a phone call from your ass."

"I ain't going to have to call you, 'cause you gon' be with me tomorrow," he replied, bending his head down to touch her lips with his.

"How you figure?" she asked, cocking her head to the side.

His brown eyes bore into hers as he touched his forehead to hers. "Cause you coming home with me tonight," he told her. His large lips plucked at hers as his hands left her arms to travel up her back. Briannah shivered; his kisses left her spine tingling.

"Yeah, I think I am." Briannah twined her arms around his neck and pressed her body tightly against his.

Tyree smiled.

Oh, shit. It's about to get real, she thought with a confused smile of her own.

Check out Little Pear Editing Services

For

I am thrilled that you decided to go through Sharae's journey with us. I Hope you enjoyed it.

XOXO  Elaine...

Elaine L. Allen is currently working on her next project.

She resides in Philadelphia with her family.

You can reach her through social media

www.perfectperceptions.wixsite.com/elainelallen

perfectperceptionspublishing@gmail.com

FB: Author Elaine Allen

Twitter and Wattpad: @MsSheWrites

IG: MsSheWrites/ or Ms_imgonnabweighless

270
Hurricane